MAKING WOLF

TADE THOMPSON

CONSTABLE

CONSTABLE

First published in Great Britain in 2020 by Constable

1 3 5 7 9 10 8 6 4 2

Copyright © Tade Thompson, 2020

The moral right of the author has been asserted.

A CIP catalogue record for this book
is available from the British Library.

ISBN: 978-1-47213-120-1

Typeset in Bembo by Photoprint, Torquay
Printed and bound in Great Britain by Clays Ltd, Elcograf S.p.A.

Papers used by Constable are from well-managed forests and other
responsible sources.

Constable
An imprint of
Little, Brown Book Group
Carmelite House
50 Victoria Embankment
London EC4Y 0DZ

An Hachette UK Company
www.hachette.co.uk

www.littlebrown.co.uk

For Beth, who puts up with my eccentricities, and David, who doesn't have to.

For Rosita Wakelin. O d'oju ala.

This happened a while ago. Some of the details are lost, others I wish I didn't remember, but read, and tell me you understand.

Tell me you forgive me.

CHAPTER 1

The lady beside me, who had spent the entire seven-hour flight reading three glossy magazines, whom I had tried to engage in conversation without success, nudged me with her elbow and thrust her jaw towards my drink.

'If you don't finish that, they'll take it from you,' she said.

She turned back to her article before I could respond. Less than a minute later, the cabin crew took my drink away.

Air travel. Never my favourite thing. Each time I had to endure descent from thirty thousand feet, I made a pact with God, and this time was no exception. Seat belt fastened, tray folded back up and locked in place, in-flight literature stowed away, back rest restored to the upright position, I gripped the armrests tightly. An announcement of some kind was not broadcast as much as beamed directly into my head. I started sweating and the landing gear struck the runway and my aunt was dead.

I held my breath until the plane was taxiing on solid ground. Dark outside, the terminal lit up like a lighthouse beacon. Other passengers undid their seat belts and started flipping on mobile phones before the plane came to a halt. I waited until the seat belt light went off and the cabin crew announced that it was all right.

Welcome to Alcacia International Airport. This is Ede.

Nobody ever welcomed you to Ede City; they just informed you that you had arrived and left you to fight or fall. Nobody

1

wanted to be here; they only travelled to Alcacia if they had to. Like UN peacekeepers. Like UNESCO. Like me.

The passport control officer required twenty bucks American folded and tucked into the photo page. He made it disappear with consummate skill. It was both horrifying and reassuring to know that Alcacia had not changed.

Blur to the luggage carousel. This served me new anxiety, but it was unfounded. I rescued my baggage. The airport appeared cleaner than I remembered, and more people wore uniforms. I was unmolested until I reached customs, where unfit officers demanded to search my bags. They found nothing, but still stood expectant, Mona Lisa smiles breaking through their sternness. Twenty bucks American each, which was twenty more than I had budgeted for this part of the journey. I could already feel the last vestiges of my inner peace leaching away.

Arrivals seethed with people and heat and intractability. The barriers pulsed, as if they were breathing. People strained to see loved ones, and a few held placards; but most just pushed and shoved. With the exception of a few South Asians, the faces were mostly black. Nobody smiled. I dove in and fought my way to the taxi rank. I used my rusty Yoruba, but it sounded odd, even to me. I needed more practice, a few days, perhaps, but I knew I wouldn't be here long enough to improve sufficiently. Silent, surly driver. Dark, windless night, no stars but abundant neon. Streetlights lined the first mile from the airport, but then became intermittent and stopped altogether. There was a savoury smell in the taxi, but I couldn't place the food. The air conditioning worked, so I counted my blessings and undid the top two buttons of my shirt.

The taxi dropped me at the Ede Marriott. The women loitering just outside were not guests. Only their smiles were free. I checked in and tipped the bellhop. As soon as he closed the door, I stripped off my clothes and turned on the shower. It did not work. I opened the tap, which did work, so I filled the bath and doused myself in cold water.

The last time I travelled from Alcacia International Airport was fifteen years ago. On that day, all the passengers ran with their suitcases and backpacks across the runway to the plane. There had been an accordion connection, but an imperfect seal had led to the fall and subsequent death of three passengers, countless others injured. Their bodies lay broken, blood-wet and mangled on the tarmac when I wheeled my luggage past.

Back then, there were gunshots from beyond the terminals and the smoke trail of a rocket-propelled grenade snaked from the ground describing an arc that just missed the communications tower and ended in the ruins of a section of roof.

I remember that I lost one of my bags, dropped it while running for an aircraft that looked like it was ready to start taxiing down the runway. I wouldn't have been surprised if the pilots took off with only a third of their passengers. I kept looking back, even though I knew it was impossible for me to spot my aunt at the terminal. I was worried. The woman was fearless but didn't know how to look out for herself. She was among hundreds of people outside the airport trying to avoid the wave of bloody revolution sweeping across Ede.

University students had been running riot for weeks. My aunt had finally saved enough money to buy me a ticket to London, England. She had packed my sister off the year before. There was widespread fear as the youths clashed with police in bloody street skirmishes that left the city fractured and charred. There were rumours of people eating fresh corpses, but it was always a friend of a friend or a distant cousin who heard it. The exodus out of the city was rapid, and people fought each other for spaces on lorries, buses and freight trains.

The students were demonstrating because the military government had promised elections and stimulated the registration of political parties, then invited the top players in all the parties to a conference, after which the conference hall just happened to blow up in a 'gas flow malfunction', killing all but eight. The result was an election suspended until further notice, widespread anger and the radicalisation of university students.

My aunt did not seem to be bothered. She just told me to be sure my passport was secure and that my books were packed. We set out at five a.m. I wore two layers of clothes. My aunt and I, we looked like looters.

'When you arrive at the airport, take off the outer layer of clothes,' she'd said. 'Igba yen ni wa wa da bi eniyan pada.' That is when you will look human again.

'Yes, ma'am,' I said.

We got into her 1980 Volkswagen Beetle and drove to the airport on the last of her hoarded petrol. Even that early in the morning, we passed four male students beating up a policeman who lay insensate on the road. They stomped on him repeatedly and blood seeped carelessly on to the tar.

Drums beating, interrupted only by gunshots and explosions. Burning cars on every street corner. My aunt drove through all of this, and, when she came to the traffic jam on the road that led to the airport, she switched off the car and left it. We walked. We pushed through the crowds with me holding my ticket high. She bullied and bribed her way through. Without a ticket, nobody could get into the terminal so I left her pressed against the glass. My eyes misted up; apart from the crowd that crushed against her there was the danger of the violence spreading. I waved. She mouthed something that did not seem tender.

At check-in, I was searched and my rectum probed for drugs. They X-rayed me for swallowed items. There was a brief interrogation. I had money for bribes laid out in packs of one hundred local dollars and had used them up when I got to the tunnel. When it fell apart, I shrank from the screams of the wounded and followed the rush to find alternative routes to the plane.

There were explosions and short-lived fires in the Duty Free shops as the revolutionaries reached the taxi rank, from where they could fire rockets at will and within range of the best parts of the terminal. Smoke burned my lungs as I ran and ran and ran to the plane that seemed too tiny for the number of people waving boarding passes. Knowing my countrymen, I was sure that most were forgeries.

The final scuttle up the emergency inflatable slide – yes, you can move in the reverse direction from its intended purpose. We scrambled up like contestants in a Japanese game show. I gripped plastic, slid a bit, stopped myself, continued, and gained the summit in inches. After me, only two passengers made it in before the attendants said, 'Sorry!' and closed the doors.

As we sped away, I looked out of the window and saw people smashing up the windows of the terminal building. I hoped my aunt had got through the crowd and home safe.

The plane's engines fired more powerfully. Gravity pressed me into my seat as the plane rose, giving me an aerial view of the city. Smoke from multiple fires. People were dying down there but I was safe. Nana was down there. My girlfriend. Her parents had fled with her to the north of Alcacia days before. I felt pangs of loneliness, but then we were in cloud and I couldn't see Ede any more.

And now, fifteen years later, I had returned because my aunt had died. There was no smoke, no rabid university undergraduates clamouring for blood and electoral representation using surface-to-air missiles. Just me in a hotel room, standing at the window dripping wet because the only way to stay cool in the infernal heat was to shower and let the water evaporate off my skin. It was a window to nowhere. It opened to the wall of the next building, and there was too much darkness to see any features. This was me in the underworld.

I sent a text message to my sister Lynn in London.

> Arrived safe. You should have made the trip instead of me. I hate it here. I'll let you know when I arrive at the ceremony. X

Her reply beeped back within thirty seconds.

> You're a Yoruba man. Alcacia is your home. You're only renting England. Stop whining, Weston. I love you. X

I only had to survive for two days. Forty-eight hours and I would be back in London living my real life.

I couldn't wait to leave.

CHAPTER 2

The next morning I set out for the funeral in a rented jeep. The satnav was erratic, but even so, I only got lost on the disorganised Ede roads three times, which I thought was impressive. I should have taken a taxi. The day was bright with subtropical sunshine and windy enough to make me squint. I found my way into the cemetery and took in the gathering. There were wooden fold-out chairs in ranks, some of which were empty. I sat in one at the very back, and although the ground was uneven, I found myself on a hump that gave me a good view of the proceedings. The guests close by glared at me. Not surprising; they either didn't know me or knew me and thought I wouldn't come.

This was my experience of the funeral: I kept running the names of the malaria parasite through my head to give me something to do while the preacher read out the eulogy. I was so scared of malaria that I double-dosed on proguanil and mefloquine. The night before, I hunted mosquitoes in my hotel room and sprayed odious chemicals on my skin to repel them.

But the funeral. The funeral was the reason I was back in the home country. My aunt had taken care of me when I was young, paid for my airline ticket to the UK, given me my start. I'd long since settled the financial obligation, but some debts just can't be settled by an online credit card transaction. There were lots of people, many of whom were here because three large cows had been tethered outside the family home for the last few days. Guaranteed food was a potent crowd draw around here.

This was the scene: Ede City, Alcacia. It was in West Africa. Former British colony, former French protectorate, former Portuguese trading post, now in its fourth decade of independence, the country of my genetic contributors. I'm British these days, but I still consider myself loyal to Alcacia.

The funeral was full of tears, a shrill, quivering warble and humongous, wobbling, semi-exposed breasts. She had a name, but I didn't know it. She was a professional mourner who worked her considerable girth, voluntary lacrimation and intimidating vocal range in the service of the more emotionally continent bereaved. The invited guests milled about or sat on headstones. Some wept quietly, privately, unusual for black Africans. We like to express our emotions freely, spread it about, communicate it to others. My tears are bigger and better than your tears. I have more grief than you. I loved her more than you.

I sat apart from everyone; I always have.

With time I recognised a face here or there from growing up. No names came to mind, though, so I just continued to roll my eyes over the crowd. Idle. They cast furtive glances at me, trying to place me, knowing me to be foreign from my clothes and demeanour. The priest finished and the mourner let rip, asking to be buried with my aunt who, if memory serves, would have frowned at her lack of self-restraint.

This graveyard was no different from the ones I'd seen in England. Except for the fences, which were there to delineate the boundaries between the quick and the dead. Vandalism was almost unknown because Alcacians were scared of ghosts, wizards and other supernatural nasties. The magical route to riches was to sleep in a graveyard for seven days and nights, at the end of which a demon would appear and reveal the secret to unlimited riches to the brave soul who had breached the taboo. I always touched my head when I passed a cemetery because I believed spirits could suck out my soul from the fontanelle at the top of the skull. Seriously, I did.

Something buzzed behind my ear and I slapped, but not too keenly; I didn't want to appear too much of an outsider. All the time I was away, telling myself every day that I'd return, telling myself that eating McDonald's and having an uninterrupted electricity supply hadn't changed me. Lynn was more realistic in her assessment and told me we would never settle back in Alcacia, but that the urge was a typical immigrant instinct, a *next year in Jerusalem* thing.

I heard someone say my name and looked around. It's difficult to recall my exact reaction but I'll go with alarm, followed by low-level anxiety bordering on panic. Here's why: Churchill Okuta. Or simply, Church. That grin. Straight out of my secondary-school nightmares. Church was the meanest person I had ever met in my life, and that is saying something. He had made my life unbearable as a child, yet here he was. I had like two inches on him now but back then he towered over me. The day I arrived in my dorm for the first time, Church took a leather belt to me 'to establish the rules and ranks'.

His nickname back then was Tippu Tip, after the notorious black Arab slave trader. He called his dormitory room Zanzibar and the activities there were notorious. 'Going to Zanzibar' became school parlance for taking a beating. Years later he was expelled for flogging, using his belt as a leash and tying a junior student to a handrail outside in the cold overnight because 'dogs shouldn't live indoors'. The boy almost died of lobar pneumonia.

Now, standing before me, he wore a shirt with a pattern of repeated kolkis on a background of deep purple. Frivolous for a funeral, but that was Church. In the microseconds before we spoke, I wondered if he and I were related, God forbid. What would Church be doing at my aunt's funeral?

'You bastard,' said Church. 'When did you get into town?' Broad grin. Church's grins were frightening as hell because he had small, even, inward-pointing teeth that reminded you of a shark. Neither was he calling me 'bastard' in a comradely fashion.

'Hello, Church,' I said. 'Nice to see you again.'

'Liar.'

'How've you been?'

'You know. Here and there, here and there.'

'How did you know Auntie Blossom?'

'Oh, I didn't know her. I just like attending funerals. I enjoy the food.'

I grunted.

'What are you doing these days? I heard you went to America.'

'London.'

'Yes, London. All is one to us. Away is away.'

'True.'

'So what do you do?'

'I'm in the police force. I'm a homicide detective with the Metropolitan Police.'

'Police. Yes.' Which was meaningless. I started to feel the familiar panic because, back in school, when Church wanted to catch you out in a lie he would make a meaningless statement, one that would coax you into embellishment and which always indicated he knew you were lying. As you talked, stammered and expatiated, painting yourself into that proverbial corner, he would start unbuckling his belt.

And I was lying, but only a little, and only because I wanted him to veer away from my orbit.

What I should have remembered is that Church did whatever he wanted, whenever he wanted. Consequences being a strange and abstract concept, the understanding of which he left to others.

Some Area Boys walked by, paying loud respect to Church by

shouting his name. He waved to them then shrugged at me, as if to say, What can I do?

Area Boys were like multi-purpose thugs for hire and private entrepreneurs. To throw a party in peace, you had to pay them in cash, food and drinks. During elections politicians hired them to disrupt the opposition's campaign. Since the opposition would have hired their own Area Boys, the result was usually a magnificent street fight or a carnival of drive-bys. Occasionally, they went on rampages in which they looted, raped and killed at random.

The ones paying homage to Church had an American street theme. Imagine five men wearing beanies and puffas in average temperatures of thirty-nine degrees Celsius and minimal wind chill. I didn't dare laugh.

'Are you going to the after-party?' Church asked.

'Yes, Auntie Blossom was—'

'Okay, see you there.'

Before I could say anything he was fiddling with his mobile phone and making his way to the exit. I can't say I wasn't pleased.

I turned my eyes and mind away from Church and back to the ceremony. Now that the preacher was finished, pallbearers lowered the coffin. There were four old men with talking drums beating away in sweet rhythms interspersed with traditional Yoruba verse, some of which were the antithesis of a Christian service.

O d'oju ala. I will see you in dreams.

The family edged closer. Well, the immediate family, because every Yoruba is related and the definition of family is broad. Up until now I had lurked at the edge of the crowd, but I started to push my way through. I became tense. I wasn't thinking of Auntie Blossom, I was thinking of the tall man wearing a massive agbada who was pouring dirt into the grave. My father, but not my dad. He must have felt something because he looked up just then and saw me. He showed no reaction except to let his eyes linger for half a minute. He had been crying. This made me sad in spite of myself. Back when I was a child this man never cried or showed emotion. He associated tears with womanly behaviour and discouraged my brother Simon and me with violence.

Beside him, with a clump of dirt in her hand and trailing a gang of children, was his new wife, the one he married after my mother. Her name escaped me. The woman looked insipid and judging from her hips and progeny, she was just a brood mare for the old man. I didn't feel fraternal towards her children. I felt unkind.

A loud bang interrupted my cruel thoughts. The songs all began with an all-powerful percussive blast, enjoyable when you weren't two inches from the drummers. I lost my hearing for a few minutes.

By the time I reached the graveside, my deafness had reduced to a constant ringing. I cried as I poured dirt on to her coffin. Two handfuls: one each for me and for my sister, even though Lynn hadn't known Auntie Blossom as long as I had. No one comforted me. I made them all uncomfortable by just being there, but I didn't care. I hadn't done anything wrong.

Later, I leaned against the stumpy palisade fence watching people leave in groups, headed for Auntie Blossom's family house to be fed and watered. A large shadow grew on the grass near my feet as someone walked up to me.

'I didn't expect to see you here,' said Dad.

'It's a funeral, Dad. Traditionally, the family attends,' I said.

'Ah, but that's the key word, isn't it? Family. The family attends. And if that's so, what are you doing here?'

Oh, we're all just comedians, aren't we?

'Dad—'

'Don't call me "Dad", Weston.'

I was still afraid of him. Lord knows why. I didn't need or want anything from him, and there was no way for him to harm me

12

or my sister any more, but here I stood with a dry mouth and a thumping heart. It was a great day for rekindling old fears.

'Auntie Blossom was my family,' I said.

'Hmf.' He cracked his neck. 'Blossom always was soft-hearted. And a little crazy to boot.' Auntie Blossom had indeed been free-range mental, but there was no way I was agreeing with the old man. 'Is Lynn here, too?'

'I don't see how that's any of your business.' I squared my shoulders.

He was quiet for a time, then he said: 'If you come to the reception you'll be treated like mo gbo, mo ya. Take one step out of line and I'll have you thrown out.' He spat and lumbered off, led by his large belly. With the warning, he had lapsed into his own dialect, which I could barely follow. A more indurate man you could never find. I didn't realise I had been shaking until he had gone and the fence began to rattle. I studied his phlegm for a while, watching it mix with the soil.

A gust of wind picked up some leaves, spun them about near my right foot and then carried them up towards the palm trees and beyond. It left a patina of dust on my clothes. I brushed my shirtsleeves off as I went to look for the hired jeep so that I could go to the reception.

CHAPTER 3

The organisers had cordoned off the street. A seven-piece juju band played off a two-foot-high stage at one end, with dancers all over the road. A few revellers, mostly male, held wads of cash and were placing individual notes on the foreheads and necks of other dancers, mostly female. The smell of expensive perfume mixed with the odour of cow shit. There was still some dung where the cows had been tethered earlier. Beer and kola nuts and jollof rice and schnapps and pounded yam and soups and stews of all kind were piled up on tables. Fireworks lit up the inky black sky.

While a funeral is for the departed, the reception is for departees.

In more ways than one, going to the reception was a mistake. I should have just gone back to the shitty hotel and waited for my flight. I think my father's threat stirred something contrary in me, something that wasn't going to be intimidated. In any case, I thought a party would cheer me up and piss him off at the same time.

Nobody was drunk, but it was early hours yet. I'd spent too long in London because I kept waiting for the police to show up after a neighbour's complaint but the neighbours were probably among the guests, and the organisers would have paid off the police and the Area Boys. Which left the military, but they were too busy fighting rebels up North. Like I did at the cemetery, I sat on the periphery, at a table where nobody admitted to knowing who I was, which suited me fine, thank you.

It looked chaotic but the set-up was obvious once you knew what to look for. The band was in full swing across from Auntie Blossom's house. The space in front of the band extending up to the gates of the house was understood to be the dance floor. On both sides of the band, tables and chairs stretched into the distance like a lecture hall without the walls and ceiling. Party lights, coloured bulbs in holders along flex cable, hung between lampposts like a night rainbow. The house itself was open, literally. All doors and windows were ajar, the command centre for the caterers, from where they dispensed food and drink.

On the bandstand, there was a man standing beside the lead singer feeding him information from prompt cards. The singer would integrate names into rehashes of popular juju songs. The people whose names were called out would be obliged to spray the bereaved family and the singer with mint-condition US dollars. Had to be crisp.

I sat watching the spectacle of rolling buttocks, elaborate gele and sweeping agbada. I drank palm wine. These were people I used to consider family. Some were doing well; others looked like they were on the verge of poverty, with their threadbare party clothes.

At the bottom of the food chain there were people who couldn't afford clothes that passed for party wear. These were the carrion-feeders of the ecosystem, waiting for scraps from the tables or notes tossed their way. They stole, begged and made the affluent feel guilty. They were mostly children, but you knew their parents were a few yards behind, feeding off the sympathy generated by the big eyes and snot-filled noses. These attendees stayed out of range of the young men wielding canes who served as sergeants-at-arms. They swatted the children away like flies periodically, horse tail swishing.

The last time I saw this number of black people in one place was at the Notting Hill Carnival. I was getting a headache so I rose and went to inspect the house where I had spent part of my childhood. A server spilled Guinness on my trouser cuff. I ignored her apologies and walked on, but then I heard her call my name.

'Weston?'

The servers wore identical white uniforms, with hats to keep their hair in check. The party lights didn't help with visibility and fifteen years had passed but still I recognised her.

'Nana?'

'Hold on a second.' Nana lowered her tray to a nearby table and served the guests three plates of rice, a large gourd of palm wine, and a pile of serviettes. Then she walked back to where I stood.

'Come with me,' she said.

I followed her into the house, past other servers, some of whom greeted her and looked at me with suspicion, past the main foyer, past the banister I used to slide down as a child, past where a nest of family wives supervised the caterers, and finally to a pantry that smelled of rice dust and flour. She bolted the door and faced me.

And kissed me.

I broke it off. 'Nana, I—'

'Are you seeing someone? Married?'

'No, but—'

She placed a finger on my lips, stroked her way to my cheek, and pulled my face to hers again. Her finger smelled of curried rice and beer. She hadn't changed much. A bit more wiry, less baby fat, but still unmistakably Nana. She kissed me like it didn't matter how I left without warning, without saying goodbye. Like it didn't matter that I didn't write, that we'd said we'd be in love for ever, that we promised, and that I broke that promise.

'We have a lot to discuss,' I said.

'No, we don't. Are you here to stay or are you returning to London soon?'

'I'm flying out at midnight tomorrow.'

'Good. We have the whole day. Call me. I have to get back to work. I'm not allowed to consort with the guests.' She passed me a card, unbolted the door and was gone. A rice weevil crawled across the rectangle of embossed paper. *Nana Hastruup. Consultant.* I wondered what that meant, but I secreted the card in my trouser pocket and left the pantry.

Nana. I thought I might run into her, and I both dreaded and anticipated the meeting. In body, she was your typical Yoruba girl – dark, round and bosomy. Her brain was at once her greatest asset and her worst shortcoming. She was lippy – I loved that about her – but a girl who didn't know when to shut up didn't get marriage proposals, and for women in Alcacia, even in the twenty-first century, marriage was all. She didn't belong there. She belonged only there.

I looked at framed photos of Auntie Blossom in the hallway. She had the same look in all of them: serene indifference. Lined thin face, deep gullies below the cheekbones, hair always wrapped in a gele. There used to be a handful of portraits by local artists – me at three, Lynn as a baby, one of Auntie Blossom, one of Auntie Anice. And there were missing pictures – Dad probably took them down.

'There you are,' said Church. He was holding two Small Boys – the 35cl Guinness – and handed me one. We clinked bottles. 'Why are you hiding here?'

'Just looking at photos.'

'Come downstairs. Meet my friends. Stop being an oyinbo.'

Church took me to a table so close to the band I could see the nose hairs of the frontman. Conversation was almost impossible. Church's friends were frightening. Three of them: Lemi, Tito, Tosin. Tito and Tosin were identical twins. None of them wore traditional clothing, which was unusual for a gathering like this. Tito wore sunglasses and had battle fatigue trousers on. Their facial expressions were grim and only Church laughed, but his laughter never had anything to do with mirth.

I drank more alcohol.

'Hey, you should give me your passport and say you lost it,' said Church.

I laughed. It was brittle, fake and excessive. 'I don't think I will.'

'No, seriously.'

'No, Church.'

'I'll pay.'

'I can't. Come on. Do you know what would happen if I were found out? Remember my job?'

'Yes. Policeman. Detective. Okay, so how about you let me photostat the first page?'

This was me back in school again refusing to give him the provisions my parents brought for me on visiting day.

I drank more alcohol.

'Tomorrow,' I said.

Church slapped my back. 'Great.' He turned to Tosin. 'This guy here, he's the only genuine original bastard that I know.' Church nudged me and yelled, 'Tell them. Go on!'

'I was a Holloway Baby,' I said, and passed out.

I remember a few things about that blackout. In my mind, I kept explaining why Church thought I was a bastard. I was unaware of my own unconsciousness.

'Tell them,' said Church. 'Go on.' His voice echoed as if my skull were cavernous.

A Holloway Baby is a particular brand of bastard.

Look. Here is the Kogi family. Here are Mummy and Daddy and three children, two boys and a girl. Aren't we all pretty in our

Sunday best and with our scrubbed faces? No, we are not. Not when Simon the older boy develops kidney failure at fourteen. Both kidneys just start to rot for no obvious reason, knocking the boy down, shrinking him, making him smell of putrefaction so bad that eyes watered from being in the same room.

Here are the mummy and daddy taking the younger son, Weston, to the white-coated doctors, where he is happily going to donate one of his kidneys. Everyone says how brave he is for a twelve-year-old. He feels a warmth in his belly whenever the elders speak of his courage. Here he is bravely bearing the massive needle for the blood test. It hurts but he just sweats a little and grits his teeth. The mummy and the daddy are happy that he does this. Here are Mummy and Daddy back from the doctors.

They are not happy with the results.

It seems young Weston failed the blood test, but Daddy is behaving like it is Mummy who failed the test. Mummy says Weston cannot give his kidney to the brother because they are not alike enough. They will have to try the sister. Lynn. But a few weeks later, Lynn's kidney is no good either. They are not alike enough.

Look at the daddy. He is livid. The babalawo comes and Mummy has to swear on a horn filled with charms about something. Look at the whole family going for blood tests. Look at the brother getting sicker and sicker. His name is Simon, and he is dying. The mummy kisses his puffy face.

The daddy no longer sleeps in the house. The mummy, who was a housewife, has to find a way to make a living. She rises while it is still dark and sells savoury dishes to the office workers in the city at lunchtime. Simon dies. Weston has nightmares about it for years. Simon has left the physical world and taken up residence in Weston's mind.

The mummy is knocked down by a car and dies instantly.

Lynn and Weston were both born in the Royal Holloway Infirmary. They are adopted by the daddy's sisters, Blossom and Anice.

I woke without a hangover. The dream left me with unpleasant after-emotions, Simon trying to tell me something but the words were indistinct.

I coughed. I'd caught a chill in the night.

Morning leaked in from an open door. On closer examination there was no door. I was half awake on a bare mattress on the floor of a hut. My feet were bare, but my shoes were beside me, socks bunched up in each one like a telescoped foreskin. I was still in my own clothes, but they felt crusty, like I'd been sweating heavily in them and the sweat had dried leaving a layer of salty grease. I rubbed the sleep sand from the corners of my eyes and wondered where the hell I was. The floor of the hut was hammered red clay. In the corner stood a rolled-up raffia mat and a mauve plastic potty. I got up from the lumpy mattress, locally made from unprocessed cotton, straw and springs fashioned from molten scrap metal, and I pissed.

Outside the doorway, there was an extinct bus blighted with rust, windows with incongruously intact glass. You could still read the legend painted on the side: NO TELEPHONE TO HEAVEN!

I patted myself down. Wallet still in place. Significant and heartfelt gratitude to the Elder Gods that I left my passport in the hotel safe. Smell of wet earth and ganja in my nostrils. Voices of men, of some irate women and of children, speaking Yoruba but in a dialect I was unfamiliar with. The speech was tainted with Portuguese, which meant I was nowhere near where I should have been. It meant I had been taken towards the east of the country while unconscious. I left the hut.

Outside, I coughed again. There had been rain overnight and my shoes squelched in the red mud. I was concerned about the suede, which was funny, considering everything else. I made my way through an alley between huts similar to the one I had woken up in. I approached an opening that probably led to a courtyard and people whom I could ask questions. I heard an engine rev and a few sharp shouts, which encouraged me.

I breached the yard.

They had a man chained to a post by his wrists and to a pick-up truck by his ankles. He screamed because the pick-up was driving away from the post. The engine went into a high whine as it strained against the muscles, tendons and bones of the man's back.

His back gave way in a mess of entrails and gore, then I was the one screaming.

CHAPTER 4

The muzzle of the rifle against my temple felt like nothing I had ever experienced before. My entire universe shrank to the cold metal against my cheek. I had absurd thoughts. I wondered if I'd feel a brief flash of heat before dying. I wondered if it would hurt. Would I shit myself? Would I beg? Would the mud stains ever come out of my clothes? What if the shooter missed and I ended up malformed but alive?

'Are you a spy?' yelled the man holding the rifle. 'Are you spying?'

His dialect was dense, impenetrable. At first, I thought he'd asked, 'Are you looking at me?' Not the right time for bizarre De Niro references. Or maybe exactly the right time.

'I'm not spying. I don't even know where I am,' I said in English, which earned me a jab. The other side of my head was in the mud, and I could already taste it in my mouth between my teeth: bland, chalky, a hint of old vegetation.

I figured that I was in one of the rebel or militia camps and cursed myself for not paying more attention to recent Alcacian politics. A crowd gathered around, and they argued among themselves about what to do with me. There were three children, two of them naked, watching me with unaffected curiosity, unimpressed by guns, violence or the bloody remains of the executed man two feet away from me. The smell of chopped meat

23

clogged my nostrils. I was still and did not say anything apart from denying that I was a spy in my best South London English, hoping it would confuse them.

'Weston, what do you think you're doing, lying in the mud?' It was Church.

I twisted my neck and saw him looking down at me. Shirtless, wearing fatigues and combat boots, laughing his nuts off. The pressure against my head lifted and I rose first to my knees then to my feet. Church stopped laughing suddenly and gave the arguing minions a look that silenced them. They seemed to find more important things to do. Church pointed at the dismembered corpse, and the one with the rifle walked towards it.

For someone I had considered overweight, Church had surprisingly muscular arms, with a big hairy gut dominating his upper torso. He was sweating. He had a pistol stuck in his waistband. He slapped me playfully with a meaty paw.

'Let's get you cleaned up.'

'Sorry about that. Some of the boys get excitable during executions,' said Church.

I left my clothes hanging off a nail close by. A halved gourd bobbed in the iron pail of water he set in front of me. I soaped myself, scooped water with the gourd and rinsed off. I worked to get the clay out of my mouth, but the water tasted of the same thing.

'Some of these people didn't go to school,' said Church. 'The Front can't be picky. We need cannon fodder.'

The Liberation Front of Alcacia, LFA. *In Guns We Trust*. This was their motto for real. Bitter enemies of the government and their main rivals, the People's Christian Army, PCA.

'What now?' I said. 'Pull my fingernails out? I don't have any politics, you know that.'

'Everybody has politics, my friend. People just need help drawing their opinions out, that's all. Give me a sharp stick and a length of rope. I'll extract politics in zero time. But never fear, Weston. You're not here because of your political beliefs. In fact, your lack of politics might be an asset on this job.'

'"Job"?'

'Someone wants to talk to you, son. As long as you don't ask stupid questions, you should be fine. Dry your scrotum and let's go. Liberation waits for no man.' Church guffawed. He obviously liked LFA rhetoric lathered with irony.

'What job, Church?' I hoped I sounded calm. The image of the dismembered man flashed across my mind's eye. I splashed water on my groin. Displaced foam fell to my feet and mixed with the mud.

'Not for me to say,' said Church.

How did the LFA even know I existed? I was nobody. 'Am I a prisoner?'

'No.'

'Then what?'

'Call it a job interview. No matter how it turns out, you go home after it's done.'

'And if I don't want to do this . . . interview?'

Church gave me a blank look, as if I'd cracked a joke in poor taste. I smiled at him, he smiled back, and all was well in the world.

As we walked through the camp, Church gave me advice about my cock. Seriously. Apparently it was not large enough.

'Not that it's small, aburo,' he said, 'but it isn't very impressive, is it? Depends, though. If your woman has never had a big one in her love tunnel? No problem. But if she has . . . I don't see how you'll satisfy her after that. There's a certain stretch—'

'I've had no complaints.'

25

'Of course you haven't. Girls are smart that way; they don't want you to know, don't want to hurt your feelings, say everything's all right. But the first chance they get, they're fucking the big dick carpenter who comes to install your cabinet.'

'Can we not discuss this?'

'Has any woman ever cheated on you? Because I bet I know why.'

I felt the sun warming my face as Church droned on. Palm trees reached over the roofs of the huts and leaned in as if to reclaim the land. A pack of dogs fought for scraps in the rapidly drying mud, each of them scarred, with the same mangy, brownish-grey coats. Nobody looked at us as we worked our way through variously sized passageways. I thought of time slipping away, and my return flight. Escape seemed an impossible concept. No idea where I was, no idea how far from civilisation, no expertise in stealing automobiles. I didn't think it possible, but I hated Church a little more at that moment.

The grogginess from the alcohol or whatever drug they fed me last night was fading. I became aware of a headache, like a hangover, except without the thirst and light sensitivity. Still, it's not my typical day to witness a death and have a gun to my head and mud in my mouth before breakfast.

We progressed to what must have been the only concrete house in the whole compound. It also gave me the first idea of the lie of the land. The camp was located on the side of a gentle rise, with tractors and heavy equipment on the edges of the clearing, green camouflage netting attached to a pulley system, ready for deployment. End to end, the settlement was about a kilometre square. Most of the buildings were a ramshackle, prefabricated nightmare of red earth, corrugated sheeting and thatch. There were some children, mostly male, toting guns or wooden replicas.

'Child soldiers?' I asked.

'These ones? We don't use them in combat. They're kept for publicity only, photo shoots, to display the effort and sacrifice the great people of Alcacia have shown in the struggle to—'

'Yes, yes, I get it.'

'It impresses the white people and gets funding. I can milk one photo of these kids for two NGOs. I don't imagine they know they are funding the wars they think they're ending. It's like printing money.'

'I'm sure.'

We came up to the door of the concrete house and the two armed guards stood aside. Matching camouflage, clean boots, identical Police sunglasses, standing to actual attention, I guessed they were a better-funded brand of guerrilla, what with guarding El Jefe, and all.

Inside, the decor was a jumble of ostentatious shit with shiny gold leaf on banisters and filigreed picture frames. A man in his early fifties stood in the middle of the receiving area on a Persian rug. He was not in military garb and he was slightly paunchy. He seemed mild mannered in his clear, circular-frame spectacles. I noticed he didn't blink much, and I made an effort to suppress my own lids. Churchill saluted in a carefree manner and the man just smiled.

'This is Weston Kogi, sir. Weston, this is His Excellency Comrade Osa Ali, leader of the Liberation Front of Alcacia.'

Ali stepped forward and offered a hand, which I shook, after which he steered me to a plush leather chair with a hand on the small of my back.

'You'll have to excuse me, Weston, I save my oratory for rabble rousing. I have no props or special effects for you, I'm afraid. Just plain talk and some palm wine, if you'll accept my humble offering.'

'It's a bit early for me,' I said. 'And I recently had a bad experience with alcohol.'

'Ah. That was necessary. But no harm done, right?'

'Well—'

'Good. Good. Our mutual friend has been telling me about you.' Church flashed a proprietary smile.

'Exaggerations,' I said. They thought I was joking. If only.

'Alcacia has a problem which you are uniquely qualified to solve. Will you do it, Weston? Will you toil in the service of the soil that spawned you?'

I thought he was saving the oratory. 'What problem? And to what qualifications do you refer?'

Church nudged me hard. 'Say, "sir" and don't ask stupid questions. Didn't I warn you about stupid questions?'

'Churchill.' The Supreme Revolutionary Leader shook his head gently. That was reassuring. What wasn't reassuring was how I was more scared of Church than the infinitely more dangerous rebel leader in front of me.

'All I'm saying is I'd like to know more about the situation before committing to it. I wouldn't want to agree to something I have no expertise in. Sir.'

'I have a rather delicate problem, Weston. I was hoping for your support. I was counting on your fortitude.'

Fortitude?

'How can I help?'

'I wish for you to find a killer,' he said with a pained expression. 'I wish for you to solve me a murder.'

CHAPTER 5

Church offered me a cigarette and sucked his teeth when I declined. He thought I was sulking and I did nothing to change this impression. The jeep returned us to civilisation in spurts – a gas station here, a few telephone poles there, a post office, a mechanic shop – until, after two hours of hesitancy, we sank into the middle of town.

Church said something, but it was lost in the noise. By the time he dropped me off in front of my hotel, we were swallowed up by the heat and smells and voices.

'I'll bring you information this evening,' he yelled as he drove off. 'Change your clothes, you look like a corpse.'

'Iya e da bi oku,' I said under my breath. *It's your mother who looks like a corpse.*

When he was out of sight, I turned and walked into the hotel. The receptionist stared, but I pretended not to care about my crumpled, sun-dried clothes, my uncombed hair and my muddy shoes.

'Three-oh-three, please,' I said.

Unperturbed. He handed me my keys. 'Breakfast is over, but the bar will open in five minutes,' he said.

'Thank you.'

I walked up three flights of stairs and entered my room. Thankfully, the corridors were designed in such a way that guests

29

rarely ran into other guests going in or coming out of their rooms. Housekeeping had been and gone. I sucked on the pillow mint while I stripped off my clothes. When I emptied the pockets a card fell out. Nana Hastruup. I turned on the television. *The Big Sleep* was on the channel that showcased old movies. I lifted the receiver beside the bed.

'Could I have an outside line, please?' I read out the number, and, while being connected, I removed my underwear and sat naked on the bed, wondering if my shoes could be salvaged.

'Hello?' Her voice was sharp, curious.

'Nana?'

'Carlos Castaneda or Kahlil Gibran?'

'What are you talking about?'

'What? Oh, sorry. I was working on a problem. Weston, how are you? What time is your flight?'

Nana had a tendency towards the surreal, even back when we were dating. It just took getting used to.

'I'm okay,' I lied. 'Can we meet?'

'Yes. Where and when?'

'I don't know where. It's your town, not mine.' I looked at my dirty fingernails. 'And I'm going to need about an hour to freshen up.'

'Heavy night, eh? Did you go home with any of those bush girls at the party? They'll give you gardnerella, you know.'

'What's gard . . . never mind. I wasn't—'

'I know. I'll be at your hotel in ninety minutes.'

'Do—'

She hung up.

I held on to the receiver for a few seconds then went into the shower. Unlike the last time, it was functional. There must have been rust in the pipes because, for some seconds, the water looked biblical, like blood rain. Then it turned orange, then clear. I stood in the stream and thought of the man I saw being killed. I think

I wept for him. Water streamed down my face, and maybe there were no tears, just the shower. Maybe I was only grieving. Maybe I wasn't grieving at all and I was just afraid for myself. I kept seeing the body rent apart – the first tear around the shoulder blades, the blood, the splat of the organs on the ground, the sudden end of the man's screams. What had he done to deserve that?

I shook it all off because I had more pressing drains on my attention. I was in trouble because of a slight problem with lying on my CV.

I was not exactly a detective with the Metropolitan Police.

I was not exactly a policeman.

I could have come clean, told them I was not what I said I was, but that would have put me at risk of playing tug of war with a pick-up truck. I could simply ignore them, leave on my flight like I had planned, which meant I would never be able to return to Alcacia. The thought didn't bother me much, now that Aunt Blossom was dead. They'd kill my family, but what family? Unless their reach extended to Camberwell, I was safe and so was Lynn.

I shampooed my hair, used the shower gel and rinsed myself off. I stood looking at my reflection, scowling at myself.

'You're an idiot.'

Nana waited at the hotel drop-off point in a maroon Mercedes 200 with the engine idling. When I emerged, the moist heat enveloped me and I felt beads of sweat appear, forced out of my pores.

'Do you want to drive?' Nana asked, pointing to the wheel.

'Only if you want to die,' I said. 'I drive on the other side of the road, and my brain hasn't been trained to switch.' The real reason was that I didn't want her to see me getting lost like I did the day before.

When I strapped on the seat belt, Nana rolled up the windows and activated the air conditioning. She looked cool and casually beautiful. As far as make-up went, she only had red lipstick on. Without the ridiculous hat of the previous night, her hair formed a black cloud around her head, like an Afro.

'When is your flight?' she asked.

My passport was in my hip pocket along with the confirmation number of my electronic ticket. 'Half past eleven,' I said.

Nana smiled. 'Plenty of time.'

'Where are we going?'

'The beach.'

We fell silent. Outside, we passed through Ede, the capital city. We drove along Xavier Avenue, which would take us to Woodgrain Beach. The streets were crowded with sweating, desperate people trying to make a living. Women carried their wares on their heads and children on their backs. They cackled non-stop while offering bolts of silk, oranges, yams, spinach, fish, spices, and other items that I no longer recognised. Muscular young men hired out their right arms and wheelbarrows for heavy lifting. A preacher spoke of Armageddon, hellfire and the salvation to be found in the blood of Jesus.

'Obo iya e n shomi!' Nana screamed at a lorry that cut her off. The lorry driver didn't take kindly to being told that his mother had an infected vagina. He commanded Sopana, the god of smallpox, to rain blindness and implausible disfigurement on Nana's family.

'Wow,' I said.

'Don't worry, we'll be through with the market in a minute, and the traffic improves.'

She was right. The crowd thinned and only the beggars remained in sight when traffic slowed. There were signal lights, but nobody paid attention to them. The beggars had mostly self-inflicted wounds, which some maintained in order to avoid work. Lost limbs, infected tsetse fly bites, massive tumours – each one had a commercial value that gave beggars a perverse incentive to avoid medical treatment.

We broke through to a palm-tree-lined boulevard with road signs pointing us to Woodgrain.

'So, how have you been?' I asked.

'Don't bore me, Weston. I haven't spoken to you in years. The least you could do is not lobotomise me with mundane pap.'

'Sorry.'

'Hey!' She smacked my shoulder. '*You* left me. I have the moral high ground here, so you don't get to give sulky apologies.'

It was all jokey and good-natured, but I could sense pain underneath it all. I didn't say anything until we pulled into the parking space. I tipped the Area Boys so they wouldn't let the air out of the tyres.

The South Atlantic blew salt and sand in my face. Nana took me by the hand and marched me across the dunes. She wore sandals but I struggled in my Hush Puppies.

Apart from a scattering of black families and white expatriates, the beach was relatively empty. Nana bought us cocktails and handed them to me, after which she led me to a green bamboo shack she had pre-rented. It had one sea-facing unframed window and a bench made of artfully arranged bamboo. She sat on the bench, took her drink from me and looked out at the waves.

'Are you hungover?' she asked.

'No.'

'You seem strained, in discomfort.'

'I'm not.'

Outside, a tired-looking horse plodded by, led by an old man with sun-blackened skin and a cigarette hanging from his lips. A boy sat on the saddle, enjoying a ride and waving in our direction. Nana waved back. From where I was sitting I could see the outline of her breasts through her white blouse. I imagined the curve creeping down and joining her hips in her jeans. I didn't know how to talk to her and she wasn't talking to me.

'Nana, do you know who Enoch Olubusi is?'

'Was. He's dead.' She looked at me. 'You have a few hours till your flight and you want to talk politics?'

'No.' I went to her.

She put her drink down and dropped a curtain over the window.

The sun had passed its zenith, and the light was not nearly as blinding nor the heat as stifling. I was still sweating, but that was from our exertions. We were on the floor and there was sand in the crack of my arse but I didn't mind. Nana was lying mostly on me and half on the blanket.

'What are you thinking?' she asked in a languid voice.

'I'm wondering what "consultant" means,' I said.

She laughed. 'It means I consult.'

'You're a caterer who drives a Mercedes, Nana.'

'An old Mercedes.'

'Nevertheless.'

'Hmm. You know what I'm thinking? I'm thinking you enjoyed the sex so much that you're wondering if my consultations involve money changing hands for carnal services.'

'Nana—'

'Let's talk about Enoch Olubusi. Why do you need to know about him? Quickly, now. I want to make love some more before you go.'

I looked down at my limp phallus. 'I'll need a minute or two. Besides, my muscles are aching.'

'You can just lie back and think of England,' she said. She

reached over me to take what was left of my drink. Her heavy breasts swung over my face.

'I met with the Liberation Front of Alcacia today, with their leader, Comrade Ali. He told me Enoch Olubusi was murdered, most likely by agents of the People's Christian Army. He hired me to prove it.'

Nana sat up. 'Are you kidding me?'

'No.'

'I don't even know where to start. How did you meet Ali? Why you? Do you have connections that I don't know about?'

I explained about Church and being drugged. Nana let loose a string of exotic swear words.

'You're an idiot,' she said.

'I know.'

'And you have no skills of crime detection whatsoever?'

'I did start a criminology course at the Open University in 2004, but it was boring so I quit after the first term.'

'What actually do you do for a living?'

'I'm a security guard at a supermarket. But I've been trying to get into the police. I was even invited for the interview. Once.'

Nana looked inwards for a while. 'The good news is you're not going back to London today. They'll have someone at the airport, and there would have been a spotter at the hotel, which means they may have followed us. The mixed news is that you will either solve the crime and live or not solve the crime and be killed. Do you have your ticket on you?'

I rooted through my clothes and handed her the confirmation slip and passport. She ripped up the confirmation slip into tiny bits and threw them into the air like confetti.

'Hey!'

'If they followed us, they know about me. If you fly away, they might come after me, Weston. I don't want that to happen because

I like being alive. I'll hold on to your passport.' She started getting dressed.

'I thought you wanted to make love again?'

'That was when I thought you were leaving today. Let's just focus on keeping you alive for the time being.'

CHAPTER 6

'Enoch Olubusi is . . . was the nearest thing to a saint this country has ever produced,' said Nana. 'In 1993, he was Desmond Tutu's main competitor for the Nobel Peace Prize.'

She had the same introspective expression on her face, as if she were a robot accessing files in her memory banks. We walked along the shore, with the sun at our backs and our shadows going before us like prophets of doom. Nana occasionally picked up bits of metal from Nigerian commercial air crashes.

'Interesting objects fetch good money on the market,' she said. A dead person's passport could be used again. A piece of fuselage could be converted into a charm for imperviousness by Ogun priests since the metal was already 'dead'. Body parts were rare since sharks and fish usually made short work of them, but a bone picked clean, especially a skull, was priceless.

Nana went back to Enoch. 'He was born in 1936 in Kinshasa of all places. Leopoldville, it was called back then. He was only there for a few months after birth. His parents moved back to Ede when Alcacians were expelled. By all accounts, his family was dirt poor, and he often spoke about the wretchedness of his early years. We don't know much about his childhood but he did go to St Bartholomew College for Boys on a scholarship from a no-name primary school. You have to understand that his father was only numerate enough to calculate the oguro tab at the local bar and his mother could neither read nor write. These factors made it highly improbable that Enoch would become the best student ever to come out of St Bart's. His old school mates say he was quiet, unassuming and helpful. Almost everyone described him as "helpful" but nobody remembers seeing him study.'

'How do you know all this?' I asked.

'I read his authorised biography two years ago for a term paper I was writing. Bland and fact-heavy but sources verified. Reliable.'

'Then why would anyone kill him?'

She threw up her hands. 'They wouldn't. He was universally loved. Didn't you see his funeral on CNN?'

'I don't watch a lot of television.'

'Considering the mess you're in right now, it might be prudent to start.'

'You move fast!' said Church. He was sitting on the steps of the hotel, waiting. His eyes were on Nana's Benz as it pulled away.

'That's just the power of Sterling, my brother. She's a professional.' I didn't look back or wave. 'Have you been waiting long?'

'I've been checking out girls, looking at their asses. Just before you arrived a hefty one passed, rolling like two footballs in a skirt.' Church stood up, feigning joint pains as if he was a world-weary old man. He held a satchel. 'You know, I thought you might have tried to leave. I have some boys at the airport.'

'Why would I leave?'

'Your passport isn't in the hotel safe.'

Everyone knew my business. Church had probably bribed the reception clerk or threatened to kill his extended family members in horrible ways.

'I just felt better with it on me, on my person.' I changed the subject. 'What's in the bag?'

'Items you will need. Let's go up. We have much to discuss, and

38

you have to change your clothes. Right now you look like the kind of person who catches his own food.'

It didn't take long to change into casuals. Church systematically emptied the mini-bar as he spoke. The first thing he brought out of the satchel was a gun. It was angular, black and cruel, and belonged nowhere near the hands of an often-intoxicated psychopath like Church. 'You know how to use this?'

I shook my head.

'You're a police officer!'

'In the UK, regular police don't carry firearms. We have armed response units.'

'Well, olopa, this is Alcacia. The woman selling roasted corn has a child on her back and a gun in her wrapper. Here.' He handed it to me and showed me the parts. 'Handle, safety catch, slide, sight, muzzle. Remember: you point the muzzle *away* from you.'

'Yes, Church, I have seen the movies.'

'You'll be surprised at the number of young revolutionaries who blow their own heads off looking down the barrel. Awon odoyo. Imbeciles! This is the ammo. A magazine of twenty-three bullets before you slot it in here.'

He shunted the rectangular clip into the hollow space in the handle, and it made a click when it rammed home.

'Now pull back the slide. What you hear is one of the rounds going into the chamber. If you pull the clip out, that bullet still remains in the chamber unless you pull the slide like so.' He racked the slide back again, and a bullet flew out of the side of the gun. 'Now it is truly unloaded. You try. Reload, rack back the slide and unload.'

I did it a few times till he was satisfied, then he handed me an efficient-looking ankle holster with a Velcro flap.

'There is only one cast-iron rule when you have to work with guns,' said Church. 'Treat every gun as if it is loaded. There is no such thing as an unloaded gun. Say it.'

'No such thing as an unloaded gun. Got it.'

Next he gave me ten thousand American dollars in crisp fifty-dollar notes.

'Church, what—'

'Don't worry, that's not your fee. This is just expenses. Holding money.'

They planned to pay me. I mean, of course they planned to pay me. What was I thinking? 'I don't have anywhere to store . . .' I trailed off when he handed me a matte-black money belt.

He rooted in the bag and picked out a manila package. This was a side of Church I had never seen – focused, tight, methodical.

'Let's talk about murder,' he said. 'First of all, Comrade Ali wants you to be absolutely clear on one thing: the LFA did not do this deed. I personally saw him swear an oath on a bull horn.'

The sacred bull horn. My mother swore on one a long time ago, when I was twelve. Consecrated first and then filled with deadly charms by the babalawo.

'Okay,' I said. 'Tell me how Enoch Olubusi died.'

I admit my tone was somewhat flippant but I was completely flabbergasted by what happened next: Churchill started crying. Real tears. From Church. Church the sociopath.

'Hey, I'm sorry if I—'

'Weston, what you are doing is important. Pa Busi was everything to us. We loved him. He shook my hand during the preliminary peace talks. He shook my hand! And somebody . . .' He handed me a photograph from the package.

In the foreground there was a body, and in the background, the charnel house aftermath of a blast with blackened, tortured metal from a jeep, body parts, ruptured earth, scattered firearms. Between the jeep and the body was bloody, disturbed sand, like the person had crawled some distance before dying.

These were the mortal remains of Enoch Olubusi.

I only knew this from the markings on the photo. Arrows pointed to the bodies (and parts) identifying each. Olubusi had burned, and there was a terrible grimace on his face, half of which had parted company from the skull. His whole body was flexed, and the explosion had shredded his clothes into rags. This was not a good death.

'Jesu!'

Church nodded. He blew out smoke. I didn't even remember him lighting up.

'Do we have autopsy reports, forensics on the jeep—'

'You're like an idiot child sometimes, you know that?' Church asked.

I exhaled, back-pedalled. 'What do we have?'

'There was no autopsy. Priority was given to the mortician who was flown in from the States to help us see that Pa Busi looked vaguely like himself. That jeep has long since been compacted and melted down.' He brought out a map of Alcacia. It was shaped like a sperm whale on the West African map, tiny, squeezed between Nigeria and Cameroon, the mouth of the whale drinking from the Atlantic.

'The East was controlled by the LFA, the West by the People's Christian Army. Other minor players, including the Federal Government, controlled the rest. Pa Busi was killed in neutral territory,' Church said.

'Where is he buried?'

'Ede. I can take you there.'

'Do we have the name of the mortician?'

'I can find out.' He dropped the packet on the bed. 'I have other details that you might find useful in here. There's a mobile phone,

41

and I took the liberty of punching in my number. If you need to go anywhere, do anything, I'm your partner.' He went to the door.

'Thanks, Church.'

'See you tomorrow.'

I had planned to go through what he'd left for me, but I must have been more tired than I realised because I dropped off almost as soon as I sat on the bed.

Two a.m.

My eyes were open, but I didn't know how long I had been awake or what woke me. Everything in the room was as I left it. My left ankle had gone to sleep because of the holster I had strapped on. I got up, stamped my foot to improve the blood flow, cleared the bed and went to piss. Each time I thought of the situation, I got a jolt of fear that quickened my heart.

There were other ways of looking at it: I had a beautiful girlfriend, I was back in the home country and I had a job where ten thousand dollars was expenses. But none of this was comforting. I thought of escape scenarios. I had money and a gun. I could bribe my way out. I constructed this elaborate mental image of me getting a car, driving on the left side of the road to Nana's house, speeding away with her in the passenger seat reloading my gun for me. Two helicopters criss-crossed the air above us and a sniper kept missing because of my fancy driving. Only one mile to the border. Nana grabbed the wheel and I twisted and shot upwards, hitting the gas tanks of the choppers, leaving them in balls of flames. Two bullets left, two border guards screaming at us to stop, Nigeria just minutes away. I shot them both in their necks and—

There was someone at the door.

Whoever it was had a key because I saw the light on the lock go red then green. The light came on and three armed men rushed in, shouting at me in Yoruba, heads covered in home-made masks. The three of them stood there, rifles trained on me. 'Weston Kogi?'

I nodded.

'Come with us,' said the nearest one.

'I have a gun,' I said.

The heavy-set one cocked his rifle. 'So do we.'

'No, I mean, I'm telling you that I have a gun so that you don't shoot me when you find it.' I pointed to my holster and waited on the bed while they removed it and searched me. When it became clear that I was cooperating, they stood at ease. They pointed their guns at the ceiling and we strolled out of the hotel. The clerk at the desk didn't even look up when we walked by, which in itself was frightening.

CHAPTER 7

We drove all night.

I sat in the back seat between two of the thugs, while one drove us. By the time the sun emerged, the kidnapper to my left snored loudly. They had taken off their masks, and it seemed reasonable to conclude that these were not Liberation Front foot soldiers because these actions weren't consistent with Church's plan for me. In the short time I had spent in Alcacia, this was the most polite abduction I had ever been involved in.

The road was narrow with the occasional pothole that would fling the car and all three of us off our seats and send the driver into peals of laughter. Even at this time of day the road was busy. We passed all-night coaches and bolekaja – modified Mercedes Benz 911 army trucks. They looked the same and were probably just as dangerous. Local mechanics gutted them, leaving only the driver's cab and engine, then replaced the back with a wooden compartment with benches designed to accommodate as many passengers as humanly possible. It was the cheapest form of fuel-based road transport in Alcacia. Riding in these death traps was a risky business. If you ever had a dispute, the hard-packed space didn't even leave room for a proper disagreement, hence the name bolekaja: *disembark and let us fight.*

There were horses, and the riders seemed to have a predilection for the middle of the road. The driver had to lean on the horn before they majestically inched to the side so we could overtake.

Then there were the police checkpoints – two five-foot barrels on both lanes where two or three tired-looking officers asked for 'particulars' but blatantly took bribes from passing motorists. Everybody in Alcacia seemed able to identify who the rebels were and we were waved past every single checkpoint.

Going by the rising sun, we were headed north-west, People's Christian Army territory.

The car slowed and found its place where other vehicles were already parked. Women fried akara in massive woks over wood or kerosene stoves on both sides of the road. My captors started pooling their money. To decide who had to do the buying, they sang:

> Mamy wata kekere kan to ko sinu omi,
> Mo n'so fun la t'owuro titi d'ojo ale,
> 'Dide soke, nu oju re nu,
> yi s'apa otun; yi s'apa osi,
> Mu eni keni to ba wun e o.'

> *Little mermaid who jumped into the water,*
> *I've been telling her all day,*
> *'get out of the water,*
> *wipe your eyes,*
> *turn right, turn left,*
> *and choose who you want.'*

It was a child's game and the snoring guy to my left lost. He looked like he was accustomed to losing.

The aroma of akara soon filled the car. They even got me some. We sliced open loaves of sweetened bread and seeded them with the akara. I was soon licking my fingers and not resenting the loss of liberty as much as I should have.

Late afternoon, we approached a collection of dwellings. It looked like a township on first glance, but there was no sign. The buildings on the outskirts were blasted, with only lizards and creeper plants living in them. Crowds of children played here and there, all holding brown paper bags and lacking footwear. Most only had on a long T-shirt which barely covered the patches of ringworm on their skin. Their ages ranged from about seven to eleven. I asked about the bags.

'Diesel,' said the man on my right.

'Some kind of drink?'

'No, it's a kind of fuel. They pour some in a can, place the can in a bag, inhale, sit back and get high.'

A few of the urchins ran alongside the car as we slowed. They laughed and sang, eyes bloodshot. Their Yoruba was mixed Igbo, Portuguese and French, and I could only understand it in a general sense. We drove through the main square where commerce reigned and the buying and selling of food seemed to be the main occupation. A Second World War era Russian tank dominated the area visually, tracks gone and the paint job a gaudy orange signifying who knows what.

There was a church – St Anselm's Catholic – although I was willing to wager there would be no nuns. A bare-chested Chinese man took about forty similarly clad soldiers through hand-to-hand techniques in the morning sun.

The people here were different from down south. They had a more ectomorphic physique than the endomorphic stature favoured in cities like Ede. Many sported deformed ears, but this was only the opinion of outsiders. Small ears were considered beautiful in this part of Alcacia, and mothers clipped off bits of their babies' ears soon after birth.

We stopped in front of a two-storey building with washing lines strung on balconies and several shoddy paint layers visible. The cement had cracked in various places. They ushered me up to the top floor and opened a flat for me.

'Don't try to run or you'll bump into patrols and vipers. If you avoid them, well, the nearest town is miles away in any direction, and they all belong to us.'

'What am I doing here?' I asked.

They smiled and left, after which I heard their boots thump down the stairs. I was in a dilapidated but clean lounge. I checked the single room; it was bare. There was a phone, but no dialling tone. I heard someone coming up so I sat on the sofa and feigned relaxation.

A tall man in a bespoke grey suit came in. He had very short hair, cropped like a carpet on his scalp. He was not sweating despite the stifling heat and the layers of fabric he had on. I envied him.

'Mr Kogi, my name is Abayomi. How d'you do?' We shook hands. 'I'm very pleased you can be here. I trust your trip was satisfactory?'

'Oh yes, the thrill of a potential gunshot wound always adds that extra bit of excitement to a journey.'

He smiled. 'Unfortunately some precautions are necessary in our line of business. We had no way of knowing if you would honour our invitation.'

'To the PCA headquarters?'

'Yes, that's right.' He seemed surprised.

'And do you, as they say, lead this rabble?'

'Lord, no. Mr Kogi, I am merely a facilitator. I also dabble in the multimedia communications for the Army.'

'You're a propaganda officer.'

'Some might call it that.'

'Tell me, Abayomi, why am I here?' I seemed to be asking everyone that. Soon I would sound like an amnestic Greek philosopher.

Abayomi produced a letter from the inside pocket of his jacket and gave it to me. It had a coat of arms that consisted of a sphinx soaring above a cross and a message that read: 'From the Office of the Supreme Commander of Our Lord's Forces'.

'You wrote this?' I asked as I tore open the envelope.

'Hey, I just make what they tell me legible,' he said. There was a certain weariness and self-mockery to his voice and manner. I decided I liked him.

Dear Mr Kogi,

Thank you for your blessed attempt to solve this most heinous crime, the murder of our beloved Pa Busi.

I shall pray for your continued success most fervently.

Whatever resources you may require, rest assured that the People's Christian Army will assist in any way. We will not rest until the true culprits are brought to swift and appropriate justice.

We are truly grateful for your impartiality in this matter. Please do not hesitate to contact me personally, should you require any assistance.

I remain yours in the Lord's service,

Field Marshall Abiodun Craig,

Supreme Commander, Our Lord's Forces, Alcacia

Instead of a signature there was a thumbprint. Perhaps he had lost his right arm in a battle.

'Hmm,' I said.

'In English,' said Abayomi, 'keep up your investigation, go through the motions and if you must find anything concrete, make sure it's the Front responsible for the kill. Then get the hell out.'

'I see.'

'No, you don't. But you will.' He took the letter and pocketed it.

'Did I have to be here to read this letter?'

'We wanted to get a look at you, and we wanted you to get a look at us. There are certain aspects to appraisal that require a personal appearance.'

'And now that you've seen me?'

'Sadly, that's for others to assess. I'm just the messenger.'

'When do I get to meet Supreme Commander Craig?'

'You don't. I'll take you to the canteen to eat. You can rest if you want, but a car will take you back to your hotel as soon as you're ready.'

'I'm not being detained?'

'We are not barbarians, Mr Kogi, regardless of what you may have heard.'

'Call me Weston,' I said. 'And let's see about that food.'

Abayomi was wrong: I did meet the Supreme Commander. I was seated next to the esteemed propaganda officer on a long wooden bench, eating iyan and spinach soup with goat's meat from beautiful china off a wooden table. We ate with our hands because it tasted better that way. My tongue was on fire because the Yoruba use the hottest chilli peppers in the world, forget what you've heard about India or that curry place in Southall.

As soon as I finished one mound of iyan, a lean uniformed woman would replace it and cast shy glances my way.

'I think she likes you,' said Abayomi.

'I'm spoken for.'

'So is she,' he said and laughed. 'Perhaps it's a good thing. If you taste her . . . iyan you probably wouldn't want to eat anything else for the rest of your life.'

I could do ribald, but all this talk made me think of Nana. She'd be worried about me by now, and I hadn't been able to phone her. 'I'm happy with my speaker, thanks,' I said. I burped. 'I can't eat any more.'

'That's all right.' He got up and went to speak to the woman who did the cooking. The dining hall was filled with tables and benches like the one we were sitting on. Four other patrons ate at the same time, all young men. My clothes made me stand out and they stole furtive glances at me. Compay Segundo played 'Chan Chan' on a loop from the most rudimentary speakers I had ever seen. On the walls of corrugated tin there were paintings of the various dishes on sale and a topless woman serving jolly patrons who all seemed to be facing the viewer and smiling in the manner of synchronised swimmers. There were posters on the wall as well. These were yellowed and some of them dated back to the 1970s. The largest one was of a startled white woman with big, blow-dried hair in a toilet, naked but for a pair of tiny panties, alarmed because a gorilla arm reached out from the toilet bowl and pulled on the panties from behind. I burped again and asked where the loo was.

Walking down a short narrow corridor, I experienced an increasingly pungent odour of urine. The loud buzzing of flies led me to the hand-painted 'Latrine' sign. The toilet was an avant-garde affair with a door much smaller than its frame. It hung by a single hinge on one side and a latch on the other. I knocked out of habit and unhooked the latch with two fingers.

From the outside the interior looked dark, but inside a single bulb hung from the ceiling next to a pull-switch. It shone grudgingly, light wavering as if it might go off at any minute. I slid home the bolt on the other side of the door with the same two fingers as before. The toilet bowl was porcelain (there was no seat), but it wasn't a water closet. There was no water level. Instead, there was a hole with a U-bend that led to a pit. The buzzing came from within said pit. Streaks of old shit outlined a path of faeces from the bowl to the final destination. No tissue paper in sight but to the left, as substitute, an ominous bucket of water with a ladle. Old fluid stains had warped and corroded the wooden floor over time. To my surprise, I didn't gag.

I undid my belt and was about to pull my trousers down when I heard loud banging behind me.

'Open up!' said a voice.

'I'm not finished,' I said in Yoruba.

'Open up, now!'

The door crashed open and into my back. I yelped brief outrage before I felt someone scuff me on the back of the head. Which I had had fucking enough of.

I kicked out behind me like a mule and spun around. He was there, lean in slimming black, narrowed eyes, no wrist watch, shaved head. He came for me in a boxer's stance, with hands raised. When he punched, I welcomed his fist into my space and grasped him at the forearm, stepped into his body and slammed my elbow into the centre of his chest. He clutched his chest and started coughing wildly, face crumpled like a wad of toilet paper. I was wondering whether to kick him in the gonads for good measure when I heard the flick of multiple safeties.

Three men pointed pistols at me, dressed like the one I had just hit and sporting similar hairstyles. I thought perhaps I should let them shoot because the way they were deployed, friendly fire was inevitable. A military man lurked behind them, decorated with epaulettes, faux medals, tassels, and the like. He had a patchy beard and a haughty look, with bland eyes lacking life or intelligence, or even malevolence.

'Take him outside,' he said, 'and burn him.'

This was, of course, Field Marshall Craig, and I was, of course, about to be grilled alive.

Abayomi appeared from behind and whispered urgently into Craig's ear. A few words filtered through to me, and a sharp *pas possible* from the Propaganda Man terminated my death sentence. Craig nodded. The men whom I presumed were his bodyguards moved away from me.

'Mr Kogi, you are welcome,' said Craig. 'Normally, nobody touches my bodyguards and lives, but I see your MI6 training has helped you overcome.'

'I'm not—'

'Your Excellency, I'm sure you are quite pressed. The toilet is free now,' said Abayomi. He came forward and pulled me by the arm. 'I also still have a few things to cover with Mr Kogi.'

'Very well. Carry on.'

Craig wore Chanel in copious amounts, and Abayomi pulled me though a cloud of it. The bodyguards shot me down several times in their heads. Back in the canteen, a heavy-set man sat in front of my plate, examining the remains of my iyan, tilting, sniffing. He wore short unruly plaits on his head. I was ready for him, blood still up from the previous confrontation, but Abayomi firmly guided me away, towards the exit.

Outside we watched fruit bats flying out of baobab trees, away from the sun, looking for food.

'You're not very bright, Weston,' Abayomi said finally.

'I'm lucky. I don't need to be bright.'

A car pulled up. Abayomi conversed with the driver and then pointed to the car. 'Your pumpkin.'

'What's your first name?' I asked.

'Abayomi Abayomi. It's a thing in my family. At least one male child has to have our surname as his forename.'

I settled in the back seat, rolled down the window. Abayomi handed me my gun and holster along with an envelope. 'Have you ever read *Ogboju Ode ninu Igbo Irunmale* by D. O. Fagunwa?'

'Vaguely remember reading it as a child. Everyone did. There's an English translation: *Forest of a Thousand Daemons* or something. Why?'

'In it the hero, Akara Ogun, goes through the enchanted forest and encounters various demons. I wrote a thesis on it in university. In this thing you're trying to do you are in a position not unlike that of Akara Ogun. A word to the wise: bright trumps lucky.'

'Perhaps,' I said. 'You do know your boy is a thug, right?'

'Some people only respond to thugs, Weston. Have a safe trip back.'

CHAPTER 8

There were twenty-two missed calls on my mobile, but I ignored them and phoned Nana.

'Hello?' Drowsy-sounding, but then, it was past midnight by the time I returned to the hotel.

'Nana?'

She yawned. 'Weston.'

'Hi.'

'People sleep at this hour, Weston.'

'I know. I'm sorry I didn't call earlier, but something happened.'

'I called the hotel. Didn't they tell you?'

'I just got in. There's only the night staff here and they probably don't know. Listen, I need you to come get me.'

'Okay. What time tomorrow?'

'Not tomorrow. Now. This instant.'

She laughed. 'Are you trying to make me hang up?'

'I'm serious, Nana. If you can't do it, tell me now so I can get a cab.'

'Calm down.' I heard bedclothes rustling and a lengthy yawn. 'Jesus, look at the time. You're going to pay for this. I have an exam in the morning.'

'Can you be here?'

'Give me forty minutes.'

She hung up. I checked my voicemails. They were all from

Church and demonstrated varying degrees of agitation and displeasure, a few threatening to decapitate me at the first opportunity. I called him back.

'Where have you been? I was worried,' he said.

'I went to see His Excellency Supreme Commander Abiodun Craig.' I forgot to add Field Marshall.

'That was fast,' Church said, not at all sounding surprised. 'I knew they'd want to talk to you, make sure you were neutral, but . . . tell me everything first.'

I did. Except I didn't mention the envelope that Abayomi gave me as I was leaving. That envelope contained fifteen thousand US dollars.

'You mixed it up with the Black Beret Brigade and lived. That's highly unusual. Craig's personal bodyguards were picked from all other forces for their brutality and fanatical dedication to the cause.' Church laughed. He was the only person I knew who was comfortable laughing to himself when in company. He didn't care that I didn't get the joke. When he caught his breath he said, 'You should be safe. We all want this murder solved so that we can go back to pushing their nyanshes back to Nigeria or Cameroon, whichever the fuck is more convenient.'

'I'll be in touch,' I said. 'I need to get some rest.'

Instead, I packed everything, strapped on my gun and waited for Nana. Soon, I got a text saying she was outside. I looked back at the room to check if I'd forgotten anything.

I used the stairs. From the lobby, I could see Nana outside in her Mercedes Benz. I placed my belongings on the floor and walked over to the dozing clerk.

I tapped the counter. 'Hey.'

'Hmm. Oh, hello, sir.' He was a kid. Neat hair, no chin fuzz, bloodshot eyes from interrupted sleep, face devoid of the lines of frustration. 'Can I help you?'

'Yes. I'm checking out,' I said. 'But I'm not checking out, you understand me?'

'I'm not quite sure what you mean, sir.'

I bent down, drew the gun and leaned its muzzle against the counter. With my other hand I spread out three twenty-dollar bills. 'As far as you're concerned, I'm still in my room and I was there all night. If they happen to *discover* my absence, it didn't happen on your watch.'

'I understand, sir.' He whisked away the money. He didn't look at the gun.

'What's your name?'

'Sulaiman, sir.'

'Sulaiman, I know you gave information to some . . . friends. This is one time you don't want to do that, s'o ngbo mi?' I wanted to be sure he got my drift.

'Mo gbo, sir.' *Understood.*

Maybe it wouldn't make any difference, but I felt better. For all I knew, he'd be on the phone the minute I drove off. I picked up my bags.

Nana's Afro was flat on one side. She looked tousled, beautiful and so completely concerned about me that I bent down to the window and kissed her hard on the lips. I felt tender towards her at that moment, like there was nothing else that mattered except her mouth on mine. Her breath tasted of saccharin and menthol from toothpaste. I felt her pull back and I opened my eyes.

'It's late, Weston. Get in the car or we'll be set upon by bandits.'

I waited a while. I could feel the pulse working on my neck. 'Thank you for coming to get me.'

She winked at me and popped the trunk. There was no moon, and the world beyond the splash of light from Nana's headlights seemed dark and forbidding.

'Don't worry, Weston,' she said when I got in. 'I will protect you.'

★ ★ ★

57

I don't remember the journey from the hotel into her arms that night. My spirit was tired and I drew comfort from her. She was wrapped in shadows and soft places, in smells of jasmine and musk, in silk and the road to Beulah Land.

The sun announced the day and illuminated a note on the pillow. Nana had gone for her exam but she'd be back immediately after. I could eat whatever I wanted, but best not to leave the flat. Three Xs. I smiled, pursed my lips in a kiss, fell back on the bed. The ceiling was patterned like a seashore, momentarily disorienting. Sand, seashells, starfish, seaweed, all above me.

There were two courses of action open to me: I could divert the considerable financial resources of the LFA and the PCA to finding a way out of this demented country or I could investigate the death of Pa Busi. I had zero curiosity about the old man's death. I literally did not give a fuck whether he stepped on a landmine by mistake or if his entourage staged an *Et tu, Brute*. From my brief interactions with the two factions, they didn't seem overly concerned with the solution, as long as the other side was found responsible. They were both paying me to find the other party guilty, which could mean either they were guilty or absolutely nothing. In other words, I couldn't infer anything from their actions or words.

So.

So, maybe they expected me to investigate indefinitely.

They could tell the press or their own people that an independent investigator, truly neutral – from London! – was looking into it. The story would die a natural death, and all involved could go back to casual genocide or whatever the hell it was that rebel factions did. All that would be required of me would be to go through the motions of an inquiry. If I could just stay alive in the process.

I thought of my life in London. No way would I be in possession of twenty-five thousand dollars, tax-free. I'd be stuck in a dank studio flat in Hammersmith, eating baked beans out of the can and watching reality television, wondering which uniform I should wear the next day to my impotent job at the supermarket where I'd have to watch crackhead shoplifters walk away with merchandise and do nothing. I'd phone Lynn once a month and pretend that it hadn't been six months since I last eyeballed her, take intoxicated women to bed or play emotion games with pseudo-Christian Nigerian girls looking for husbands or sperm-donors, take a series of useless courses at the Open University, telling myself it was improving my chances at self-advancement but knowing deep inside that I was marking time, waiting for my real life to begin. But this *was* my real life.

Jandon la wa yi. *This is London we live in.*

I'd need to organise some kind of identification, get whatever passed for a permit in Alcacia. Print business cards, something flashy to impress receptionists.

Thus, lying on the downiest pillows I had ever experienced in my life, I decided to take the job.

CHAPTER 9

I worked all morning, sorting through the data on Pa Busi, everything spread out on Nana's dining table. I had one pile for what was common, freely available knowledge garnered from newspaper clippings and such, one for restricted access information, and a final pile for conjecture and doodles. I needed to be convincing in case anyone enquired about my progress.

The ambient noise was disorienting. The faint buzz of mosquitoes trying to escape the flat after a hard night's bloodsucking, chickens clucking their hunger, two women arguing over conjugal rights with their shared husband, a few traders melodiously calling out their wares – Oyin l'adun osan: These oranges are sweet like honey.

This is what it looked like: Pa Busi, elder statesman of Alcacia, had been acting as peacemaker between warring rebel factions. The two major groups had arisen more or less simultaneously a decade ago at a time of particularly harsh economic hardship. The PCA appealed to the largely Christian populace, emphasising the godlessness of the current regime, but having no qualms about alliances with communist foreign powers for weapons and finance. The Liberation Front laid no claim to such lofty ideals. The original leader (revered, but rumoured to be HIV-positive and long since beheaded by Federal troops) cited the Baader-Meinhof Gang as inspiration. The Front seemed dedicated to mayhem. Pa

Busí was a conduit between these two steady thorns and an exasperated Federal Government. All three lived in an unsteady equilibrium but the extensive property damage, if anything, served to keep the government in power, and the defence budget tripled each year, favouring foreign powers who wished to sell the products of their death factories.

Then there was an incident that some say State Security engineered. PCA troops killed eleven unarmed LFA soldiers. PCA said the LFA fired first and, after killing them, stripped the LFA of their weapons, for the 'war effort'. This was when the rebels began to fight each other.

Recently, the battles and explosions had become bloodier and more sinister, with forced auto-cannibalism, rape and the ubiquitous ethnocide. One government official was quoted as saying, 'The enemy of my enemy in this case is still my enemy, but, by God, I love it when they cancel each other out like this!'

Public and international outcry led the government to start the INTERN-POL initiative, which was basically a death squad that ran seek-and-destroy missions against both rebel sides. Minor rebel groups based on flawed pseudo-Islamic ideologies were quashed within weeks and the major factions suffered heavy losses. The blood flowed wild and free.

Enter Pa Busi, who came out of retirement to serve his people one last time. As soon as he declared his intentions, Supreme Commander Craig declared an immediate ceasefire pending the conclusion of talks. The Front stopped all hostilities. They talked, they made progress on all items of discussion, and peace was in sight. But in neutral territory, during a time of relative peace, Pa Busi was blown up by unknown persons.

I went over the police reports and photos. It was dull, intensely dense technical prose that might make sense to an expert in ballistics or forensics. In summation, it came to this: an explosive, possibly a mine, detonated under the jeep carrying Pa Busi and his entourage. He survived long enough to crawl a short distance from the burning wreckage and died. All the other men in the jeep died, too. From shrapnel wounds.

I scribbled in my conjecture notes: *Why was there a mine in a so-called neutral zone? Talk to mortician. See post-mortem for occupants of jeep. Speak to witnesses. Unanswered questions: Who discovered the wreckage? What were the last communications on all the occupants' mobile phones?*

Next was a file that detailed Pa Busi's survivors. He had a young wife, his second. She was thirty years old and something of a local celebrity. Active in charities and civil rights right up until the death of her husband, after which she dropped from the public eye. I looked at her photo: exceptionally beautiful in a European way – clear, fair skin, pointed nose, large eyes with light-brown irises, slender, long hair straightened, mouth kept slightly open. She was heavily made-up, but in a good way, like the women we used to lust after in Indian films. I thought she might have some white blood a few generations back. Her name was Diane Olubusi.

Interview Diane Olubusi. Trace Pa Busi's finances. Children? First wife?

Nana announced her return with slamming doors and singing. I stopped scribbling and put the pen down since I was fatigued in any case. She fluttered into the dining room and beamed when she saw me.

'How was the exam?'

'Easy. A minus.'

'Sure?'

'Yes. Done it many times before.' She dropped her bags on the floor and urgently started unbuttoning her blouse. 'Now, come over here and fuck me.'

'I've been thinking about communication,' said Nana.

I sat on the floor of the dining room, against the wall, knees drawn up but parted. Nana was between my legs, back to me, resting her head on my arm which embraced her. I grunted, signalling her to continue.

'They say most of our communication is non-verbal, right? I hear seventy to ninety per cent. I'd like to know how they conducted the studies that yielded those results—'

'You're drifting.'

'Yes. I am. Are we in a hurry?'

I kissed her hair.

'That's what I thought.' She continued: 'So, if communication is mostly non-verbal, certain actions have to be considered the height of communication.'

'Such as?'

'Murder. Sex. Hugging. Spitting. Defenestration. Anything people do at crisis point. Critical mass action . . .' She leaped up and rummaged through her bag until she found a pencil and notepad. Then she wrote furiously, frowning but completely immersed in the moment. Her backside jiggled softly and she bit her lower lip and dogs fought outside the window and I loved her.

'How is it that you're this intelligent, yet you keep failing the exam you went for?'

'I have never failed an exam,' said Nana.

'But you said—'

'I said I'd taken it many times, not that I'd ever failed it.'

'You know, it's strange,' I said, 'I could have sworn this conversation started out in Yoruba. Now it's in gibberish.'

'Weston does sarcasm!' She stopped writing and came back to me. 'I take examinations for people in the universities. And some of the polytechnics. For money.'

'You impersonate students in exams?'

'I also write theses, term papers, essays and miscellaneous assignments, yes.'

'Does it pay well?'

'You have no idea. I've been living off this for a while.'

'What courses do you specialise in?'

'Anything at all.'

'Examples?'

'History, literature, physics, advanced maths, philosophy. You name it, I've done it. I've done pre-med twice.' She twisted around and looked into my eyes. 'I know everything. I have a third eye and it sees all.'

She did know everything; she always had.

'You have no ethical problems with that?' I asked.

'Do you?'

'I'm not sure.'

'It's Alcacia, Weston. It's survival. I have a lot of raw information in my head. I can tell you about the October Revolution or the Treaty of Utrecht, or recite all the monologues of *King Lear*, but the difficult bit is toning it down, tailoring it to the academic level of the clients. I have to make it look hard. I have to add errors of grammar and syntax. That part of it is exhausting.' She turned back and continued jotting on the pad.

'But your hard work goes unrecognised. Doesn't that matter to you?'

'In what sense?'

'You do the work, but others get the glory. You're a ghost writer. Wouldn't you rather have your own name on an essay or book or . . . I don't know, win some prizes? Isn't this a kind of half-life?'

'The last time I cared about shit like that was my first year of university. I started what I thought would be the first of many degrees. For my term paper I wrote an eight-thousand-word essay titled "I, Rastafari", which was an examination of the sociocultural effects of the black African Diaspora on the adopted identity of the individual on the Caribbean Islands. It was brilliant. My professor said it was years ahead of what someone of my experience should be writing. He said I'd easily graduate with a first. And then he stood up from behind his desk, dropped his trousers and asked me to fellate him.'

'What?'

'Don't be shocked, Weston. It's really quite rampant. Nobody bats an eyelid at these things any more. Even crusty old academics have to get obo somehow. I never liked formal education anyhow. Too prescriptive; too restrictive.'

Nana always complained about school when we were younger. She read more than anyone I had ever known before or since, but nothing relevant to school work. When we first met, she was reading an astrophysics textbook that she barely understood. She was twelve. I was thirteen and completely fucked up from my family being torn to bits and my mother's recent death. I was the new boy at school since I had just moved to Aunt Blossom's house. I remember sitting by myself at lunch for weeks. One day, she came and sat next to me, holding a book that strained her forearm muscles. 'Are you retarded?' She nudged me. 'People say you don't talk to anyone because you're retarded.'

And that was how we began to talk.

Evening.

The unholy ball of fire in the sky had retreated far enough that I didn't feel scorched, sweaty or scared. Brave, pioneer mosquitoes had started buzzing about. Nana made some eba, and we ate on the veranda.

'It can be done,' said Nana. 'Just takes cash.'

'I have cash.'

'Okay, but then there are still delays. You can't just walk into the ministry and ask for a private detective licence. There are forms to be filled, procedures to be performed, clearances. You must be stamped, triplicated, filed. You must lose your head and get angry at least once. You must experience the bureaucracy and the bureaucracy must experience you.'

'Can't I bypass that with more cash?'

'Maybe a whole lot of it, more than your sponsors are willing to pay. It's better if you know someone.'

The soup was spinach, tomato paste, red peppers, red onions, palm oil and stock fish sold so dry that you had to saw it into pieces before softening it with boiling water. I licked my fingers and asked for the washing bowl. When I had cleaned and dried my hands, I phoned Abayomi Abayomi.

'Akara Ogun!' he said into the phone. 'How goes the demon-slaying? Still feeling lucky?'

I watched Nana clear the dishes against my hand-gesture protests. 'Very much so. Listen, d'you know anyone at the Ministry of Justice?' I explained the problem. He gave me a name but could not talk much afterwards. We exchanged pleasantries and he was gone.

Nana said, 'Do you want to see something cool?'

Dogs howled at the full moon, took a break, then howled some more. People came out on raffia mats, deckchairs and carved stools. Children ran around the central wood-fed fire, squealing their delight and roasting wild mushrooms on dirty sticks. Wasps, sand flies, stick insects, confused termites and other arthropods flew into the flames for one shining moment before dying. Chickens roosted on rooftops or the low branches of surrounding trees. Sheep clustered together, chewing regurgitated grass and warily observing everything.

An old man told stories of Ijapa, the tortoise, considered the most cunning of animals in Yoruba folklore, but often unlucky in his schemes. The old man wore a soft fila on his head and sat serenely on a black stool, his voice a soft monotone that

threatened to send me to sleep. He was skinny, asthenic enough
to be painful to look at, his face riddled with wrinkles. I wondered how old he was. His stories were familiar and comforting.
There were no surprise endings. Many of his sentences were
completed by others and garnished with laughter from all.
Children sat cross-legged on the ground, adults knelt or stood.
Nana and I listened from the edge of the circle.

I whispered to Nana, 'This is nice and quaint. It warms my
heart several times over. But I don't see—'

'Shh. Just wait till the end.'

The old man finished with a tale of Ijapa tricking a whole
village into staying awake all night by telling them the moon was
actually the sun, only very pale and sick. By this time, many of
the children were asleep and mothers carried them away. As the
listeners dispersed, Nana and I approached.

'Papa,' said Nana, 'might we see?'

He nodded.

'Put some money in his hand,' Nana said to me, and I gave him
ten dollars, wondering what I was paying for.

The old man took off the fila and leaned towards us, showing
his bald head.

He wasn't bald. A large sheet of scar tissue covered his crown,
an unusual smoothness broken only by a bishop's fringe of white
hair at the margins.

'Accident?' I asked.

'No,' said Nana, who had obviously seen it before. 'This man
was scalped.'

'Where? How?'

'Papa, tell us your story, please,' said Nana. To me she said, 'Give
him more money.'

He first took water from a canteen beside his stool, wiped his
mouth with the back of his hand and exhaled. He had no teeth;
just gums and a glistening tongue. This close, I could see every

blood vessel crawling over the whites of his eyes. He began to speak in Yoruba with the same unaffected monotone with which he had delivered the moonlight tales.

'I was fifteen years old, an apprentice roof mender working with my father. The village prospered in those days. The Por-tu-gii developed it because of the gold mine that had served them for years. Usually, only about a dozen of them stood around with their guns and slaves who carted the gold to the coast. They were so selfish that they even made slaves shower so that the gold dust would not benefit the families who had lost the right arm of a son. Is that not evil? Does not the Book say, *Thou shalt not muzzle the ox when he treadeth out the corn*?'

'It does, Papa,' said Nana.

'One day, marauders invaded the village, slaughtered the Por-tu-gii and stole all the gold. They took a few of the young women, but they left most of the villagers alone. Slaves escaped and the marauders scattered into the forest to neighbouring encampments. After seven days, new Por-tu-gii arrived. They scourged us for the massacre, for letting it happen. For each dead white man, they scalped every tenth male in the tribe, as evidence of retribution. They would have killed us all, but they needed slaves.'

'And you survived this?' I asked.

He looked at me with sad eyes. 'Never stand between a white man and gold.'

We were mostly silent on the way back home, Nana and I. I thought of the things I'd heard.

'What a lonely man he must have been,' I said.

'Lonely?'

'Yes, with the scar and all . . .'

'You're kidding, right? He's outlived two wives and has tons of children and grandchildren. People say he was marked by the gods for survival, so they want a piece of that. It's like the mark of Cain: nobody can kill him, no disease afflicts him. Plus, he makes a lot of money from tourists showing off his absent scalp. I mean, he's sweet, and it's a shame what happened to the village men eighty-odd years ago, but the fucking Portuguese did him a favour.'

My phone rang. It was Church. I didn't quite feel like speaking to him or explaining why I wasn't at the hotel. I sent the call to voicemail and powered the phone down.

CHAPTER 10

The Ministry of Justice was situated in an ugly brutalist building that seemed to have been designed with the sole purpose of making supplicants feel unwelcome. Each layer of security required a swipe card and created delays for visitors. I finally arrived in a waiting room where I was to see a man called George Elemo, Abayomi's man.

I waited in an antiseptic room, white, and surveilled by a rude camera in the exact centre of the ceiling, one of those black hemidomes that look like the eye of God. I hated not knowing who was looking at me or recording my image but, living in London, the city with the most cameras per person in the world and the spiritual inspiration for Big Brother, I was used to it. Orwell was right.

Elemo came in and sat next to me without saying a word. He was a slight, fair-skinned man who wore delicate glasses and looked nervous. This was misleading because he was all confidence when he began to speak.

'Payment,' he said.

I paid him two hundred American dollars, which he counted.

'Documents.' He gave me a bundle of papers.

I checked. It had a licence drenched in grandiloquent language, the bottom line of which was that I could operate within the borders of Alcacia as a private operative. It had the name and number of a police liaison officer as well as a badge.

'If, in the process of an investigation, you uncover a crime, you are obliged to report it. Should the police require information from you about a case, my advice is that you give it to them. Otherwise, your annual renewal will not happen.'

'I see.'

'If anyone asks you, it took two months to get your licence.'

'But I've only been in country for a few days.'

'Then you asked a friend to apply for you because you are a forward-thinking individual.'

Did Mr Terse just crack a joke?

'That's it. Go. I do not want to be seen with you.'

I pointed to the camera.

'I switched it off beforehand. Goodbye, Mr Kogi. I don't want to see you again.'

While waiting for a taxi I called Church.

'Where have you been? I thought you'd been taken again,' he said.

'No, I left the hotel, but I'm fine. Listen: do you have the details of the mortician who spruced up Pa Busi?'

'Yeah. Hold on.' There was a short delay. 'Here. His name is Olaf Johansson. He's back in America. Here's the number . . .'

I wrote it down and hung up on Church just as he was constructing questions about my whereabouts. I wanted him off balance for a while.

A taxi arrived and I got in. It had two amazingly life-like plastic testicles dangling from the rear-view mirror.

'Where to, Oga?' said the driver.

'A place to shop for men's clothes.'

'Designer wear? I have a cousin who can—'

'I really don't care. I just want to buy some clothes.'

He shrugged and turned up his akpala music and started singing along. I phoned Nana. It went to voicemail. I thought of calling Olaf What's-his-face but I wasn't sure about the time difference. It felt like the humid air was slowly steaming me.

'You must be an Englishman,' the driver said.

'Why do you say that?'

'Oh, that's easy. You're not chatty, and your Yoruba is . . . slow. Tourist?'

'Hmm.' I had to be vague. The less these people knew the better. The traffic slowed and I signalled one of the kids selling bottled water.

'I wouldn't do that,' said the driver.

'Why? I'm thirsty.'

'Yes, but you'll get cholera from this "pure" water.'

Three Area Boys walked in front of the car, all in large sunglasses and sleeveless white shirts. One of them banged on the bonnet. The driver bowed meekly. They sneered at us, perhaps considering whether to cause more trouble. They were everywhere, ubiquitous like moss, like weeds, like dandruff.

I had been so engrossed in my spanking new papers that I didn't keep an eye on our progress. Instead of heading for the shopping district, we seemed to be passing through a low-income residential area. The roads were bumpy, untarred, with deep, mud-filled gutters on both sides.

'Driver, where are we going?'

'To buy clothes now. Like you said.'

'This doesn't look like the way.'

'We're going to my cousin, remember?'

The houses flattened to single-storeys, lost paint jobs, became shanties. People stood or squatted on roofs staring at me as the taxi trundled past. I saw a man slice open the neck of a chicken, then dip the carcass in boiling water while it was still twitching. Steam rising off it, he plucked the feathers off skilfully. The children in the red dust were all barefoot and the adults who were shod wore thongs. The flat, hard-packed ground was only interrupted by the occasional banana tree, clustered around yards but never near dwellings. The Yoruba believe witches slumber in the branches at night.

I knew this place. It was called Ileri and everything I'd heard about the district was bad. I was therefore not entirely surprised when the taxi driver stopped between two shacks, turned around and pointed a gun at my head.

Careless.

They stripped me down to my boxer shorts and I faced a corner in a room that had held other prisoners. I knew this because of the human jawbone on the floor.

The taxi driver did, in fact, have a cousin. They argued with each other behind me, trying to decide whether to kill me. I hadn't brought my own gun because it wouldn't have made it past the metal detectors in the ministry. They had taken my phone. I hadn't memorised any numbers, so even if I escaped somehow, I wouldn't be able to phone for help. They had taken about a thousand dollars plus change. They had taken my private investigator papers because they looked like they would be worth something on the black market.

It was opportunistic bullshit. I had made myself a target by acting like a visitor, an original JJC, Johnny Just Come, asking to be taken to a shopping centre, not caring where, talking like money was no object, careless.

Ileri was so notorious that the police never came in except

during the most violent of military coups, and even then, only to hide out till the rampaging soldiers lost their bloodlust.

Careless and stupid.

They beat me twice with bamboo sticks and electrical cables and fists. My face felt lumpy, I could still see out of my left eye but only partially from the right. I had lost a molar and a few caps. The first time I fought back, but this was futile and stirred them into a frenzy. They made me take off my boxers and threatened me. They were going to kill me. I had skirted death around the most murderous rebels, only to be killed by petty criminals with a grudge against affluence.

I was afraid and they knew it. They whispered to each other, wondering what to do next. They made international calls on my mobile. The taxi driver called Antigua. He said he didn't even know anyone in Antigua. They charged other people to use the phone, and a queue formed. Children came into the room to stare, slack-jawed. They left, giggling.

The criminals decided that since I was so fresh from England, I must have relatives in Alcacia with some money to pay a ransom.

'Who do you wish to call to bail you out?' said the taxi driver, pointing the gun at me. 'If they pay a reasonable amount, you'll be gone in no time.'

'Churchill,' I said.

I could not understand some of their behaviour. One man spent an entire hour prodding me with a stick. Not a sharpened one, just a regular stick broken off a tree somewhere. It did not hurt, but I could not relax because I wondered what the point was and when the more harmful implements would come out. He went away without saying anything.

The taxi driver returned with his cousin.

In laboured English, the cousin said, 'Weston Kogi, you are going to die and I am going to have to get rid of your body. We don't personally mean you any harm. We are just making wolf.'

Making wolf? What the fuck was making wolf?

'Weston Kogi, turn around.'

I did. The taxi driver shoved my mobile phone in my face. 'Speak.'

'Hello?' I said.

'You bastard,' said Churchill. Different from usual, softer. 'Have they harmed you?'

'Nothing permanent.'

'Hold on,' he said. 'I'm coming. Give the phone to that mother-loving whoreson.'

They discussed terms while I tongued my broken teeth and swallowed my own blood. Soon, they left me alone again.

It is possible to sleep standing up.

They did not water or feed me. I pissed on the ground and watched it sink into the earth. Flies investigated my vicinity but left unimpressed.

'It means you are not dead, yet,' I said to myself aloud, but with the dryness of my throat and the shreds that were left of my lips, my voice sounded like a croak.

Hours passed, or maybe minutes. It was hard to tell.

The taxi driver's cousin came in with a stool, waving the lone revolver around for emphasis.

'Do you like Jill Scott?' he asked, but I could tell it was rhetorical. 'Big woman. So, so beautiful. Hips like that would go all night.'

He went on.

I collapsed, but woke up with him whacking the pistol handle against my skull.

'Wake up, wake up, do not die yet. You are money, hot money. Owo gbona. Are you still alive? Stand up!'

I stood and faced my corner, feeling more warm fluid drip down my neck. I wanted to die from the pain and humiliation, and to deprive them of the ransom.

I heard a door open, and the taxi driver's cousin said, 'I—' After which there was a loud report. For a few seconds I thought he had shot me, but as I wasn't bleeding any more than before, I turned around.

In the fading light I saw Church standing over the corpse of the taxi driver's cousin, now headless because Churchill's shotgun had atomised whatever existed above the neck stump. The red mess spread in a fan pattern on the wall away from Church. He turned to me, but I couldn't make out his expression.

'I'm here to liberate you,' he said. 'I'm your fucking Statue of Liberty, you bastard. Come with me.'

'Bullet holes are freckles on the neck of Lady Liberty,' I said.

'What?'

'Nothing.' I staggered after him.

CHAPTER 11

I had to spend some time in hospital. Nothing elaborate, just a couple of weeks for X-rays, some dental and maxillofacial work, lots of painkillers. I discovered an allergy to all opium derivatives, which was a shame because the first dose gave me such absorbing hallucinations for hours on end, along with delayed but near-fatal anaphylaxis.

I didn't see Nana while I was in hospital because Churchill was there. I wanted to keep them separate for as long as possible. Churchill should be filed under 'Creatures That Go Bump in the Night'. There must have been terrible portents the night before he was born. He didn't tell me what transpired that night when he dragged me out of Ileri, but I read the newspapers over the next couple of days and wondered if he acted alone or with foot soldiers. Two-thirds of Ileri was burned to the ground. I don't think it was his intention but the shanties were too close together. The fire swept quickly through the district before being stopped by a natural firebreak where the ground dipped too steeply to build on. Church shot the four members of the taxi driver's family he could find. The newspapers mentioned that the victims who died from gunshot wounds were related, but the reason was a mystery to them. The phrase 'police are baffled' was used liberally. I felt complicit, but pleased, and then disgusted with myself.

I had had enough. I took the gun with me everywhere,

including the shower. I was prepared to use it, too. No more hilarious kidnappings.

We were all just making wolf.

Nana's house.

Nana had changed her hair while I was in hospital. She wore these long braids that reached down to the middle of her back. Each lock was garlanded with multicoloured beads that clicked against each other when she moved. When she spun around she sounded like a Geiger counter.

'You're beautiful,' I said.

'Is that all you can say? I'm more than beautiful.'

'You're right. Words are inadequate to capture your essence.'

The loudest parts of an argument from the flat below came in through the open window. It was the man with two wives again. One of the wives had gonorrhoea but nobody owned up to how she got it. I just hoped the wet, smacking sounds were the wife beating on her own chest in proving her innocence and not the husband meting out swift and bloody punishment. Most likely, the husband brought it to the household.

The phone rang, an international call: Olaf Johansson. Good a time as any to get back on the horse of detection.

'I understand you've been looking for me,' he said. I'd expected a kind of Eurotrash accent, not Tennessee by way of Manhattan.

'Yes, Mr Johansson. I understand you're the mortician who worked on Mr Olubusi after his tragic death.'

'Funeral director.'

'Excuse me?'

'The preferred term is funeral director. And, yes, I did the restoration on Mr Enoch Olubusi.'

I stroked my gun while I thought about what to ask him. 'Did you find anything odd?'

'Could you be more specific? With Mr Olubusi in fifteen separate and badly burned parts, it would be easier to discuss what wasn't odd.'

'Tell me what you had to do, then.'

He sighed. 'I flew in first class. I was a bit put out because they did not give me time to bring my own materials. I had to work in a government facility, a teaching hospital. There was this major in the room with me all the way through. I started work, which was essentially reconstructing Olubusi from scratch using photographs and video recordings as source material. There was nothing left after the fire. Just a very good skull, which provided an excellent template, I must say, despite the exit wound. Most of—'

'Hold on, Mr Johansson. Did you say "exit wound"?'

'Yes.'

'In the skull? You're saying he was shot in the head?'

'I'm sorry, what agency did you say you work with again? I assumed you were part of the investigative team.'

I explained who I was. He ruminated for a bit.

'I counted five puncture wounds that I thought might be bullet wounds: one on the skull, the rest on the abdomen. Various other wounds could have been shrapnel, but I'm not a medical examiner. I recovered one deformed bullet and some suspicious fragments. The major took these from me and asked me to forget about it.'

'Do you have any idea when he was shot, before or after the blast?'

'Mr Kogi, I don't think the blast killed him. I wrote a strongly worded letter to the government asking for a full investigation, but you know how these things go.'

'Hang on. If the explosion didn't kill him, how do you explain him crawling out of the jeep afterwards?'

'He did not crawl, Mr Kogi. He was carried. I could see places

81

where the skin had separated during the lifting. But you're talking to the wrong person. Perhaps you want to talk to the witnesses, his bodyguards and such.'

'They were all killed in the attack,' I said.

'Were they?'

'They weren't?' asked Nana, while starting the car.

'Apparently not. There were two survivors,' I said. I checked the magazine on my gun before applying the seat belt.

'Hmm. How is it that this never leaked, though? I mean, we know how often the Head of State uses Viagra, but no one knows that Pa Busi was shot or that a couple of his bodyguards survived?' She shifted into first gear. 'Where to?'

I recoiled. She reminded me of the taxi driver saying 'Where to, Oga?' and I found myself leaning away from her into the passenger door, feeling again the punches and kicks and beating. Shaking, unable to stop, until she placed a hand on my cheek.

'It's Nana,' she said. '*I, who have loved you; I, who have washed your face with water and blood. Be calm, Akande, my soul speaks to yours.*'

I was amazed that she could remember. *Akande* was my oriki, my praisename, which is a kind of poem each Yoruba has that speaks directly to his or her spirit or soul. Mothers use them to quieten squalling babies.

'You still know that?' I said.

She nodded, stroking my face. 'What's our destination?'

'Arodan.'

Arodan was a village in south-west Alcacia, about an hour's drive from Ede, population about ten, fifteen thousand. This was before I was born. In 1963, something happened there and it just dried up overnight. All the inhabitants disappeared. Some of the buildings showed slight structural damage, but otherwise they were all intact. Arodan featured in an episode of *Arthur C. Clarke's Mysterious World* in 1981, and there was still no explanation that didn't involve alien abduction or Roswell-style secret government experiments.

When proposals came for a new asylum in 1970, Arodan was the natural choice, and paradoxically a town sprang up around the asylum as a kind of support system for the families of those who worked there. Arodan lived again.

'Once upon a time, there was a witch in my village, a very wicked one, and she died. Natural causes. Most unfair. For days afterwards travellers reported seeing her at the intersection of footpaths where she would beat them up and drink some of their blood. The elders finally ordered the young men of the village to exhume her body, chop it into little pieces and scatter them over a wide area for the birds of the air and the beasts of the field to eat. After that, the sightings stopped,' said Nana.

'Okay,' I said. 'Why are you telling me this?'

'I'm just saying: strange things happen.'

'Like whole villages disappearing without a trace.'

'Yes.'

'You know, it's entirely possible that the real culprit saw the desecration of the witch's body and decided to stop.'

'Yes, it's possible, and even probable, but nobody's going to believe that, Weston. It's not a good story.'

Journeys in Alcacia were all the same. I had never noticed this when I was young. You left a conurbation and experienced hypnotic green sameness for a time, and then you got to the next human settlement. With Arodan the difference was in the ruins of the old village. The buildings were there, falling apart, deserted. Even forest fauna left it alone. I stared as we drove past, a touristy sign proclaiming it as Old Arodan. The houses reminded me of the kind of sun-bleached bones you find in deserts. None of them had roofs, and any colour had long since succumbed to the elements. One hut stood away from the rest.

'A hermit,' said Nana when I asked her. 'Or a witch, or a leper, or a man enamoured of *Walden*, which he read while on a scholarship to America. Or a lunatic.'

The Arodan Asylum dominated the view because of its size and also because it was built along the lines of similar Victorian-era establishments and was therefore different from all the structures around. About a mile to the place, the road straightened and turned to grey-blue gravel. The walls of the asylum loomed, and I estimated the drive would take a few minutes.

'Prepare your engines of war,' said Nana.

'We're not here to make war. We're here to solicit information. I plan to be obnoxious.'

'Oh, fun. Can I be obnoxious too?'

'As long as you do it in the car park. You're not coming in with me.'

'Weston—'

'I don't want anyone to see or remember you,' I said, and she went quiet. I needed to get the courage to drive on Alcacian roads in order to keep her out of my business. I sometimes thought of what would have happened if she had been with me on that taxi ride and shivered.

The walls of the asylum were like twelve, thirteen feet high with impressive barbed-wire decorations. We drove through a freestanding horseshoe arch before reaching the gate where two men smoked and casually waved us along. I guess they figured if we had driven this far we had to have legitimate business in the asylum.

We parked. Nana started reading Julian Jaynes, possibly sulking. I kissed her cheek.

'Are you going to be okay?' I asked.

'I have knowledge,' she said. 'I have been studying so much that knowledge is dripping from my pores. I have wisdom breath. I have erudition-meme-bomb farts. My gonads are pulsing with education. I have datavision and information-snot. Yes, I am going to be okay.'

My girlfriend is strange beyond belief.

No CCTV cameras, no warnings absolving the organisation of blame should the car be broken into. A few other cars parked in no particular order. I suppressed a brief impulse to turn back and invite Nana along. I opened large mahogany doors and 'California Dreamin'' hit me, The Mamas & the Papas. Just hearing the song made me think of the sun, blonde Californians on a beach, hippies, weed, bongs, flower power and, strangely, Bruce Lee.

Short walk to reception. No sign of the mentally ill, just a woman with cornrows behind a counter ticking boxes on a tete sheet. A gambler. I wondered what sporting event she was plac- ing her bet on. She didn't look the sort when I tried to picture her in one of those tete halls scattered all over poorer districts.

She looked up at me, frowned briefly, then brightened up. 'Eka 'san, o. Can I help?'

I returned the greeting in Yoruba and told her who I was, flashing the badge like it meant something, allowing her to fondle it and to extract the fifty dollars folded within.

'I need to see a patient called Afolabi Akinrinde. I also want photocopies of all his psychiatric records. I need this right now.'

'Records are confidential, Oga.'

'So am I. My job requires me to be confidential. Do you want to see how confidential I can be?' I showed her confidentiality in the form of an extra fifty dollars.

She put down her tete. Her badge identified her as Bola, Reception Assistant. She narrowed her eyes. 'You're a Holloway Baby, aren't you?'

'I don't like to talk about it.'

'I do. The whole topic fascinates me. There was a documentary on it a year ago where they gathered all the living Holloway Babies under one roof.'

I remembered that. I did not know how they found out my address, but they sent me stuff. Invitation, first-class air ticket, five hundred dollars non-refundable expenses. All to participate in a freak show. I returned it all.

'Do you like talking about menstruation to total strangers? Not the general science of it but your own periods, the kind of tampons you use, the accidents that lead to the staining of your favourite jeans. Do you?'

She shook her head and looked at me with distaste.

'I do. The whole topic fascinates me. D'you know, if three or more women live in the same building their periods synchronise? Of course you do. It's probably happened to you, right?'

After that, she fell silent and went through a database on the screen in front of her. She twisted her mouth to one side and poked a little finger into her right nostril while she worked.

'What do you prefer to do first? See the patient or the documents?'

The documents would probably provide context and help me understand Afolabi better, and I told Bola this. She took me to a reading room devoid of any personal touch whatsoever. Desk, seat, telephone, filing cabinet, all polished metal except the phone. The walls were white and bore not even a calendar. There was no window, and light came from fluorescent tubes on the ceiling. They hummed like lightsabres in *Star Wars* films. Presently, Bola came in with several files.

'When you're done, pick up the receiver. You don't have to say anything.' She left. I began to read.

The earliest files did not identify Afolabi by name. There was a number: 56232. Every page had the seal of the Federal Government, indicating the need for secrecy. The censorship and medical jargon conspired against my full comprehension of the first few folders. I could tell that Afolabi sustained serious injuries during the assassination, injuries from which he was not expected to survive. The family had already been notified of his death during what was thought to be a terminal coma. Afolabi did not die. Ten days after the event, he started breathing spontaneously. In a month he was opening his eyes and attempting speech. Within six months he was ambulant, though violently psychotic. It was determined that Afolabi could not live independently because of associated brain damage. When his physical wounds healed, the government dispatched him to Arodan.

There was no mention of Pa Busi in the files. There were allusions to Afolabi's military background, especially on the risk assessment forms surrounding his violent outbursts. In the first few weeks of his stay, he hospitalised seven nurses despite being narcotised with bucketloads of very serious chemicals. He appeared to go through alternating periods of quiescence and excitement. Later assessments held the opinion that he might not be psychotic at all but had just sustained damage to his frontal lobe, whatever that meant. I wrote it down for Nana to explain it to me later.

There were no transcripts of analysis; there *was* no analysis or therapy. The documents did not help much, especially with random parts redacted. There were seventeen pages that had been entirely blacked out. I had to see the man himself.

Afolabi Akinrinde had transmogrified into a mountain of soft fat.

From his file I already knew he was over six feet and in his youth had won kickboxing trophies. The man before me could barely breathe, and did so in intermittent wheezes and with all the drama of an Olympic weightlifting event. His head was inexpertly shaven. His eyes were pits because of the fat of his cheeks. He drooled saliva constantly from open lips and, at intervals, the nurse who watched over him would dab a cloth across his mouth. He had large scars around the head and face that I thought probably came from the explosion and surgery. The tunic of his pyjamas held wet food stains and ballooned out over his gut, which was the largest I had ever seen. Each movement made him look like a fluid-filled sac rather than a being of flesh, blood and bone. He stank of excrement and fermented sweat. His left hand shook, and he would reach across his double-wide chest with his right hand to still it at times.

His nurse, a Nigerian man with a hostile face, stared at me like I had disturbed an interesting and no doubt sexual dream to which he would like to return.

'Mr Akinrinde,' I said. I sat two feet across from him.

He did not respond.

'Mr Akinrinde, my name is Weston Kogi, and I'm a detective. Can you hear me?'

'He can hear you,' said the nurse.

'I'm talking to Mr Akinrinde,' I said. 'Please let him respond.' *And shut the fuck up.* 'I would like to talk about Pa Busi.'

He looked at me then, the whites of his eyes barely visible within the dark, comma-shaped holes of his fat face, and it was like being gazed upon by a Buddha, but without the serenity or mirth. I had registered on his consciousness, but he still wasn't talking.

'Do you remember anything about the day he was killed?'

Akinrinde took a deep breath and exhaled blowhole fashion, aerosolising saliva in the process. He frowned, facial muscles straining to shift the adipose. He opened his mouth, and a cough came out. He put his fist to his chest, burped and tried again. He said, 'I have tried everything, and only nothing works.' Droplets of spit flew from his mouth and landed on my face. I resisted the urge to wipe them away.

'Can you try to remember what happened?' I said.

'I do remember. Nothing works.'

I looked at the nurse, but he only shrugged.

'The contingent consisted of four agents,' Akinrinde said in a crisp, clear voice that surprised both me and the nurse.

'Idris Wallace, Antoine Adebowale, Junior Alao and myself. Idris was a special agent, and we were instructed to follow his lead.

'We bivouacked in the Imperial Hotel, six hundred yards from the subject's residence, the evening before. Adebowale and I did several sweeps of the surrounding streets while Alao familiarised himself with the vehicle we would be using. At oh eight hundred hours the next day, we relieved the night detail, which consisted of one agent.' He stopped to swallow spit. It occurred to me that he thought this was a debriefing.

'There was no heightened security? No alert about threats against his life?'

'Negative. The four agents were there because of his negotiations with the rebel factions. He planned to make a journey into territory that was considered hostile. At oh nine hundred hours the subject entered the vehicle, and we set off.'

'Destination?' I was taking notes at a demonic speed.

'The People's Christian Army camp. It was a relatively low-risk time. There was no active conflict and most combatants respected the ceasefire. Intelligence suggested that it was a safe period in a difficult zone. There was no chatter and we were not expected. The journey was uneventful. The subject insisted on stopping for akara at thirteen thirty-two hours.'

My mouth watered as I remembered my own experience of the savoury snack. 'Thirteen thirty-two exactly? Not thirty-one or thirty-four.'

'Thirteen thirty-two. I checked.'

'I see. Did Pa Busi . . . the subject, did he seem tense? Fearful?'

'Negative. He was calm, cheerful, looking forward to engaging the rebel leadership in dialogue. He started a discussion with Wallace, but the rest of us remained silent as per protocol.'

'What did they discuss?'

'Philosophy. *The Meditations*. Bertrand Russell. Others whom I cannot remember.'

'Was it a heated discussion?'

'Negative. There was a lot of laughter. Special Agent Wallace was diplomatic and obsequious.'

Which he seemed not to approve of. I wondered what else he thought of Wallace.

'Had you known Special Agent Wallace for long?'

'Negative. I met him for the first time three days prior. He was involved in selecting the personnel for the assignment.'

'Did he mention why he selected you?'

'Negative.'

'What did you think of him?'

'He was a competent—'

'Personally. What did you think of him personally?'

His face crumpled up and he appeared to be on the verge of apoplexy. Maybe he didn't want to break discipline and speak against a superior officer.

'Disregard the question. What happened next?'

'At sixteen hundred hours Agent Alao lost control of the vehicle and veered off the road into a ditch.'

'Sixteen hundred hours on the dot?'

'Affirmative.'

There was no mention of that in the official report, which was now taking on the appearance of a whitewash. 'Continue.'

'There were two gun reports. One high-velocity rifle, one handgun. The handgun was inside the vehicle, but I did not observe who fired because of the explosion. I can tell you that the subject was hit on the trunk. This ends the report.'

'Afolabi, are you saying your people returned fire when you heard the shot?'

'Negative. I am saying one of the persons inside the jeep shot the subject.'

Nana was sitting in the car, leg on the dashboard but otherwise pretty much how I left her.

'You all right there?' I asked.

'I'm fine,' she said.

'Were you bored?'

'Hardly. I made up a one-act play and populated the set with well-known thespians after vigorous casting-couch sex. It was diverting.'

'I'm happy for you. Shall we go?'

CHAPTER 12

The car in front dragged a strange trailer. The boot was open and a man sat inside, half of his upper torso extended out of the boot, and he held on to the two arms of a dark green wheelbarrow. Inside the wheelbarrow sat three children, all facing me. They stared with expressionless faces. The man in the boot stared as well, sweating, muscles straining with the undulations of the road. The car itself was sardine-packed with people and rode low with the excess weight. I thought the tyres would give out at any minute, but they didn't. Given the surfacing of the road, the barrow was surprisingly stable.

Nana drove in silence this time, one of those companionable silences that follow a long conversation in which all participants agree, a basking silence.

The second man to survive the bombing of Enoch Olubusi was Idris Wallace.

His address was listed in the files handed to me, but, when I called the number, it had been disconnected and the current occupants of his house had never heard of him. They had moved in a year after Pa Busi died. Just to be sure I spent two weeks outside the property watching the comings and goings. Nothing. I looked for him the old-fashioned way.

There were seventeen 'Idris Wallace' entries in the Ede City telephone book. If I made the search wider, there were five 'Wallace, I.' entries and ten other uses of the surname only. By posing as a solicitor trying to locate Idris for some disability money coming to him, I was able to eliminate all but three after making hundreds of telephone calls and dozens of house calls. People in Alcacia do not like strangers telephoning them or showing up on their doorsteps is what I learned from this exercise.

'If Wallace was sitting beside Pa Busi when the bomb went off, how did he survive?' Nana asked.

'I have no idea. Apparently these things happen. He was severely injured but not on the critical list, it seems.' I thought of the twisted wreck of the jeep again and wondered.

Idris Wallace did not live at the address we were on our way to. Aaron Wallace, motor mechanic, father of five and self-professed first cousin to Idris, did. This had happened before. Once a person got a whiff of money, they tried to fake being Wallace or being related to him. I had checked each one out to be sure.

'This is the street,' said Nana.

'Drive through to the next one and park, then I'll continue on foot. Stay in the car until I call you.'

She mock saluted. 'You've become more and more sexist, Weston.'

'I'm sorry. This country is a bad influence. I'll do better.'

Aaron's children looked like small clones of him and clustered around his chair, listening to our conversation and whispering to each other. They were all boys and seemed to be the same age, which was about seven or eight, no older than nine. He himself greeted me in a white singlet and khaki shorts. Red flip-flops slapped against the floor as he walked.

'Do you want a drink, Mr Kogi?'

'I've just eaten, thank you.'

'Nonsense. Let me offer you a soft drink.' He gestured to one of the children who brought me a frosty bottle of Coke and a glass and placed it on a nested table beside my seat.

'Thank you.' I took a sip to be polite. 'You say you know where Idris is?'

'Yes, he's dead.'

'Dead?'

Aaron nodded. He reached for a box folder beside him. He had spindly arms and a gaunt look with a tendency to talk and move slowly. He was about forty-five or fifty, and there was no sign of a wife. His house was barely furnished and had a smell that I didn't care for.

'I want the disability payout,' said Aaron. 'For that you can have this box.'

'What's in the box?'

'Proof of what I will tell you, after you pay me for it.'

'The money was for Idris. If he's dead—'

'Mr Kogi, let me be plain with you. I know you are not here peddling a disability allowance. If that were the case you would have found someone to impersonate him and split the money. I don't even believe your real name is Kogi. Now, all I'm asking is for some money for me and my boys in exchange for information on my cousin. Surely, this is fair?' His upper incisors were all cracked and I wondered how it was that they didn't cut his tongue when he spoke.

'One hundred dollars. If I like what you have, another hundred afterwards.'

'No, sir. Two hundred now, two hundred afterwards, whether you like it or not. But you will like what I have to say, sure banker.' He cracked a smile. One of the boys scratched his own belly, showing such indolence that I wondered if there wasn't something wrong with him, neurologically.

I counted off the bills and handed them to him. He carefully verified the amount then slowly put the cash in his pocket. He gave me the box and began to speak.

'Idris was my cousin on my father's side, first cousin, brothers like. He was the most successful member of our clan and, as a result, the one we all went to if we needed help. When he went into law enforcement, everybody derided him, and his mother wondered—'

'Mr Wallace, I don't want a biography. I want to know what happened to him.'

'Yes, well, he and I were close. I came from our village in Okun to live with him in Ede when he got that government job. He was always paranoid. He would check locks and alarms and telephone me several times a day to make sure I hadn't broken any of his many security rules or noticed anything out of the ordinary. I would tell him that the Good Book says, *Unless the Lord watches the house*—'

'—*the watchmen watch in vain*,' I completed. Psalm 127. Until that moment I didn't even know I remembered the Bible verse, but they drill that shit into you in primary school here.

'Yes. Idris did not derive comfort from that. He said I was a superstitious bush man and spouted blasphemies about our Lord.'

'He was a philosopher, I have heard.'

Aaron shrugged. 'He read some books; broke his mother's heart when he stopped attending church. She prayed for him every day and begged me to help him.'

I nodded. Deep interior Alcacians understand apostasy as long as it involved taking up another religion like Islam or even Hinduism. What filled most of them with terror is the idea of living without any religion. How could one live without any obeisance to the spirit world, however rudimentary?

'How was he on the days leading up to the explosion?'

'He was his usual self. He gave me advice since I was looking for a job at the time. There were a couple of days that he spent away from home. I got the impression that he'd found a lover.'

'What made you think that?'

'I'm not sure.' He thought for a minute. 'Perfume. He started spraying perfume and bought and wore a designer white shirt rather than the regulation one they are meant to wear under their regulation suit. He checked the crease of his trousers.'

'Do you have any idea who he might have been seeing?'

'No. His job didn't leave him much time for dating. Irregular hours. And his poor mother. She was worried that he was getting old without children.'

'What happened on the day of the assassination?'

'I heard about it in the news like everybody else, but I was detained for a week and interrogated because of how close I was to Idris. I was treated well compared to some. It was three months before I next saw him.'

'What was he like?'

'Scared. He became even more paranoid than before, especially after the official story came out that Pa Busi's entire retinue had perished in the explosion. He rarely left the house and spent the day at the windows looking out of the blinds with binoculars and making notes of his observations. He bought animal traps and placed them around the entrances to the house. If I wanted to urinate at night, I had to be careful. He rifled through my things every day, looking for evidence of my betrayal. Once, I woke up with a gun to my head and him, sweating profusely, eyes wide as oranges, screaming at me to confess.'

'Confess to what?'

'To working for some agency that was out to kill him, that was monitoring him. He was crazy. I wanted to pack up and go back to the village, but my mission in the city was to get a good job and bring over my wife and children. I couldn't just leave. He threatened to torture me to get at *the truth*. He spent a lot of time calling a number but being frustrated because nobody picked up the phone. He made me swear that if anything happened to him I would burn all his property. This went on for months.'

'How did he die?'

'Suicide. I went to work one day, came back in the evening and he had shot himself in the face.'

'I see.'

'It's not that simple. He had stockpiled weapons over those months. At night, he would sit beside the window with an array of loaded guns, grenades and spare ammunition laid out on the ledge, ready for action. But I don't believe he wanted to die, Mr Kogi. There was no suicide note, this from a man who wrote obsessively in his notebook. I came back to find the house in an awful mess. All the animal traps were sprung. It was . . . unusual.'

'You think he was murdered but made to look like suicide?'

'I don't know that, but after he died, I feared for my own life as well. But only for a short time. As you can see, I am still here and so are my boys. The elders say, *As the crab walks, so do its children.*'

'True talk, true talk.'

'The secret police came and "sterilised" the scene. It did not get into the papers. I was warned against discussing the matter, and I never did until I got your phone call.'

The box contained papers, photos, a mobile phone and other random bits.

'How goes your job?'

'I lost the job, but my wife found one that pays enough, so I stay and look after the children.'

'That's very modern of you,' I said.

'I had no choice in the matter.'

I paid him the balance and left with all that remained of Idris Wallace.

★ ★ ★

The next day I was up early, like four a.m., and at the desk, going over my notes. Apart from the occasional cricket, there was silence. Muggy weather, but not unbearable since the sun was not out yet. The air carried a residual odour from cooking, but I could not place the dish.

Nana cried in the bedroom. Three times we tried to make love and three times I went soft inside her. I was aroused to start with but the moment I began thrusting, thoughts of the assassination crowded my head. She thought I was growing tired of her and that I was preparing to leave.

'In your mind you're already gone, like before. Your body is simply following your thoughts.'

'Not true. Come on, you think this isn't embarrassing for me? I'm just tired,' I said.

'Yes, you are. Tired of me.'

I could not ever play word games with her and win, so I got up and worked on my case. No longer did I consider it a chore. I started paying more attention to Nana's thesis on Pa Busi. Afolabi's testimony – hell, Afolabi's *existence* – spelled conspiracy, and Idris's experience confirmed it.

The car slowed down, fell into a ditch.

One high-powered rifle shot.

One handgun report from close quarters.

One explosion.

They wanted to be sure.

Whoever *they* were. Elements within the government? Why? As a political force, Pa Busi was spent. He would never run for president because an election just wouldn't happen in his non-senile lifetime. The rebels? Pa Busi dying at either of their hands had led to the current problem. Both the Front and the Christian Army needed legitimacy and good public relations was a part of that. Assassination of a well-liked statesman was not good public relations. That was why both groups were paying me money to blame the other.

Could it have been a case of mistaken identity? A random sniper saw a shiny four-by-four and decided to take potshots? That combined with an accidental discharge from the secret service and a landmine going off? Right. Accidental assassination, simultaneous manslaughter with incidental bomb detonation. Happens all the time.

There were a few things to follow up from the strange case of Idris Wallace. I needed to get the telephone numbers off Idris's mobile phone. Who had he been trying to reach? What had scared him so much? And his death: suicide or homicide? Did he fire the shot inside the jeep? Was that why he became increasingly paranoid? I wanted to speak to someone in the secret police about the cause of death.

I'd seen the so-called survivors, or rather, one survivor and one ghost. I needed to see the scene. I'd have to contact Churchill and get him to drive me.

I stretched, got up and massaged my temples. They were moist – I had started sweating. The cock crowed and I began my day.

When I stood near the window, I saw a man standing in the street. Using the parked cars as reference, I'd say he was rather short, with a shaved head and wearing a plain blue shirt hanging loose with the sleeves rolled up. He slouched away when he spotted me.

I checked the gun clip. Paranoia was addictive.

Nana left for work without speaking to me. The emotional backwash almost drove me to drink.

Nana had taken the car and I wasn't going to take a taxi after my last experience, so I caught a danfo – a bus whose factory-installed seats had been taken out, except for the driver and two passenger seats. It was painted yellow and wooden benches replaced the seats, increasing the capacity to twenty-five. The trade-off was poor ventilation.

There were no bus stops per se, just arbitrary patches of street or tarmac where people had agreed to congregate over the years. The conductor, a poorly dressed minor, rattled off a list of idio-syncratic bus stops with names like Anthony, Hoseni, Shosh (church), Town Planning, John Holt, Costain, Ede Central, and so on.

I met Church at Town Planning. There wasn't a draughtsman or bureaucrat in sight. The sun blazed with a whiteness that seared my eyes. In the emotional maelstrom of my fight with Nana, I had forgotten my sunglasses.

Churchill was wearing a red suit with a white, open-collar shirt. His shoes were crocodile-skin.

'Church.'

'Yeah, yeah, my brother.'

'I thought we were going to the interior?'

'We are.'

'You're dressed like we're off to a party.'

'Relax, aburo. All will become clear.' He patted me on the shoulder paternally, then stood facing the road.

We watched the cars go by in silence for seven minutes (I timed it).

'This is relaxing, Church, but what are we waiting for?' I asked.

'That.' Church pointed to a slow-moving column of black cars with hazard lights blinking: a funeral procession.

Only the first vehicle was a hearse. The others were family cars, overflowing with grieving friends and family, many of them weeping. As they passed us, doing like fifteen or twenty, Church started to run in their direction, so I did what he did. The last car was an old Citroën saloon, empty save the driver, and it slowed for us. Church got in the passenger seat and I got in the back.

'Weston, meet Dami. Dami's a grave digger. Dami, Weston. Old boy from school.'

'Bawo ni?' asked Dami. *How are things?*

'O nlo,' I said. *It goes, it goes.*

'Who's the client?' asked Church. He lit a cigarette and leaned his elbow out of the window.

'Malcolm Jaiyesinmi-Ojo. He dreamed he was eating at a banquet in his village. Dead the next morning, not a mark on him.'

'Just so I'm clear: Jaiyesinmi-Ojo is dead because he ate in a dream? That's the cause of death?' I asked.

Church and Dami looked at each other briefly and burst out laughing. 'He's been away,' said Church, to explain my ignorance.

'Aburo, there are two things you don't want to do in your dreams. One of them is to eat food,' said Church.

'The other is to fuck,' said Dami seriously. The tip of his right index finger was missing.

'True talk,' said Church.

'I'll have to bow to your experience in the matter,' I said.

They laughed. Dami nodded without irony. '*A man who pays respect to the great paves the way for his own greatness*, or so our elders say.'

I had forgotten the proverb thing. Yoruba people love proverbs and the appearance of wisdom gained by using a proverb in speech. Attributing the wisdom to Our Elders gains extra points so that in addition to being wise the speaker is also considered humble. It was tiring.

I said to Church, 'Why do we need to attend the funeral of Matthew Jaiyesinmi-Ojo?'

'Malcolm,' said Dami, wagging a finger.

'Malcolm,' I said. 'So why?'

Church turned and smiled at me, toothy and lupine. 'Funerals are lucky for you and I, aren't they?'

After the ceremony, the friends and family of the dearly departed departed and it was left to Dami to fill in the grave. All through the service and the caterwauling, Church smoked and told me about a fellow rebel called D'Jango. Legendary. A fierce 'warrior', according to Church. D'Jango took his name from a cowboy film.

'*Django*. Franco Nero. 1966. It was on TV a lot when we were young. You remember it?'

'Vaguely,' I said.

'D'Jango went at government troops with a hard-on, and I mean that literally, bro. He went into battle stark naked with his dick and his gun pointed at the enemy. Scariest thing I've ever had to behold.'

'I just knew the conversation would get to penises sooner or later,' I said.

'He said it was what the medicine man told him to do. Said as long as he didn't put clothes on, bullets would not find him. It worked, too.'

Dami kept digging, even though the sun was making its way down, time being about five in the afternoon. He had stripped to his shorts and rivulets of sweat trickled down his muscles. He had almost finished, the hole full, the cement work all but done. It felt odd not helping out, Church chain-smoking and me just hanging about. A few times my phone vibrated in my pocket but I ignored it, knowing it was Nana and that she would misunderstand my reasons for not answering.

'What happened to him? D'Jango?' I asked Church, since he was not answering any questions about our purported trip to the bush.

Church waved his cigarette in circles, terrorising the swarm of gnats that had gathered around him. 'Ambushed by government troops, captured, tortured. He could be dead, languishing in a gulag or rotting in a hole somewhere in the bush. Anything is possible.'

Dami took Polaroids of the completed tombstone and gravesite, slowly walking around to get shots from various angles. When he finished, he arranged his tools carefully on the ground and said, 'Wait till nightfall before you start anything. I mean it, Churchill, I don't want to hear any stories. I like this job.'

Church brought out a bottle of Gordon's Gin, unscrewed the cap and poured the clear liquid over the new gravestone.

'Ile'n tile.' *What is of the ground belongs to the ground.*

He handed Dami a wad of cash and I felt for my own money belt. It was reassuringly snug. Exit Dami.

Church drank the gin and passed me the bottle. He asked for it back when I had taken two long swallows. The gin went down like sulphur. I would bet that it was local gin in the bottle and not Gordon's. I told Church so.

'Of course it isn't Gordon's. Do you know how much it costs to buy the original? No, this is bottled somewhere outside Atakunmosa by a friend of mine, sells them to me half-price.' He glanced about and picked up the pickaxe.

'Time to start work.'

'Work doing what?'

'Resurrection.'

Grave robbing was a new low for me. Church, I could tell, had done this before.

A bus arrived to pick us up. Church phoned for one like a general calling for an air strike. He still refused to answer any of my questions and I still refused to answer any of the phone calls from Nana. The driver of the bus said nothing, but he did wrap the corpse in tarpaulin before helping us lift it on to the bus. Church was in a good mood, and I wanted to kill him, but I owed him my life. Of course, my life wouldn't have been in danger in the first place if he hadn't put me in harm's way, but those were just details. I decided to check my voicemails to distract from the lolling of the sheet-wrapped body.

Meep: 'Hey, loverboy. Sorry about the hormonal blah blah this morning. I'll make it up to you, okay? Call me back.'

Meep: 'I just got fired from a job. It stings a bit, you know. Not still angry, are you?'

Meep: 'Oh, never mind. Sulk then.'

Our next stop was a strip of dirt road in the middle of nowhere. Church called it Black Market. There were women hanging around and men floating by in various automobiles. The women were painted like masquerade performers and bared as much flesh as they could without being naked.

'Prostitutes?' I said.

'To be sure,' said Church.

A mixed-race worker appeared in the headlights. She had short spiky hair that reminded me of the hide of a cactus.

Meep: 'Call me back.'

'That one's name is Lilliana Oil. Not like Popeye's bitch. Proper oil,' said Church. 'Stop the vehicle.'

The light revealed a tattoo of a blade on the side of Lillian's neck.

Meep: 'I had a dream last night. I was walking through this Nigerian market. I needed to buy stuff and there was all sorts on sale – gari, yam flour, cassava, spinach, okra, pepper – but the stalls were empty. Fully stocked, but empty. I walked through, not taking anything. In the meat section the cutlets were all there, along with the electric saws and the machetes, but there were no butchers.

The poultry baskets were in place but the chickens and turkeys were dead. I stood among the offal. Four vultures descended on me. One even started to tug at my flesh. I looked at them in turn and said, "I wouldn't do that if I were you. Don't you know I'm an initiate?" They scattered like I had thrown stones at them. When I turned back to the market, it was full of people, and I woke up. Call me.'

The driver offered me gum, which I accepted. Church went out and talked to Lilliana, cajoling her towards the van. Off to the left, a man coupled furiously with a skinny girl who could not have been older than thirteen. He held her up against a tree and pumped away. Her eyes were open, and it looked like she was staring at me. That couldn't be true because it was dark in the van.

She looked dead, like the man was fucking a cadaver.

I looked away.

Church opened the back of the van and Lilliana giggled in, followed by a cloud of cheap perfume that almost choked me. Church didn't come in, leaving me, Lilliana and the corpse of Malcolm Jaiyesinmi-Ojo in the back.

'Take me to Bangkok,' said Church to the driver. 'At once.'

We narrowly missed crushing a buxom girl in a painted-on purple dress with knee-high black felt boots.

Meep: 'I'm contemplating Zsa Zsa Gabor, thinking of the social milieu that led her to think it was acceptable behaviour to slap a black cop. Too much hashish or simply an inevitable effect of the Hollywood studio system?'

The night swallowed us progressively. Lilliana had gone silent since Church broke a vial of amyl nitrate under her nose. *What the fuck am I doing here? Why am I with these people?* I could feel myself becoming inured to what was happening and, like Nana pointed out, losing my own values.

We thundered through some checkpoints. Indignant police officers yelled after us most times. One took a potshot that zinged past us. Church became incandescent and fired his revolver in the general direction of the gorodom over and over, even though the driver kept saying we were out of range. The noise woke Lillian from her chemical stupor and she started giggling again. God, I wished she would stop.

We slowed down, stopped.

We were at the gates of a guarded compound. It was similar to Arodan, except that there were armed guards and a tower with searchlights. Affectionately called Bangkok, it was a prison.

'Wait,' said Church, unnecessarily. He walked up to one of the guards – a fat policeman who was apparently expecting him. Money changed hands. The gates opened and the guards waved us in. Church joined us inside the parking area and the guard stood a few yards away.

'Lilliana, you stay here. Weston, bring the body.' For the first time Church seemed tense, nervous even.

'I can't. Not by myself,' I said.

'You're making me look bad,' said Church. 'These people know me.'

Lilliana laughed.

Church took the head end while I carried the legs. The fat cop led us into one of the main buildings. We met a few people on the way, but they looked in different directions as if some cloud protected us from their gaze. We stopped at Cell Block H, by which time my muscles were rigid with fatigue.

The cells had thick metal doors, the kind that absorb sound when you strike them. The fat cop drew back the slider to a small rectangular eye-slot in the door.

'Step the fuck away from the door,' he said. To Church he muttered, 'The fool has a habit of leaning against the eye slot so that all you can see is his diseased yellow eye. I've had to poke it once or twice myself.' Fat Cop punctuated his sentence with a fart, which immediately filled the corridor space with a sulphurous smell. He opened the cell door. A wiry, bearded man in prison blues stood in the exact middle of the room.

'Be quick,' said Fat Cop.

The man in the cell stripped off quickly, with an urgency that seemed more frantic because of the silence. Church and I took the clothes off Jaiyesinmi-Ojo.

'I got you a nice suit, Nine,' said Church.

It was difficult getting the clothes off a dead weight. It was even more difficult dressing one up in prison clothes. We dragged the body into the cell.

'*Habeas corpus*,' said Church to Fat Cop. 'You may have the body.'

Fat Cop rolled the corpse over so that it was prone. After which, he steadied it with his foot and fired a pistol into the back of its head. He placed the revolver in the right hand of the twice-dead man.

'How the hell is he supposed to have shot himself there?' I asked.

'It worked for Andreas Baader,' said Church. 'Come on. I want to show Nine his other present.'

In the back of the van, Nine fucked Lilliana on the bench opposite me while I tried not to look.

Church explained that Nine was D'Jango. When the government agents arrested him, they didn't realise who they had, and D'Jango took the identity of a lesser rebel known as Nine.

'He will take us where we need to go, like a guide,' Church said.

D'Jango-Nine climaxed loudly.

'Tomorrow,' Church said.

★ ★ ★

Nana hugged me for a long time. You'd think I'd just told her about a routine day at the office instead of a mad odyssey with a hooker, a corpse and an insane rebel.

'I lost my job,' she said.

'I know. You said so in your message. Which one?'

'It doesn't matter,' she said.

Later, as we made love, an image of the skinny hooker being banged against the tree came unbidden to my mind. I saw her eyes open, focused on me, and I ejaculated immediately, violently. Nana stroked my head as if I were her child, and I slept.

CHAPTER 13

'Your father wants to see you,' said Nana.

'That's impossible,' I said, then thought I might have been too hasty in answering. 'Sorry, I didn't catch your meaning. Are you saying that in a general sense, subconsciously, in a moral way, that he must *want* to see me?'

Heavy rain drummed down on the windows while a Korean film played out its drama on the bedroom TV. There were no subtitles, and Nana did not speak Korean. We had fun imposing our own meaning on the words and actions, taking turns to narrate each scene. Nana lay across my chest.

'No, I'm saying he sent one of his guys to the campus yesterday to search for me in order to give a message to you, the message being that he wants to see you pronto.'

'How did he know you would know where to find me?'

'I have no idea. I didn't ask.'

'The guy he sent . . . tall guy, shaven head, prominent occiput?'

'That's the one.'

'That's Bolaji Taiwo. You should know him. God, he must be really old by now, like in his fifties or sixties.'

'He did seem a bit old for messenger work. I thought there was something familiar about him, but I was distracted.'

Bolaji Taiwo – or Mister Taiwo, as he insisted we call him from when we were kids – was my father's main go-to guy and had been for the last twenty-five or so years. He was a real in-betweener, a dangerous interstitial guy. Nobody but my dad knew what his job description was or how much he got paid, but if I had to guess, I'd say he was a family fixer. My sister and I hated him because he was intimately involved in putting my mother out after the whole kidney business with my brother. He was brutish, muscular and primitive-looking, with greater prognathism than most, and longer arms. Apelike, in short. But nobody would tell him that to his face. I once heard my dad saying Mister Taiwo was the only survivor of a long line of abiku, which could mean anything from multiple dead siblings to sickle cell disease.

Nana yawned, stretched, covered me with her stale morning breath. In the Korean film, a sad child was explaining a deep and soulful poem to a clueless adult. The child might have been a ghost. At least that's what it seemed like to me.

'Must be serious for him to send Mister Taiwo,' I said casually, though my belly seemed to become heavy, like it was full of pebbles.

'He flogged me once, you know,' she said.

'Really? Mister Taiwo?'

'No, silly. Your dad.'

'What did you do?'

'I think I was eight. One afternoon I was chasing a butterfly across our compound—'

'I remember you used to love doing that. You had this weird collection with labels and all that.'

'Yes, well, I was chasing a butterfly and became very single-minded about it; so much so that I crossed over into your compound without even registering that I had climbed over the fence. I just wanted the butterfly. I was filthy from all the running. I bumped into your father. He seemed like a giant, an ill-tempered one, wearing white lace – white lace that now had a Nana-shaped dirt stain on the front. He was furious. I remember his face contorting slowly, and his big belly rising and falling from heavy breathing. He grabbed my wrist, lifted me off the ground by my left arm, and spanked my tushy with the other. The pain was so much that I wet myself and he dropped me in disgust.'

'Yes,' I said. 'Sounds like him. Didn't your parents do anything? I mean, it wasn't even his house. He was probably visiting Aunt Blossom.'

She twisted her head towards me and stared. The movement unsettled me. It was as if her neck was bent into an abnormal angle and the look was cadaverous. After what I felt was too long an interval, she turned back to the Korean film and said, 'I didn't tell them.'

We watched in silence after that but I couldn't shake the feeling that I had missed something in her look, something I was meant to know, something important, and that she was disappointed that I didn't.

I fell asleep and woke up with Nana gone and my phone ring-ing. The TV was off but the bedding beside me was warm, so it could not have been long since she got up. I hunted for my phone. The ringtone was a part of a Nina Simone song that I had been fond of, but had become tiresome since I heard it so often. The phone hid in a tangle of sheets and stopped ringing the moment I found it, number withheld. A few seconds later it beeped with the voicemail notification.

'Good afternoon, sir. I hope this is the voicemail of Mr Weston Kogi. Mr Weston Kogi who is the private detective. I wish to engage your services. You see, my husband is missing. I wish for you to find him. I can pay a lot of money for this. Please call me back, sir. Thank you.'

What?

Her voice sounded mellifluous, even though the English was

halting second-language stuff. How the hell was I supposed to call her back without her name or number? How did she get my number? Who told her that I was a private detective? I was barely detecting anything, plus I hadn't advertised. I should have paid attention and worried more about the answers to those questions, but I didn't.

My father's office was a grandiose affair. He had a seventies Bond-villain desk: six feet wide, polished glass top resting on a mahogany base. A window took up the whole of the wall behind his desk, giving a view of the bay. It did not open, and the room was ventilated by air conditioning. Knowing my father, he liked the window because it placed visitors at a disadvantage by allowing the brilliant sunshine to dazzle them. There were blinds, but he only drew them for VIPs. I was not a VIP. Not that I cared. I had sunglasses on and had no intention of taking them off.

On the other walls were extravagant reproductions of Cara-vaggio. Art in Alcacia was a tricky thing. There were talented artists to be sure, even accomplished painters. The problem was that generations of middle-class children had been exposed to imperialist education and they grew up with money in their pockets and a taste for the work of classic masters. The bulk of oil painters in Alcacia spent more time copying Sandro Botticelli than creating original work.

My father grunted when he saw me. He pointed to the seat, but I remained standing.

'What do you want?' I asked.

'Is that how you greet your father?' he snapped, as if I were twelve.

'Oh, you're my father now?'

He glared.

'Fine. Good afternoon, Father. I hope you're well. How is the family? The wife? The children? The dog? All well? Grand. What the fuck do you want?'

'Why are you being so hostile?'

'Do you actually want me to answer that?'

'I understand you are associating with the rebel faction.'

'And?'.

'Your grandfather would . . .' He sucked his teeth and said something under his breath.

I pushed my sunglasses down the bridge of my nose and peered over the top of the lenses. 'I notice you said "grandfather".'

'Slip of the tongue.'

'Slip of something—'

'You listen to me. You may be a Holloway bastard, but you still bear my name and people associate you with me. I've come to terms with the idea that I can't stop you or your sister from using the Kogi name.'

'What's your point?'

'This . . . affiliation with these insurgents and their heretical ideas – this thing of yours – could affect my business, might even get me arrested. Our family could be ruined.'

'*Our* family?'

'You know what I mean.'

'No. I don't. My family is my sister and me.'

'Weston—'

I got up. 'If that's all you have to say—'

'Sit down.'

He still had enough command in his voice and I had enough residual fear that I obeyed. He opened a drawer and extracted an envelope that he tossed to me. There were two glossy black-and-white photographs of two men in dark suits. The photos were grainy and taken from above, security camera footage. They had identical close-cropped haircuts.

'Friends of yours?' I asked.

'They came here to ask questions about you. I had the stills taken from the reception feed.'

'Who are they?'

'They had State Security IDs but I don't remember their names. They refused to sign in. Whatever you are doing is generating attention from the wrong quarters. I know how State Security works. They shoot first and investigate later. If you see them, run the other way.'

'You sound like someone out of a movie, and why do you care, anyway? *Father?*'

'Because I am a businessman and I cannot do business from a cell in one of the many gulags owned and scattered around by our beloved government. Look, I know the whole business with Holloway wasn't your fault—'

'Don't. Don't ever.' I got up and left. I didn't close the door.

He had always hated that.

Outside, four cyclists rode slowly in tandem on the main road, causing a grievous tailback that snaked west in an unending line of automobiles. They must have been Area Boys, otherwise someone would have lent them brutal wisdom by now. As I watched, a bolekaja rumbled from the opposite direction and mowed into the riders, launching them into short-lived arcs that ended in broken bodies and blood. It was nearly comical. I looked for a taxi as one of them bled on to the tarmac.

I composed myself on the side of the road. Talking to my father always unsettled me and left me in a bad mood.

I found the interest of the secret police bothersome, scary, even. I had heard the tales. I called Nana but there was no response. I had a missed call from Church, but I didn't want to talk to him yet. A mad prophet whispered to me desperate analyses of three chapters of the book of Jeremiah. His breath intimated at several rotting teeth and dying gums. Partly to get away from this, I walked along the bay to the wharf. The sky was now cloudless. The sun bleached colour out of everything. The air was still, and sweat was my cologne. I took some shade near a buka and phoned Abayomi Abayomi, then I hung up. I didn't want to talk to him either.

The wharf was more like a market or bazaar than anything else. As I walked I saw ships in the distance – or at least their radar masts. A mass of people crawled all over like ants on a corpse. Steel containers were everywhere, and customs officials milled about like a sprawling immune system, overweight, every single one of them – full of the bribes from innumerable smugglers and desperate legitimate businessmen. I saw cranes and carriers, lorries, Area Boys and sellers. Unsavoury types cracked open unclaimed containers and sold the contents at low prices to opportunistic punters. Items were bought at less than cost or given away as extras on a larger purchase.

A man blew gently into a crudely made flute, playing Miles Davis. I stopped to listen and gave him a dollar. His happiness at the reward lifted my spirits a little.

Brief and brutal fights broke out every hour or so, brutal because of the monetary stakes, brief because of the coldly efficient clubs and nightsticks of the customs officials. Commerce had to continue at all costs. The rights or emotions of puny humans like me meant nothing. Customs jobs were at a premium. The officers were monomaniacal in their pursuit of bribes because they had a quota to pay upwards to their bosses, who in turn had to feed their own bosses. Anything that clogged that flow was dealt with swiftly.

The tarred ground looked muddy because of dirt accumulated over the years. Molue and bolekaja brought in increasing numbers of people yet took very few away. At the waterline I saw a corpse buffeted by waves, bloated with gases, rhythmically hitting the hull of a ship as if knocking to enter, the loneliest corpse in the world. Nobody did anything about it.

I walked past a fish stall where gutted sturgeon was on careless display. A meaty woman separated fish heads from bodies and intermittently hurled abuse at a boy who knelt beside her snivelling. Around his neck hung a placard that read: 'OLE', which meant *thief*. I mused idly – could a child ever truly steal from a parent?

I was hot, sweaty and feeling sorry for myself. I wanted to extract my gun and fire it into the air, scare the people out of their mindless transactionalism.

There were no taxis, but other than the buses, a whole fleet of okada serviced the wharf. These motorcycles were great for manoeuvring through traffic and getting to places in a hurry. Of course, they were unregulated, untaxed and unsafe, and most of the drivers were unlicensed. Everyone knew someone who had perished on an okada.

I hailed the nearest one.

When your earliest memory is being on a motorcycle, holding on to your nanny's boyfriend's torso for dear life, moving at what seemed at that age to be the speed of light, you always approach such vehicles with childlike wonder. A little regression never hurt anyone. Well, maybe it did, but not this time. People fly out of your way when you're on a motorcycle with a mad pilot. Mine looked like the fucking Red Baron, if the Red Baron were a short man wearing a First World War pilot's helmet, goggles and sporting three days of grey unshaven glory. Several times during our journey, a few globs of saliva would break free from his mouth and spray me. He barely spoke English and his body odour could kill any number of forest animals, but I had to grab hold of him. Before long, we were riding through Ede's richer quarter. I told him to slow down. It took six attempts to get the message into his illiterate brain.

The houses were beautiful, palatial and quiet, with no cars parked on the streets. The nice Audis and Beamers were inside the sometimes electrified fences. No stalls or shops in evidence. This was the anti-commerce district, the place where the commerce bore fruit. The streets were paved, even and clean, with no open gutters, which meant decent sewerage. No poles bearing electric cables, which meant underground wiring. Gatehouses, which meant guards, which meant money to spare. Most of the guards were Fulani men armed with charms or bows and arrows or clubs or just their big dangling dicks. They weren't hired to offer serious opposition to intruders.

Here lived the Four-One-Nine warlords and the former military rulers and the big smugglers and the drug kingpins and minor ex-presidents of forgotten African republics who took too much money and ran. Interpol knew where these people lived but had no idea how to operate in a country like Alcacia.

When I was young, one night a few friends told me that the police would be coming to arrest one of our neighbours the very next day, so none of us went to school. We all camped outside in deckchairs sucking on lollipops, wearing cowboy hats while waiting for the police to arrive. Before noon four black Range Rovers with tinted windows rolled up and serious-looking men in black suits with guns rushed out and broke their way in. Tumult. Shouting. Gunshots. The result? None dead, none arrested, frustrated Interpol agents milling about. The house was empty and I heard it was so denuded of property that even the light fixtures were removed and the naked wires taped over.

Foreigners. They know nothing. How can any Alcacian cooperate fully with international authorities when we still blame any

Western nation for colonisation? Sure, we'd grass our criminals, but then we'd warn them that they'd been grassed because, ultimately, it was always an us-versus-them situation where white people were involved.

The real rich, the legitimately wealthy, the genuine old money and the Alcacian version of aristocracy could not afford to live in these quarters any more. Many families were given the bullet treatment in the many wars and rebel attacks. Some ran away but a few persisted, living in large, decaying family properties with no furniture or valuables. They hung on like the tough fleck of goat meat that you can't loosen from between your teeth after a heavy meal.

There was a cloud lifting from my mind as I admired the swimming pools. Something about the street, something I had read in the case files Church gave me—

'Stop!' I yelled.

'What?' asked the pilot.

'Stop the okada now!'

I paid an indeterminate amount to the pilot and ignored his response, which was lost in the smoky whine of his engine at any rate. When he was gone, the street seemed quiet. Many of the houses bore no number, but the name had leaped out at me. This was Tunji Braithwaite Street. I knew it because Pa Busi's widow lived there. I just did not know which number. I walked around a bit, up the street first, then down. Not a soul to be encountered, not a car to be seen. No noises. Or perhaps the noise was well contained. Oh, to be rich. I looked at my striped shirt – still relatively presentable. The trousers had a sheen of dust around the cuffs but still looked pressed. Nothing could be done about the shoes. I had walked in mud, and caked mud on leather requires a special kind of attention. Fuck it. I hammered on the nearest gate.

It was scarlet, about ten feet high and made of steel. A slot slid back to reveal a rectangular opening and a guard looked out at me.

120

'Uh, hu?' he said, the kind of grunt that meant, *What do you want?*

'Olubusi,' I said.

'Four houses down, opposite side of the road. Green roof.'

I thanked him and set off.

Four houses down in London is nothing, five minutes' walk at the most, and that's if you're stopping to admire the finish of the roofs. Four palatial houses take longer, especially in the noon sun. The Olubusis' gate was made of bars rather than sheets of metal, so as soon as I stood outside it, a uniformed man came out of the gatehouse.

'May I help you?'

Educated guards, uniforms with logos, politeness. I was impressed.

'I'm here to see Mrs Olubusi,' I said.

'Is she expecting you?' His eyes dropped meaningfully to my clothes and back to my face.

'Give her this.' I handed over my ID. 'Tell her I won't take much of her time.'

'Perhaps you'd like to come back another time. She is not at home. I will tell her you called.'

Standard bullshit. 'Perhaps I'll wait for her to return.'

'She has travelled. It will take some time.'

'I have time, and it is important.'

I toyed with the idea of a bribe, but discarded it. This kind of person took the job seriously and would need a magnificent amount of money for corrupting. He stared at me for some minutes.

I smiled.

'Wait here.'

I did.

A hawk glided overhead and the cowboy song 'Old Turkey

Buzzard' played briefly in my mind. The movie was *Mackenna's Gold*, I think. I remembered it from my childhood.

The guard disappeared into the gatehouse. I imagined him telephoning the staff at the main house asking Mrs Olubusi if she was accepting callers, especially ones dressed like they lived in a tip. Presently, I heard a beep and a mechanical click, after which the gate opened and the guard waved me in from his cubby hole.

I sat in an armchair with a cold glass of freshly squeezed orange juice and ice shavings in my hand. Piano music drifted towards me from somewhere in the house, but not the professional kind. More like someone was taking lessons. On the flatscreen affixed to the wall two Asian men stalked each other in a ring, kicking and punching, volume turned down low, perhaps because of the piano practice? A commercial break told me it was Thai kick-boxing, robbed of intensity by the absence of sound. One of the walls had shots of Pa Busi, one with Olusegun Obasanjo, two-time president of Nigeria. A few photo opportunities were with major and minor diplomats, the Spice Girls, Wesley Snipes, Miriam Makeba, people like that. He appeared benevolent, his demeanour more priest than high-powered politician. He rarely smiled for any of the photos, and his wife was not in any of them.

I set my drink down on a coaster and got up to get a closer look at the wall.

'Would you like me to talk you through it?' a voice said behind me.

So this was Diane Olubusi.

It's difficult to describe meeting her. It was as if she was so slight that reality parted to let her exist, but only barely. She was fair-skinned, slender, with a long neck and prominent forehead. But that was wrong. She could not be reduced to body parts. Her skin shone, glowed with an inner light. I had never been in the presence of such a woman in my life. Her photographs did no justice to the actuality of her. My mouth was not moist enough to form words.

She gave the impression of lightness. She was the opposite of having the weight of the world on her shoulders, and, given a strong enough wind, she might take off. She stood in a doorway the way a doe would stand. She smelled like a gardener had pulled new leaves from a shrub, crumpled them and let them dance through the air. Her hair was pulled back and clasped at the crown of her head but a few tendrils tumbled carelessly down her back. It was not black, but dark brown — either treated or evidence of mixed heritage, which would explain her European looks.

I became aware that time had lapsed.

'Mrs Olubusi?'

'Yes.' She sat down on one of the chairs, crossing the weight-less legs. 'And you must be Weston Kogi, the private investigator.'

'Yes, ma'am.'

'Please. I dare say we are about the same age. Are you related to the owner of Kogi Imports?'

'My father.'

'Aderele is your father? Odd. I cannot see the resemblance and his wife seemed a little young to be your mother.'

'That woman is the second Mrs Kogi.'

'Oh, hang on. I know this.' She leaned forward in her seat — I obviously held new interest. 'Your mother died, did she not?'

'I really do not wish to speak about it.' I sat down opposite her. 'Please.'

'Such a long time ago. Bad memories?'

'I'd just rather not.'

She shrugged, the most elegant shoulder movement I had ever seen. 'I have met your father. He attended one of my fundraisers. I forget the wife's name. A bit passive.'

I did not like the direction of the conversation or the fact that she knew my father.

'That's . . . I mean, I'm here to talk about your husband,' I said.

'That hardly seems fair. You wish to talk about an intimate family member of mine, deceased, God bless his soul, yet you do not want to talk about an intimate family member of your own, also deceased, God bless her soul. You see the problem I have with that?'

Where the hell was my spit? It felt like I had walked into a trap.

'Tell me about your mother.' She settled back into her chair.

'I—'

'All I am asking is that you tell me about yourself. Then maybe I'll tell you what you want to know about me. Or my husband.'

That was how I told a complete stranger about my mother.

'To understand my mother's death you need to know about the Royal Holloway Infirmary scandal of 1972. Are you familiar with it?'

'Vaguely, but tell me like you would a stranger.'

'From 1969 to 1971, a gynaecologist called Olurombi Roy, apropos of nothing, began to systematically abuse his patients. Sexually. Any woman who came in for a consultation was given an internal, a vaginal exam. He would deposit some semen in them by means of a syringe while the victim would be none the wiser.'

'His semen?'

'His semen. It's estimated that he impregnated hundreds this way. Nobody knows the exact number, and nobody really wants to know. The resulting offspring were known as Holloway Babies.'

'Were you – are you a Holloway Baby?'

'I'm the first. My sister Lynn and I were the first-discovered Holloway Babies. There used to be three of us – me, Lynn and our older brother Simon. Simon got sick and the doctors said he needed a kidney transplant. I volunteered to be the donor, but even preliminary tests showed that Simon and I were not genetically similar enough. Then they tested Lynn, and the result was the same.' I sipped my juice to cool down the inside of my mouth. The ice was melting fast. 'My father did other tests, including getting a babalawo to test the auguries, to see if my mother had been unfaithful.'

'And the verdict was that she played away?'

'Yes.'

'What did your father do?'

'Drove my mother out without any financial support. I want to . . . I need the toilet . . .'

'Through there.' She aimed me and I staggered away.

When I locked the door, I vomited.

I cleaned up as best I could and returned to the living room. 'I can't do this, Mrs Olubusi. I'm sorry. I . . . we . . . I want to leave now.'

She stood up, seemed concerned.

'You look unwell.'

'Goodbye.'

Leaving Ma Busi's house like that was most unwise. It found its place among a long line of unwise moves I had made that day. Going there without preparation was daft. Going there after seeing my father? That was the kind of demented move I could only attribute to heat stroke. The pièce de résistance was leaving without having them call me a cab. It took forty-five minutes to get to the nearest bus stop, which, you will recall, had a tendency to be unmarked in Alcacia. I saw people clotted together, and I joined in. Not many buses were required in the rich quarters except to bring the impoverished workers.

I rode the bus in silence even though my phone rang twice. The second time it was insistent and people stared with irritation. I just looked out of the window. There was a shanty town growing under the bridge intersection we were approaching. Dirty children played in the abundant mud, no piano lessons required.

I waited a few minutes outside the apartment before Nana returned.

'What happened to you?' she asked.

'Freudian ambush,' said I, taking shopping bags from her.

'Tell.'

'Maybe later. I need a shower and clean clothes right now.'

I washed in tepid water.

Nana hammered out an essay while I cleaned myself. I felt less miserable after some soap and sympathy. I thought it was a good idea to leave the Widow Busi for another time.

I called Church.

'Yeah?'

'It's me,' I said.

'Hey, brother. How you dey?'

'Worried about D'Jango.'

'Oh, that. Tell me where you are; I'll come and get you.'

'Nope. Tell me the pick-up point. I'll find my way there.'

'Haba, are you still hiding your location? Brothers don't behave like this towards each other.'

'You are so right. Brothers don't.'

'I'll call you back with the details. I'm in the middle of something.' He hung up and I pictured him sticking a rusty screwdriver into someone's middle.

While getting dressed I received another phone call.

'Hello?'

'Is that Mr Weston?' A familiar female voice.

'Who are you?'

'I left a message for you before, sir. About a job, sir. I am looking for my husband.'

Right. 'Leave a number. I'll call you back. I'm in the middle of something right now.' I was using Church's words. Shudder.

'Okay, sir.'

She read out a number. I did not copy it down and put her out of my mind. I wore a pullover on top of jeans. I put the gun in my waistband at the back – I'd rather accidentally shoot my arse than my balls. It was getting to evening and the sting of the sun was less potent.

Nana crept up on me and hugged me from behind. She noticed the hardness of the gun and removed herself.

'Where are you going?'

'To check out the place where Pa Busi died.'

'To what end?'

'Officially, to get clues as to where any assassins could shoot from and see if there's evidence to be gathered.'

'And unofficially?'

'I'm just justifying my fee, marking the time so I have something to report.'

'You are a bad man.'

'Just giving the people what they want.'

Church called.

This time it was obvious that we were going to the interior. We went in a jeep, and Churchill had on military boots. There were four of us – me, Church, Tosin, one of the guys who kidnapped me, and D'Jango. We careered along the V8, the main expressway connecting south with north-west. Leaving Ede would not be an easy thing for three rebels and a private investigator. There were random and arbitrary checkpoints. The police and customs were easy; they could be discouraged by simple stern looks from Church. The real problem lay with the army, although it seemed like they were more concerned about inbound rebels than a contingent like ours.

'It's easy. We go into the fighting zone armed, and we come out as refugees. I do it three times a week,' said Churchill. The others nodded assent.

'What do you do about army checkpoints?' I asked.

They all looked at one another and then at me.

'If you are about to be captured, shoot yourself,' said D'Jango.

I looked at him. 'I can't help noticing that you didn't do that when your time came. You allowed yourself to be taken.'

'Are you calling me a liar?'

'No, a hypocrite. There's a difference.'

'Long as you're not calling me a liar.'

'When we come to an army checkpoint keep your trigger finger ready,' said Church. 'We can't brazen our way.'

As it turned out, we only came to one checkpoint, and it was the Customs and Excise boys.

We travelled for three hours. There was no stopping for food, which made all of us tense. Tosin had a skin condition that made him itch and the rest of us worried about contagion. His skin flaked off and floated in the air-conditioned interior before being sucked out or recirculated.

We had our guns on the floor. D'Jango had the safety on his machine gun off, which caused me to sweat. I knew he was like a talisman to the rebels, thought to be unstoppable and invulnerable with a keen sense of survival, but one bump in the road, the right kind of bump, could mean the end for all of us. Or at least those of us sitting in front of D'Jango. He had his eyes closed, but I knew he hadn't dozed off because he was blinking under his eyelids. Church brought him to all incursions for good luck and guidance, but D'Jango, I was sure, survived at the expense of others. I would have to watch him.

We paid our way through a tollbooth. Children shoved food items at us and we bought some puff-puff and Coca-Cola.

After continuing along the slightly narrower V8, Church turned into a side road, then off the road entirely. D'Jango held his gun off the floor, eyes still closed. Tosin stopped scratching and seemed alert, and I just copied them with no clue about what I would do.

The jeep came to an abrupt stop and Church jumped out. 'Change,' he said. He opened the trunk and stripped off his clothes. We were all to wear camouflage fatigues. They looked like Federal troop uniforms, and I said so. 'Yes,' said Church. 'You can be an officer.'

'I'd say a Hail Mary first,' said Tosin.

'Pull the stripes off,' said D'Jango. 'Makes you a target.'

I did.

'All right, march,' said Church. He had a rifle slung over his shoulder and magically acquired military bearing. 'No singing, though.'

We went through the bush in a direction that seemed random to me. There was no real footpath, just Tosin clearing the way with a cutlass. The undergrowth was not dense, and it was clearly a path they had used before. Mosquitoes fed on me constantly. I tried to remember if I'd taken anti-malarials that day.

We were in a column with Tosin on point, Church behind him, me and then D'Jango at the rear. Church whispered to me occasionally.

'The thing is the rebel positions are surrounded by Federal troops. The Feddies have no intention of quashing the rebels, but they will fiercely resist any kind of advance towards populated areas. No, sorry, I mean areas of financial import. The point is, we're unlikely to encounter any fighting. Once we get past the

Federal positions we bury these uniforms and change into civilian wear again.'

'I don't recall any Federal positions when I was taken before,' I said.

'Those were camps, base camps, not areas we were fighting for. Nobody truly cares about a half-dead conurbation or some land peeled off the side of a mountain. Start moving towards a dam or an oil refinery and see how animated and explosive the army gets.'

Animal traps left by hunters and trappers slowed us down, making the journey irritating. Tosin refused to destroy the livelihood of another man.

'Strange,' said Church. 'Mass destruction of government property through armed struggle he doesn't mind, but clear a few traps and he becomes reverent of downtrodden peasant heroes. I give you Tosin, hero of the proletariat. Still, it's good. It will ensure we arrive at night.'

I had not realised we'd be spending the night, and Church had ordered all mobile phones off as part of a communications blackout. Nana would worry, but it was too late for me to do anything about it.

I was musing on this when a big explosion turned everything bright and hot. Foliage and clumps of earth and chips of wood that used to be trees and grass and debris fell to the ground like perverse rain. I was already flat, prone, unable to breathe because my nose and mouth were pressed into wetness by something heavy on my back. A high-pitched whistle had been activated, and it was loud and constant. The Feddies were signalling each other. I had to shift the weight behind me or I would drown on dry land. I cleared the dirt from my eyes only to discover the wetness as blood. I retched, panicked, flailing like a pinned bug. I tried to roll, called for help, but the infernal ringing drowned out my voice. Someone helped me and I scrambled to my feet. The weight that used to be on me was Tosin's smouldering torso. His arms, legs and head were gone and his blood was in my mouth. Church and D'Jango were talking but the whistle was too loud for me to hear them.

Then it occurred to me that there was no whistle, and the sound was my ears ringing, a threnody for Tosin. My gun was still in place. I pulled it and cocked it like Church pantomimed for my benefit.

We ran.

'Can you hear again?' asked Church.

I nodded.

He patted me on the shoulder. 'Would have been an old landmine. Fuck knows who planted it: us, them or some other fatherless motherfuckers. Fuck knows when it was laid. Poor Tosin.'

My muscles stiffened and sweat poured off me as we slowed to a forced march. There were some gunshots behind us or in front of us – we couldn't tell with any certainty because of the acoustics and reverberations. I had a few minor cuts, but the Kevlar and extra steel plate stopped anything potentially fatal. I had Tosin's rifle, but I was concerned about blast damage to its action and thus did not feel it was an advantage. Besides, I had never trained on a rifle.

Church had lost his compass and we had no idea where the fuck we were.

And it was dark.

Not pitch, because we could still see each other and avoid rocks and trees, but torches were a no-no unless we wanted to be seen. Even I knew this and I'd never been in the bush. D'Jango kept moving his head as if he were trying to look everywhere at once, trying to swing his muzzle in the same direction as his eyes but failing. He did not inspire confidence.

'I know I'm a novice here,' I said in a fierce whisper, 'but this situation looks to be one that requires us to stay still and find our fucking bearings.'

Church looked at D'Jango, who shrugged.

'We wait, then,' said Church, but he didn't say what we would be waiting for. We each picked a tree and sat at the base, covering ourselves with elephant grass and leaves.

'Most of the snakes won't crawl up your trouser legs here,' said D'Jango. 'Usually they drop from the trees. The thing to worry about is the scorpions. A bit dry for leeches, so count your blessings, but the dry weather makes the scorpions' poison more concentrated.' He tucked everything tight into his boots and cradled his rifle.

Fireflies floated out from their hiding places and worked like cheap fireworks. It was all depressing. I could tell Churchill was embarrassed because he did not speak much, and when he did there was no cavalier humour or lewdness.

I dozed off.

I had a dream of an empty marketplace, like the one Nana told me about, now mine. I waded through the stalls until I reached the butcher's where the meat was all laid out as if the butcher had just left mid-cleave, knives laid out as if in use. Cow's blood flowed off the table into a bucket. There were no flies, no carrion birds, nothing alive.

Tosin's severed head rested on a slab. He blinked at me and smiled. He wore wrap-around shades like the night I first met him. His neck ended in a jagged wound and the remnants of his windpipe curled outwards, occasionally letting forth bubbles.

'I'm not pretty, eh?' he said.

'No,' I said. I took off his sunglasses.

'Will you learn anything from all this?'

'I don't know. Am I meant to?'

'Abo oro la nso f'omo luwabi. To ba de inu e, a di odindi.' *A hint is all you need give a good person. It grows into full knowledge inside them.*

'Do you know?'

'Me? Why ask me? I'm dead.' He looked around him with restless eyes, at the chopping block, back to me, up to the sky. 'Do you know, when you dress an animal you have to avoid cutting into the gall bladder at all costs?'

'It stores bile, and bile makes the rest of the meat bitter. Yes, I know.'

'Good. It's time for me to leave now. I don't think it's a good idea for me to keep my ancestors waiting.'

Heavy wings flapped and I saw vultures descending, about a dozen or so. They covered his head as he was trying to say something else.

I woke up with Church kicking my side.

'We're moving,' he said.

D'Jango had made moves while I slept. He found the rebel position and a path through the Feddies. We marched, and I ached along. My entire body was pain and I just placed one foot ahead of the other, hardly paying attention to where I was going, what was going on around me, or if I wanted to fucking survive or not. How loud is a racing heart? Can people around you not hear? I can't say how long it took while I was in that zone, but we stopped.

Not in a clearing, more like improvised trenches. Along with the others, I descended as the denuded ground dipped. The soldiers here all wore dark green helmets festooned with grass and twigs. Frontline troops, stinking of shit and urine and violence, staring at us with mistrust. The three of us sat and caught our wind, drinking water and chewing on bush meat – smoked antelope dried out till there was an almost wooden consistency to it. You chewed till your teeth ached and your jaws were on fire. There was a hint of rot to the taste but I was so hungry that I didn't care. False dawn was upon us and the frontliners faded away. The crickets seemed louder, but already the night had lost its mystical glamour. I wondered where Nana was or what the Widow Busi was up to.

'Five minutes,' said D'Jango.

The frontliners had left an elongated pit which was five feet in depth. Here they had slept and cooked. You could light a fire and through a complex system of bellows and ducts direct the smoke elsewhere. They had coal for this purpose. We buried our clothes and changed into variously coloured khakis. Church gave D'Jango and I Red Cross armbands. 'It makes soldiers hesitate, and sometimes that's all you need.'

He allowed us to use our phones while he radioed for transport. I sent a text message to Nana, but did not bother retrieving my voicemail.

Soon, a jeep arrived and we were ferried to the ambush point.

It did not look like the photographs because of different seasons, and a road that had been resurfaced a number of times, but residual similarity convinced me this was the place. D'Jango had not hesitated as he steered us there, which impressed me in spite of myself. The only hairy moment had been when we burst into a clearing and found seven rusty and ruptured hazardous chemical cylinders with Cyrillic writing on them. The vegetation had grown around them so we figured whatever toxic waste they had contained was long gone. Hopefully. I decided I wouldn't think about it.

Church and D'Jango stepped away from me as if I was a mystic trying to divine truths from the site using magic, whereas I had no idea what I was looking for.

'Which direction would Pa Busi's jeep have been facing on that day?' I asked. They pointed.

Well-planned ambush. There was a curve to the road at the

precise point which would offer some protection from curious eyes. As it was, no cars passed us, which didn't really mean much because traffic patterns could have changed over the years. The spot was in a depression as well, lower ground. A person with a sniper's perch in the trees could take his time as the car slowed into the curve. Especially if one of the occupants shoots as well. The trees were mostly palms, some of which had calabashes for sap collection, which would later be used to make emu or oguro.

Which meant—

'Is there a village close by?' I asked.

'A hamlet, more like,' said D'Jango. 'Ekuro. They are basket weavers. It is a small place.'

'Take me there,' I said.

Ekuro boasted no tarred road, no post office, no electric wires. All the houses were made from blocks of baked red clay and only a few had tin roofs. Meat hung from hooks for curing and dry tobacco leaves left an intoxicating smell in the air. Livestock roamed free and did not fear us. A she-goat shat right in front of me and my curses did not impress her.

'She likes you,' said Church.

'Funny,' I said. Why did everybody keep saying that?

'What are we looking for?' D'Jango asked.

'The palm wine tapper. Or tappers. I need to speak to every palm wine tapper in the village.'

There were three and the interviews were short because what I needed was there. We had a problem with their dialect, but the fact is everybody speaks violence, sex and money. I used money.

'Well?' said Church. He had a gourd of palm wine halfway to his lips and there was some dribble from the left angle of his mouth.

'I know what the assassin looks like,' I said. 'Let's go home.'

CHAPTER 14

I caught up with my voicemail.

Meep: 'Boy, where are you? Said you'd call when you got there. I miss you.' Nana.

Meep: 'Mr Weston Kogi, I am just calling to find out when you will call so we can talk about my husband. Please call me back soon. Thank you. Oh, and money is not a problem. Thank you, sir. Bye.' Strange woman looking for help with missing husband. What was her name again? Blegh.

Meep: 'Weston, I saw a missed call from you. Get in touch.' Abayomi Abayomi.

Meep: 'Mr Kogi, this is Diane Olubusi. I am not pleased at how we parted. It looked like you were sick. I feel awful about it and wish you would call. Just so I can see that you are all right. And, so that I can answer the questions that you put to me. The number is—'

Meep: 'Loverman, what a g'wan witcha? Why are ya late? Come to me, loverman. Come fill me up, loverman. I need you now.' Nana, singing the lyrics of a popular Nigerian reggae song.

Meep: 'Is this Sheun's number? Sheun, don't forget to pick up the amplifier and get a gorodom for the ice. And be fast because the ice is melting already.' What the fuck?

Meep: '. . . [breathing] . . . [breathing] . . .'

Meep: 'Boy, I'm worried about you. I know you'll turn up, but I'm tired. Call me when you can.' Nana.

Meep: 'End of messages.'

CHAPTER 15

Back to civilisation. In a few minutes Church would drop me bang in the middle of Ede.

'I still don't understand what we just did,' said D'Jango.

'Okay, listen: Pa Busi wasn't just blown up. He was also shot with a high-powered rifle. The palm wine tappers would have the best vantage points from their palm trees. I was looking for any witness on the day of the assassination. Did they see anyone on the trees that was new? That sort of thing. What we got was even better. Our guy said one of the tappers was taken by the forest on the exact date Pa Busi died. They also saw a stranger lurking around days before. I'm betting that's our man.'

'What's he look like?' asked Church.

'That information is . . . more modest. Tall man, hunched, dreadlocks, complexion uncertain. But it's a step closer, though.'

'Ore, for all we know he could be a mercenary imported from Nigeria for that very purpose. And he probably went back to Nigeria immediately after. Then what? You gonna go to Nigeria and find him? Hmm? Interview all the Rastas?'

'One hundred and seventy million Nigerians in Nigeria alone, man. Not counting the ones spread far and wide like gypsum seeds. Tall man ma bombo claart.'

'Hang on, do you guys find the description familiar? Are you trying to tell me something? Is this where I'm supposed to fol-low another line of inquiry?'

Church and D'Jango looked at each other and guffawed.

'Wankers,' I said.

Home.

It bothered me that Nana wasn't there. I don't think she received any of my messages, so she didn't know I had no way of calling her back during Churchill's communication blackout. Maybe she was out looking for me somewhere. I called her but it went to voicemail.

'Hey, baby. I'm back. Listen, I didn't know I'd be out overnight. Church never told me beforehand. I wasn't able to phone either. I've missed you. Call me back.'

It seemed inadequate. I felt like calling again, leaving a fluffier message, saying I loved her, but I didn't bother. I planned to buy her an expensive dinner later to make up for it, maybe go to a club.

I put the phone in the power cradle, stripped off and showered, my skin bumpy with insect bites and scratches. Some of the cuts from the bomb blast opened again and blood mixed with the water and dirt at my feet. My bones felt old. If this job didn't kill me it would definitely take years off my life. I sliced up a papaya and ate it while making notes on the dining table. Knowing a vague description of the assassin wasn't much. It did not tell me, for example, who paid the piper, which was more important. Why would a Rasta even kill Pa Busi, or anyone at all for that matter? Dreads are too distinctive. You'd think a Rasta would take enough time to disguise themselves, pack the hair in a special way. Except if the person was not a true Rasta in the first place and put on a dreadlock wig to avoid detection. The permutations were mad-dening. So, really, all I had was a tall black male. Hunched was neither here nor there and hairstyle was unreliable. Still, I thought I had caught a scent, and that would have to do.

I called up Abayomi.

'Hi.'

'Hello, Weston. How goes everything?' he said. He was outside and though the connection was good there seemed to be a multitude around him and that made him difficult to hear.

'Managing. Surviving. Listen, should we meet for an update and a beer?'

'Not an easy thing to manage, *mon frère*. I'm negotiating a deal that will take a lot of time. If you can come over here I'm sure I can squeeze some time, though.'

'Sure. Tell me where you are. Wait: I forgot something. Listen, there are some secret police guys sniffing about, trying to pick up my trail. I might lead them to you.'

'I'm not worried about those clowns, Weston. Get over here if you can.'

'Where are you?'

'The docks.'

'That cesspit? I was there yesterday. Nothing but shit and sinners. Pass.'

'No, I'm on a nice ship. Tell me when you arrive and I'll send a skiff for you.'

'Define "nice".'

'Women with huge cup sizes and the skins of movie stars are feeding me grapes and dripping honey in my mouth.'

'Liar.'

'Give me at least one hour to sort something out. See you soon.'

A speedboat makes any large body of water seem romantic. Cutting through the Atlantic from the docks to a luxury liner where Abayomi Abayomi waited, I had to restrain myself from opening my mouth to the spray. That way lies hepatitis A.

The liner was called *The Bernice* and it was crawling with thin, tall men carrying AK-47s and RPGs. Oh, fuck, of course. They were Somali pirates. What were they doing docking in Alcacia? And what did Abayomi have to do with them?

He was waiting for me at the end of the gangplank, arms spread out like a party host and flanked by his own armed guards, who were definitely Alcacian.

'Weston! Omo nla! Welcome. What would you like to drink?'

He led me to a starboard deckchair and I had an iced ginger ale while he sipped a shitty-looking cocktail. He sighed after the cool liquid went down his throat, then he looked at me.

'I know what you're thinking. You're thinking, What's he doing with Somalians? That *is* what you're thinking, right?'

I nodded.

'I won't lie to you. Ten per cent of a couple million dollars is a large number and the revolution is always hungry for cash.'

'So you're doing it for the money?'

'Money is the reason the pirates exist.'

'The wrath of the nations will be poured out on them, Abayomi. NATO and their third-world puppets don't like their oil tankers and pleasure yachts molested.'

'Who do you think is responsible for— Oh, sit and listen, little one, for I am wise and shall tutor you well.'

'Heh. Speak.'

'Somalia hasn't had a proper central government for years. A bunch of sun-toughened warlords rule with the gun and machete and the UN turns its back. Why? Because of money. Somalia has nothing to export except beautiful women with high foreheads. They have no oil, or what they have is not even worth speculating over under the current conditions. They have no diamonds, no cobalt, no uranium. America made an excursion, lost two Black

Hawk helicopters and ran crying to their mamas. The world turned away; after all, it's a tough, brutal place. Let them kill each other, one less nigger nation.'

'They grant those who need asylum a place to go, Abayomi. At least in the UK.'

'Pennies. They did not tackle the root cause. Sorting out the lack of organised government in Somalia would have prevented or at least alleviated the emergence of pirates. Do not forget that the pirates started out as fishermen. The lack of government meant no coastguard, meaning trawler fishers from Western nations could come to their seas unmolested and unregulated. This was their livelihood. Since they couldn't fish in their own territory, they armed themselves and started attacking ships first to protect their fishing grounds, then to rob, then to demand ransom, which turned out to be lucrative.'

'It seems to me like you consider them patriots.'

Abayomi paused, thought for a few seconds and shrugged. 'The outcome of their actions is attention focused on their tortured country. Some do that by writing articles, some by fighting, others by piracy. The end result is the same: Somalia moves closer to democracy.'

'Or a few pirates get blown into atoms by a frigate sent by the French or British.'

'Acceptable risk, acceptable outcome.'

'Jesus, you *are* a lawyer.'

'Every day of the week, baby. Look, I know. These are just thugs, and they would steal no matter what the status quo was. Working with them is mad. The ringleaders are half psychotic on khat most of the time.'

Abayomi looked fit and prosperous. The revolution worked well for hired mouthpieces, it seemed. Never had to lift a gun. Again he was in a suit, brown, with beautiful brown leather court shoes. A gold chain glittered on his neck, but it was tucked in and most of it was hidden by the white shirt he had on. He looked cool, untouched by the heat. I envied him that. Me, I felt like I'd been on a slow roast since arrival at Alcacia International.

'Now that they have a taste for it getting them to stop will be difficult. The oil companies pay the ransom for their jacked ships because it's cheaper to pay two million in exchange for a two-hundred-million cargo. That's just good business sense, but only in the short term. It gets the freighters back, but rewards and hence encourages further piracy.

'Can you believe these fuckheads wanted to shoot a music video on board? No, really. I had to tell them that piracy is a crime and Interpol would find them because the video would qualify as photographic evidence. Don't ask me: someone's cousin is a musician, a rapper. Wants a place to have bling and big bottoms and merlot and weed, all mixing to the beat of his baseline. Guns too.'

'How did they manage to take this vessel?'

'Audacity and deadly weapons. This boat has no big guns – it's a pleasure craft. Passengers are locked in cabins. All the crew had by way of defence was a water hose. Crew tried to blow the pirates off as they in turn tried to board with grappling hooks. I imagine it was comical and frightening at the same time.'

Despite the cavalier attitude, Abayomi was tired. A day's growth of beard, a rim of spidery blood-vessels around his iris all pointed to near exhaustion.

'Should I get out of your hair, then?' I asked. 'Give you my report?'

Abayomi nodded at his bodyguards and they stepped back. 'In Yoruba.'

Using my halting command of the language I outlined what I had learned and gave him my description of the killer.

'You've gone far,' said Abayomi.

'Still far to go,' I said.

'One would almost think you didn't care about your retainer.'

Now, why would he say that?

'I like the retainer very much,' I said. 'Can you point me in any directions?'

'That kind of assassin would be expensive. Most likely there were initial tentative approaches to other top players in the field. I'll give you a name; you ask if he or anyone he knows was offered the contract.'

'And the secret police guys?'

'I'll ask around. Leave that to me.'

'One more thing. Should I . . . would you be bothered if I took minor assignments from others?'

'No. You've exceeded my expectations already. If you have opportunities go for them.'

We talked some more, but nothing of significance, so I left just as the Somali interpreter started to get antsy. I watched every single Rasta who walked past me. This was ridiculous. It wasn't even paranoia. It was more a morbid curiosity or something undefinable. I stopped a street vendor and bought fried yams, plantain and sun-dried fish. An enterprising young Igbo boy brought me a bottle of Coke so I bought that too. People went by. The cars raised hell with their horns, but nobody could clear Ede streets in the middle of a working day. I sat on an empty stall and ate my lunch. I felt like pouring the Coke over my head, but instead I drank some and placed the cool bottle on my forehead. I was lying to myself, pretending to think, but I knew what I really wanted.

I called the Widow Busi.

I hadn't seen the Oduduwa Wall in many years. It was about forty years old. The mad idea behind it was some pseudo-scientist woke up one day and said there was a rapid decline in the amount of sand on the beach. This, he said, had to do with erosion and wash-off by the sea. The solution he proposed was to build a sea wall, a twenty-mile-long construction that would keep the sand in and the sea out. He was able to convince the government of the day and they built all of two miles before funding ran out or civil war started in Nigeria or the architect was the victim of cholera or witchcraft. The project lay dormant and time passed. Then, over the years, graffiti artists began work. The quality varied from crude to amazing, but every inch of the land side of the wall (which tended to be leeward in most wind conditions) was covered in writing or paintings. The subject matter varied, but it chronicled a simplified and condensed version of mostly Western popular culture. I used to love walking there and was delighted when the widow suggested this as a place to meet.

There were few people walking along the wall. The insurgents tended to limit tourist activity. I drifted westward. She said she'd find me, the widow did. A teenager ambled up to me and tried to sell me a wood chip from the One True Cross. This was because Joseph of Arimathea who donated his tomb for the interment of Jesus's body found bits of wood there. He is said to have removed wooden splinters of the cross that became embedded in Christ's body while dragging it to Golgotha. This particular splinter had found its way to Alcacia by way of the Ethiopian eunuch converted by St Philip. It was an interesting tale and the boy tried to add value by saying the wood had healing properties, but I waved him on.

An eleha stood ahead of me. Eleha were married Muslim women in shapeless black garb similar to a burka covering their entire body from head to toe. Netting resembling a fencing mask covered the face, and you could not see the figure of the woman beneath because of the bulbous design. The alternative to wearing it was to stay at home. When I was a boy they scared me more than Darth Vader.

I faced the wall and tried to get lost in the graffiti, which was easy. I walked past a black-and-white rendering of King Kong holding Fay Wray while climbing the Empire State Building, biplanes circling overhead; Sean Connery as James Bond; a colour painting of Muhammad Ali, one hand aloft in a victory salute, one foot on a red demon labelled as George Foreman with the caption 'ALI, BOMA YE' repeated six times in blue; a pyramid showing Elizabeth Taylor atop it sporting unnaturally huge breasts and big green eyes; Bugs Bunny; an Aston Martin; *The Spy Who Came in from the Cold*; a crude American flag; an ode to Kingsway Stores; *Casablanca*; Ed Wood; Spider-Man in mid-swing; James Coburn as Our Man Flint; *Space Shuttle Challenger* in flames; multiple drawings and paintings of Rambo; Chuck D; Christopher Reeve; Albert Einstein. And on it went.

The eleha drew near me and she smelled pretty nice, like expensive perfume. I was about to excuse myself when she started talking.

'Do you not wish this place did not stink of urine?' It was the widow.

I recovered quickly. 'A wall is a wall, I guess. No wall is immune to being pissed against.'

'I wonder if anyone does this to the Great Wall of China.'

'Of course they must.' I faced her. 'Mrs Olubusi. A pleasure to see you again.'

'All mine, I assure you. Forgive me for not shaking hands. It would look odd to observers.'

'I didn't know you were a Muslim.'

'I am not.'

'Oh . . .'

'Are you feeling better? The other day—'

'I'm fantastic. Do you wish for us to stand still or walk while we talk?'

'Let us walk along the wall and you can ask me what it is you

147

want to know.' She paused at a drawing of a slim white man with a Viking hat, a red singlet and a moustache, but holding a microphone. 'Who is this supposed to be?'

'That's Freddie Mercury,' I said. 'From Queen.'

'Ah. I see.' She was like an old woman in the black enveloping material. 'Do you like the theatre, Mr Kogi?' she asked.

'No, and before you start, I do not want to go either. This is not going to be one of those scenarios where you save the underclasses by introducing them to culture.'

'I think you are far from representative of the underclasses.'

'Oh, I'm not like the others, yes? I'm a good nigger.'

'You are being rude, Mr Kogi. Why?' She stopped.

'I'm sorry.'

'Apologies do not interest me. I asked why you were being like that.'

I scratched my head and looked out at some dunes. 'I'm not sure. I'm intimidated by you, I guess. I was trying to even things out by being crude. I really am sorry.'

She appeared to consider this.

'What would you like to know?' she asked at length.

'Tell me about your relationship with Pa Busi.'

'We were married.'

'I know that.'

'That should tell you everything.'

'Not really. It tells me he paid your bride price, met your family and probably had lawful carnal knowledge of you.'

'As you say.'

'Were you in love?'

'Please.'

'Did you get along?'

'Are you married, Mr Kogi?'

'No.'

'Pity. I do know some fine single women who would find you

an acceptable match. At any rate if you were married you would know that husbands and wives exist in a state of truce most of the time, with conflict and ecstasy pulling and pushing against each other.'

'In your relationship with your husband, did conflict dominate?'

'No.' She sighed. 'I was his second wife and there were quite a few years between us. He treated me like a silly little girl whenever I took issue with his behaviour, and this was not always a bad thing. He could be quite indulgent. He would walk away rather than argue and concede as many points as were within reason. I confess, I did push the boundaries of reason at times.'

'How did you meet?'

'We met in Italy, at Sorrento. I was looking at the cliffs and the Bay of Naples, considering whether to take a speedboat to Capri, making notes and sketches, when I heard Yoruba spoken behind me. I recognised him immediately.'

'Did he notice you?'

'With all humility, Mr Kogi, everyone notices me and they will continue to do so until gravity and time finally win the battle we commenced at puberty. He asked if he could use the viewer after me and I said we could share. His entourage faded away and we pointed things out to each other in turn. He kept feeding coins and that is how we started talking.'

'Were you attracted to him?'

'Not at first, but it did happen over the next few hours.'

'Hard to believe given the age gap.'

'You learn to look past the obvious after some time. All sorts of men ask me out till this very day. They either tell me I'm beautiful or begin the primate display of virility. I do not mean literally—'

'I know what you're referring to. They tell you precisely what makes them a superior choice of mate.'

'Yes. He did not do that. Instead, we talked about shellfish. Or jellyfish. Some marine organism. He was very well-spoken, very articulate. I was entranced. Mr Kogi, people, men especially, do not know or understand the value of good conversation, of erudition. This man did.'

'This might sound rude, but it's not meant to be. Did his financial status have anything to do with how articulate you found him? With your relationship?'

'Why do you ask?'

'Well, you've alluded to not loving him, but you were attracted to him. That's not necessarily contradictory, but when an ayounge like you is involved with an arugbo like him finance is often involved.'

'Some women just prefer older men.'

'I'm sure they do.' I wiped my damp brow with the back of my hand. 'Are you one of them?'

'No.'

'But you weren't dating him for the money.'

'I did not need the money. My family originates from Ife, the cradle of the Yoruba, in Nigeria. We are moneyed folk. Of old.'

'But you did inherit a lot after his death.'

'You think I killed him for his money?'

'Did you?'

'Be reasonable, Mr Kogi. If I had done, I would not tell you. If I had not, I would simply say "no", but it would change none of your suspicions.'

'True. Why'd you ask me if I liked the theatre? Do I look like a Philistine?'

'Ask me again in a few minutes.'

'Why?'

'I have to make up my mind about you.'

'Fine. Did your husband have life insurance?'

'He did. Paid out, investigated thoroughly by claims departments, all above board.'

'Which company?'

'Gentian Alliance.'

'Value?'

'Sixteen million dollars.'

'US?'

'Yes.'

I swallowed.

'Mrs Olubusi, who would want your husband dead?'

'Not a soul. He had no enemies.'

'You do realise that's not helpful.'

'It's the truth. It could have been a random rebel attack. He was in rebel territory. Mistaken identity.'

'Possible.'

'You sound unconvinced.'

'Yes, do I not?'

Her fingers traced a sunken-relief lettering of Buffy the Vampire Slayer. 'Is that a detecting technique? Eternal scepticism?' She asked this in a low voice.

'I have no techniques,' I answered truthfully. 'Did you have a lover while he was alive?'

She didn't answer and I didn't push it. She walked towards the dunes after dropping a greeting card from the folds of her cloth. Inside was a theatre ticket.

On the way back I phoned Nana and left a voicemail.

'Getting a bit worried now. If you can't phone send a text to say you're okay, Nana. I miss you. Bye.'

Back home I stripped off, wiped my armpits and genitals with a damp cloth and put on fresh boxer shorts. I had a small rash around my waist where the money belt made contact, and the skin there looked like the underbelly of a fish. I used some of Nana's talcum powder and strapped the belt back on. I quartered a papaya and ate it minus the rind. I wrote in my journal for an hour to get everything straight in my head.

Officially, Pa Busi's murder remained unsolved. Jeep blown up, no survivors. No known enemies. No autopsy, fast-track embalming and state burial.

I had uncovered two survivors, one in an insane asylum, the other suicided. From my conversation with the mortician and the surviving bodyguard, Pa Busi was shot at least twice before the jeep blew up and dragged out of it, probably to make it seem like he lived for some minutes after the blast. It stank of conspiracy. The non-insane bodyguard, Wallace, makes furtive contact with someone, becomes intensely paranoid, shoots himself, even though his cousin doesn't believe it's suicide.

Rewind. The wife. Inherits sixteen million. Good motive, except she was already 'moneyed, of old'. Confessed to arguments, but the claim had been investigated. I did not see Diane doing it. Besides, how would she arrange it? She was too well-known to contact a hit man directly. I made a note to look into her associates, see if there was anyone unsavoury. One place to start was my father, seeing as he's shady and she mentioned knowing him. Hmm. There was the lover, too.

The secret police were following me. Were they trying to maintain the seal on their conspiracy? Did the government kill Pa Busi? Nobody believed he had any enemies, but maybe the government benefited from the conflict with the rebels and did not want an elder statesman mucking about with the status quo.

I had to be careful. Abayomi did not like the fact that I'd made progress. I decided not to update him any more. I had to keep reminding myself that my aim was to live through this without pissing off any of my homicidal paymasters or shadowy state police. I had to slow down, wait for Nana, run it by her. And by 'slow' I meant stop.

The phone rang. I closed my journal and answered it.

'Mr Weston Kogi?'

'Wait, don't tell me: your husband.'

'Yes, sir. You did not call me back.'

'What is your name?'

'Clara. Mrs Clara Efriti.'

I exhaled, not caring if she heard.

'If I could just meet you to explain. No obligation to take the case,' said Clara. 'I can pay you to take the meeting, sir.'

Not like I had anything else to do, and it did look like she was offering me money here.

'Okay. Where will you be?'

Clara Efriti was late.

We had agreed to meet at the central Ede bus station where scores of danfo, bolekaja, molue, okada and taxis converged in a sweet and noisy chaos which they and the habitual passengers appeared to understand perfectly. There was no edifice to orient me, no fixed point. It was simply a wide-open space like a football field bang in the middle of town. Area Boys and agbero roamed about, sometimes shouting, but in a good-natured way. Agbero were literally the 'gatherers of crowds' and their job was to corral passengers for the buses since there was no real queue system. They were loud and affected aggressiveness because they had to at least seem capable of violence to discourage fare dodgers.

Thankfully, there was no mud that day. I had to fend off the usual street traders, religion peddlers and hooligans. It did not help that no one was in any kind of uniform, unless you counted the white robes of the ascension prophets. You could only tell the passengers apart by their purposeful manner. I stood at the edge of the boiling mass near the road, waiting for Efriti. I wouldn't be there if Nana hadn't taken off somewhere and it was a sure bet that she was angry with me. I had my back to the street, keeping my eye scanning the terminus, so I was surprised when a voice called to me from behind.

'Mr Kogi!'

I turned to the voice, spun and started running away the second I saw a gun pointing out of a car window.

I ran into the crowd, which now convulsed and became a mass of panicked people because of gunshots. I remember it was a Renault of some sort – red, window down, a man in the passenger seat aiming a black revolver my way. He was black and wore sunglasses. I did not, at first, see the driver. I weaved through the fear-crazed people with my head low as bullets hit buses, shattered windows, but missed me. I hid behind a molue and peered back. The car had turned into the terminus and was negotiating the obstacle course of abandoned mass-transit vehicles. No active shooting. I darted from cover to cover, silent as possible. It then occurred to me that *I also had a gun* and with shaking hands I drew my weapon from the ankle holster.

I was sweating all over, including my palms. The grip I had on the gun was laughable, but I wasn't amused. I crouched behind a danfo and peeped out. The Renault had stopped, but the engine was still running. The man with the sunglasses was out and walking towards me with intent. I flipped the safety, took four quick breaths, broke cover and fired five times at him. I saw his mouth open wide and he dropped to the floor and rolled to the left, out of sight behind a diesel storage drum. I missed him outright but one of the Renault's headlights exploded, spraying glass on the tarmac. I was back behind cover, mouth-breathing and wiping my hands dry on my trouser thighs. My heart would not slow. My right elbow and shoulder hurt from the recoil. I could feel the adrenalin in each one of my blood vessels, down to the capillaries in my eyes. I sidled to another vehicle and fired random shots in their general direction, each blast pumping testosterone into me, making me feel invulnerable. I was going to kill them both, and after they were dead I would still empty my clip into their bodies, and even then I'd fuck the larger of the bullet holes so that my jism would follow their spirits down to whatever hell awaited them.

Then I heard two rapid reports and an abbreviated scream. I risked a look. The sunglasses guy was on the ground, supine, his lower torso hidden behind the diesel drum. There was a hole in the windscreen of the Renault on the driver's side, blood splashed on the inner surface. *A man walked towards the car.* He looked plump but he was tall and wore braids tied into a knot. He opened the driver's door, aimed and fired once. The person inside twitched and went still. The man reached in to touch something, then he turned to my direction and looked right at me. His face was odd, completely asymmetrical with one eye narrow and one slightly large. There were too many teeth in his mouth, which was slightly open. His face was pock-marked and textured with pimples. He dropped the handgun he had in his hand and walked away.

What in the name of all the copulating deities . . . ?

Numbers.

I have always found them calming. It is not sorcery. I read somewhere that they occupy the mind, prevent it from focusing on anxiety or the source of it.

Two by two is four.

I was surely anxious.

Julius Caesar was stabbed twenty-three times.

I took deliberate breaths, drank my beer, sweated in the booth.

There are fourteen books in the Old Testament Apocrypha.

I could not reach Nana. Ditto Clara Efriti. On the seat beside me my gun was cocked and ready.

Twelve mug stains on the table I was using.

It must have been Clara, whoever the fuck she really was.

Six hundred and sixty-six, the number of The Beast, for buying and selling, forehead and right hand, don't leave home without it.

After the stranger killed my would-be assassin I ran, ended up in a bar, the Night Flash Point, it was called. There was a black-and-white cathode-ray television that played *The Exorcist*. A Chinese man sat at the bar talking to the listless barman, but otherwise the place was empty and shrouded in darkness.

Two. The number of secret policemen who failed to protect me from the attack.

On TV, a news bulletin interrupted Linda Blair's antics. Police all over the bus terminus. Close-ups of the two dead people. One male, one female. No mention of me or my mystery protector. I was willing to bet the woman was Clara.

Where the fuck was Nana?

Seven. The number of seconds into the news bulletin when they showed the identity card of one of the victims. The male, Farayola Ifriti, private detective.

I had seen that kind of ID before.

I phoned Church.

'Bi oju ba ko oju, aala yoo to,' said Church. Matters are best sorted out face-to-face.

'One, two, buckle my shoe,' I said.

'What?'

'Nothing. I'm thinking about numbers.'

'You're fucking insane.'

'Maybe.'

George Elemo, cog in the Ministry of Justice wheel, issuer of my PI licence, the person Church and I were waiting for, this person who is the link between me and Clara Efriti.

'You don't know of any killer in braids or dreads, Church? Don't hold back from me now.'

'It is a myth that major players are known to each other, aburo. Or that they are generally known. The expiration business thrives on secrecy. So, no, I do not know your mystery saviour.'

Church and I were waiting outside the ministry for George Elemo to emerge.

'We'll have to kill him if your theory is correct,' said Church.

'I know,' I said. 'I know.'

People, workers, started leaving the ministry by four thirty. I kept my gaze fixed on the employees. Church spent his time rating the women's breasts and buttocks. He thought I was too grim. The rage inside me was white hot, but glacier cool on the outside. You'd think we were just a couple of layabouts staring at chicks, sitting in a car.

'Is that him?' asked Church.

It was. He slipped from one of the side doors and made his unobtrusive way to the parking space.

'Yes, that's George.'

'Skinny one, isn't he?'

'Let's pick him up.'

'You *are* insane. There are security cameras and ogberi all around. We're going to follow him and wait for the most favourable time.'

Which is what we did. The stories Church regaled me with while we followed Elemo were too disgusting to recount. Taking the guy was a simple affair. Traffic slowed on our lane. Church left the car, sprinted up to George's car, reached in and switched off his engine, all without concern for witnesses, which kind of invalidated his earlier speech, but Churchill's actions didn't always make sense. George made no fuss and followed Church to our car. He did not seem surprised to see me. Church got into the back seat with George and said to me, 'Make a U-turn, aburo.'

'Hello, George,' I said, looking into the rear-view. I hate driving outside London, but necessity, invention, et cetera. 'I know you don't want to be seen with me, so this will be a short meeting.'

'I hope so,' said George. 'I liked that car. It was a present.' He was irritated. Not exactly the fear and trembling I expected.

Church poked him. 'You won't need it after today.'

'I surely will. I can't walk to work,' George said.

Fuck this.

I stopped the car, drew my gun and pointed it at his nose. Still no fear. I cocked the weapon. He raised his arms defensively and turned his head away. 'You can't kill me,' he said rapidly. 'You can't. Think about it, you mongoloid Holloway shit.'

Church punched him on the left ear, then clouted him from behind. George cowered, but not as much as I would have if I knew my time was up. I was curious.

You can't kill me, George had said.

'Why? Why can I not kill you?' I hated his calm. I wanted to abandon reason and shoot. I'd never shot anyone before, but then I'd never been this angry before. Assassination attempts will do that to a man.

Elemo smiled. 'What do you think you know about me, Weston Kogi?'

I pressed the gun under his chin, dimpling the skin. 'I know that you gave my details to Efriti, probably for money. Efriti is . . . was a private detective who saw me as a rival. He probably had you looking out for PI registration applications. That way he could find out who his competition was and take them out of the market by scaring them off or shooting them. Keeps his monopoly alive. Everybody in Ede goes to him, I expect. He probably ran his usual scam: get his wife Clara to make a bogus plea about a missing husband, set up the new PI, me; except it didn't quite work and I'm still fucking here.'

George spat out of the window. 'You did not start the story at the beginning, Mr Kogi. You left out the part where I am identified as an asset *in situ* to the People's Christian Army. You cannot touch me, boy.'

I looked at Church who had stopped smiling. He shrugged but said nothing.

'You should count yourself lucky. I'm out of pocket with Efriti dead and his steady gratuity gone. There's also the matter of my car. I could go right to Supreme Commander Craig to demand compensation of you. But I am understanding. I realise you have just escaped death and your blood is hot.'

'Understanding?' I said.

'Remove your firearm, then take me back to where I left my car.'

'I—' I started but Church gently pushed the barrel aside.

'No, he's right,' Church said. He smiled, a tight-lipped grimace. His eyes were narrow. 'We apologise for the inconvenience.'

That night, as I prepared to attend the theatre, I heard a news bulletin on the radio.

'In a bizarre twist to the story of the terminus shootings earlier today, George Elemo, a middle-level worker in the Ministry of Justice, was bludgeoned to death while being detained by police. This is the twenty-seventh death in custody this year in Ede City.

'Elemo was arrested earlier today based on an anonymous tip that he had been connected to the murdered private investigator Efriti who was found shot dead with his wife Clara earlier today. Eyewitnesses state that Efriti himself had been firing shots at an unidentified male before being himself shot dead. It is unclear if his intended victim was responsible for his death.

'It is also unclear what Elemo's exact involvement was, but before he could be questioned another detainee beat him to death with a pestle. Police sources have—'

I had no idea what Churchill had done, but I didn't really care. I wasn't sorry Elemo was dead.

I wasn't sorry for anything.

CHAPTER 16

A taxi dropped me at the main entrance of the National Theatre. The percussion coming from inside was seismic. I was on time so I knew it was a curtain-raiser act rather than the main event. Hands and drumsticks assaulted tight animal skins with a frenzied, manic energy. It was not full of people – theatre was not a top priority in a land of struggling masses. At the ticket hall they took one look at my reservation and sent a tightly gowned Chinese woman to lead me away through a side door. She asked me in Yoruba if I would like some champagne and I said yes. What the hell, I had just survived an assassination attempt. I deserved to celebrate. Her Yoruba was educated, fluent, like she had lived here all her life except for the absence of regional accent. Before I could ask any questions she ushered me into a small room with vases, statuettes, sofas, heavy curtains and Diane Olubusi.

'Thank you, April,' she said.

'Good evening, Mrs Olubusi,' I said.

'I believe in this informal atmosphere first names are called for. If you have no objections, that is.'

'I have none.' I sat on the adjacent chair.

She wore a low-cut white dress, designed in such a way to give the impression of a woman wrapped in a bolt of silk which was about to slip off. She smelled like a botanical garden with all the flowers in full bloom. On her left wrist she wore a single gold bracelet. Nothing on her neck but creamy fair skin devoid of spot or blemish.

April brought me a long-stemmed glass of bubbly and I tipped it towards Diane who raised her glass in an ultra-feminine gesture. Her slender fingers ended in black fingernails.

'Shall we see the rest of the opening act?' she said.

I nodded and she led me to a balcony which could seat ten. The sound assaulted us as soon as she opened the door. There was a man in ofi underwear and nothing else playing a saxophone solo reminiscent of and obviously channelling Fela Kuti. Diane was rapt even though the whole scene seemed too perseverative to me. Then it was over and I dutifully clapped. April refreshed our drinks.

The play was titled *Mother of All* and I should probably have recognised the main players but I didn't. I had never really liked theatre.

'Are you familiar with the legend of Moremi?' she asked.

'I vaguely remember being told about it in school and by my mother.'

'*Mother of All* is a dramatisation of it.'

'Should be fun.'

Then it started.

Moremi is a fact-based myth from Ife, the birthplace of the Yoruba in Nigeria. It might be based on history, but who knows what drunken eunuch was taking history down in those days or, in fact, who rewrote it? Ife suffered several raids from the Igbo, who appeared inhuman to the Yoruba because they garlanded themselves in raffia and other leaves.

Unable to defend themselves from the otherworldly invaders, the people of Ife suffered numerous attacks until a married mother-of-one, Moremi, decided to let herself get captured in order to learn the secret of the Igbos, their weakness, their flaws. When captured she was given to the Igbo king as a slave but she was so noble and wise that they made her the queen. She discovered that the Igbo were human and owed their fearsome appearance to foliage and were afraid of catching fire during battle. Moremi escaped back to Ife and told of what she knew. The next raid had a different outcome as the Ife warriors ran among the Igbos with lit torches and thus set fire to them. This victory stopped the raids and made a hero out of Moremi. The tragedy was that Moremi had promised a river goddess her only son if she succeeded. The goddess demanded that she kill her son. After some futile negotiation she had to comply. The whole of Ife shared her sorrow and declared that she was now a mother in perpetuity to them all.

'Some versions of the story say the son was not dead and that he woke up on the riverbank and was taken up into heaven,' whispered Diane. Her lips were close to my ear and I could smell the fruity champagne on her breath. I was aware of nothing else but her lips and the skin of her neck at that moment. I gripped the armrests of my chair so tight to stop me from misbehaving. I turned to her and in the light reflected from the stage I saw her pupils turn my way. Her mouth was slightly open as if in mid-speech.

'You're going to have to let me enjoy the play, Diane,' I said, but my voice was not my own as so often happens when I'm stressed.

I turned back to the scene playing out. Moremi, in bed with her husband, explained why she must go with the Igbo invaders. Her husband brought up the slight problem of gang-rape.

Diane was silent. During the intermission we discussed inconsequential things, irrelevances delivered with polite smiles. During a scene where the Igbo king first made love to Moremi, however, she placed her hand on my thigh. I was not sure if she was aware of it. She seemed genuinely aroused by the stylised sex scene unfolding. I did not move and her hand remained there until the end of the play.

Following Diane home was a bad idea. Unfortunately, I did not have a what-would-Jesus-do state of mind. In a way there was nothing I could have done to prevent it. I was not equipped to resist creatures like Diane Olubusi; neither did I want to.

At three forty-five a.m. I thought of Nana but immediately pushed her out of my mind.

At six a.m. Diane finally fell asleep. I remember thinking Moremi could not have loved her husband or child that much to set off on a spy mission without caring about the consequences to her family. What motives could she have had? Was he abusive to her? Had she even wanted a family in the first place?

At eight a.m. I checked my phone messages. Nothing from Nana. A missed call from Abayomi Abayomi. One message from Churchill.

'Bawo ni, brother? Listen, wherever you are don't go out tomorrow. Stay at home and watch television. That's all I have to say. And keep this to yourself. Ire, o.'

Whatever that meant.

It was daylight. Did I have enough time to rush home and hunker down?

* * *

Diane was calling my name from far, far away. I woke up again.

'What time is it?' I asked. I wasn't fully sure where I was.

'Ten o'clock or thereabouts. Listen to the news. Look at what has happened.'

This, then, was what Church meant. Ede market was on fire.

Several blazes, all from different parts of the same sprawling market. The report said it was unlikely to be accidental in origin because witnesses reported explosions in the early hours. There was no effective fire brigade service in Alcacia. The fire engines were wide American beasts, cast-offs without a functioning water hydrant infrastructure to support their operation. Roofing blackened and rolled back, wooden framework glowed orange and produced steady burning flames or persisted as embers, the occasional gas cylinder popped and caused secondary local eruptions. Pathetic locals used buckets to try to put out small areas of the fire. They were not successful. Mobile phone footage showed one man on fire after trying to retrieve goods from a store. It was unclear if the person was looting or trying to rescue his stock. Reporters interviewed tearful men and women who mourned the loss of their livelihood.

Ede market covered one square mile. From a distance it seemed to have been constructed by a six-year-old given limitless supplies of corrugated iron and wooden support beams. The shops were all the same – box constructs with storage in the back and stalls in front where goods could be displayed to customers who walked down narrow aisles. They were all tightly packed and there was a saying: you touch one shop, you touch them all. It would not have been difficult to raze the market. A message from the Liberation Front of Alcacia followed the conflagration footage.

It was a grainy image of three men, only the middle one sitting. The other two held in turn an AK-47 and a rocket launcher. All were masked and none looked like Church in stature. The rhetoric was not broadcast. Clever. The public would know who to blame since LFA had taken responsibility, but not why. Instead, the chief of police gave an interview.

Diane rose from the bed, ethereal and unreal to me. She moved like her feet did not touch the ground, like she was borne on a cushion of air or clouds. She got dressed.

'Will you be all right on your own?' she asked.

'Where are you going?' I said.

'To the household prayer. My staff are quite religious and they feel calmer when I'm present.'

'Do you want me to leave?'

'God, no.' She leaned in and squeezed my penis under the sheets. 'I want more of this.'

She put on a chaste dress and tied a scarf.

'Do you have any books I can read?' I asked.

'There's a library downstairs. The corridor next to the dining room will take you there.'

She left.

I rolled in the sheets and stretched. Silk feels different. It's the kind of sensation that makes me decide being rich is a good thing.

I went to take a piss and looked in the medicine cabinet. Antidepressants, sedatives, Senna, painkillers. What's she depressed about? I wandered about aimlessly at first. I touched curtains, blew dust off busts of Roman generals.

I did not plan to look through Diane's things but I found the empty house irresistible. I rummaged like a gentle hurricane, a good and nosy private detective. First, I went to the library and selected a translation of *Arabian Nights*. The books were all hardcover and looked new. It was more the size of a community centre library than privately owned. The titles said nothing to me – I got the feeling they were picked by an interior decorator. I searched several of the rooms, an unrewarding task.

I took digital photos of family snaps for later comparison. I perused correspondence, but it meant nothing to me as I had no context. There was routine, bill-paying shit as well as supplications for funds or appearances at charity events or schools. Useless. I found a study on the first floor. Routine as well. Computer. Desk. File cabinet. M. C. Escher print. There were four books on the shelf, all written by Pa Busi. It occurred to me that this was his study. I could imagine him sitting down writing one of the manuscripts, haemorrhoid cushion in place on the seat. I carefully went over every inch, photographing any important-looking documents. My soundtrack was the singing from the prayer service. I imagined Diane singing, imagined her lips, imagined kissing her and . . . *Focus!* No diary. Nothing locked, which was a good thing. In one drawer I found a pretty impressive and distressing stash of porn. Extreme humiliation, simulated non-consent, pain. I supposed nobody could be good natured all of the time, and he was an adult. Why was it still here, though, all this time after his death? I understood why online material would be difficult for someone of Pa Busi's generation, but I didn't understand why Diane hadn't cleared out the desk.

I searched some more and returned to the bedroom with my book. My heartbeat was steady, meaning I was getting used to this private detective shit. I put on the TV. The news told of how none of the city beggars who usually slept in or around the market were harmed. A local government politician made an incredibly offensive remark about beggars being like animals, able to sense danger. From the news commentary nobody registered offence.

The crescendo of a chorus reached me briefly, the result of a transient acoustic anomaly. Presently, Diane returned and we fucked.

Towards the evening Diane became strangely morose and I left – in a cab. I kept my gun unholstered and chambered this time. The streets were stable although there were many more police checkpoints than usual. They focused more on getting bribes than searching the taxi, which was good for me since I didn't fancy explaining my handgun or money belt.

The house was empty, no sign of Nana. A couple of envelopes had been slipped under the door. Each had a number written on it. I opened them. Cash. The same amount in each envelope. I figured they were rent payments and left them on the table. I sat down and spent fifteen minutes phoning Nana several times. Straight to voicemail without negotiation.

This time a sense of dread hit me with heavy finality and I became certain of one thing: Nana was missing. Why had it taken me so long to reach the obvious conclusion? Given the country and town I was in there were a whole range of possibilities. She could have been abducted, raped or killed at random. Someone might have offered up her body parts to their juju god. The secret police might have taken her either for a random, arbitrary offence or because of her association with me. One of the rebel groups could have taken her. Efriti might have arranged to have her killed as part of getting to me. But he and Elemo were dead and gone now, so there was no one to question. She could have been in a car accident. She could be in hospital from amoebic dysentery. E fucking T could have taken her home. Alcacia held limitless possibilities for swallowing people into her maw and not spitting out the bones.

Think.

Shit.

Think.

I didn't know any of her friends or where she went for fun except that village with the scalped old storyteller. I knew she sometimes took catering jobs, but I couldn't well scour through Ede stopping at each party to examine the servers. I didn't know who to ask.

I rummaged through the cupboards and bookshelves until I found a rudimentary street map for Ede. This was a yellowed book whose pages were warped and filthy with thumbprints. I circled all the hospitals and then made an expensive call to directory enquiries.

'Operator.'

'Hello. I'd like the telephone numbers of the following hospitals and health centres please . . .'

An hour later I had been through all the Casualty departments of all the hospitals on the map and none of them had a Nana Hastruup in attendance. Three had young women matching her description, but further probing ruled them out. Dead end.

I dialled for a taxi, but hung up when I realised I had no idea where the storyteller's village was.

Rising panic mixed with guilt over Diane.

Think.

I called my father's office. His PA put me through to Mister Taiwo.

'Hello,' he said. His voice was the sound of a cement mixer. Here was a person who always meant business.

'Good evening, Mister Taiwo.'

'Weston. How are you?'

'We thank God; we thank God. How is the family?' Did he even *have* a family?

'Everybody is fine. Do you hear from your sister?'

This verbal perambulation continued for a minute and a half. The Yoruba love to meander before getting to the crux of the matter, the koko oro. There is no getting around it, especially if there is an age gradient to consider.

'Mister Taiwo, I wanted to ask my dad something.'

'He is busy. What is it you want to know?'

'It's a father–son conversation.'

169

'Haba, Weston. You know he does not like that paternity business.'

Mister Taiwo's voice lacked variation or cadence. He was like a Vulcan from *Star Trek* except twenty times uglier and scarier.

'Very well,' I said. 'Can you tell me how to contact the Hastruup family?'

'Hastruup? Who are they?'

Difficult to tell if he intended this to be irony or he seriously expected me to believe he did not remember or know them even though he had been to see Nana just a few days earlier. My heart went into red alert.

'They lived next to us, next to Auntie Blossom's house, when I was young.'

'Blossom. She was crazy, wasn't she?'

'*She was not.*' Easy. Tread fucking carefully.

'Either way. I do not know how to reach the . . . what did you call them?'

'The Hastruups.'

'The Hastruups. Yes. I do not know how to reach them.'

'Can you ask—'

'And neither does Chief Kogi.'

'Okay. Well. Thank you.'

'I will tell Chief you called.'

He hung up.

Maybe my father and Mister Taiwo had something to do with Nana's disappearance. Shit, I did not think the old goat hated me that much. In fact, I didn't think he hated me at all. I should not have been more than a minor embarrassment. Strictly speaking, a Holloway child is not evidence of a cuckold, but Yoruba men do not see it that way. In fact, the Yoruba went to extreme lengths to avoid even the appearance of it. There is a fetish charm called magun, which means 'do not mount', supplied by the babalawo. It comes in the form of a single strand of raffia or broom thistle.

It is laid across the threshold of the main entrance of the matrimonial home and the wife unknowingly steps over it. If she should be unfaithful after this, the man involved would crow like a cock three times and then die. I wondered where Nana was, what she was doing, if she was even alive.

The man downstairs was arguing with his wife again. I closed the window.

CHAPTER 17

I laid my head on the table for a minute, but it lasted all night and the dawn chorus woke me.

Every muscle in my neck and upper back ached like I had run a marathon. I staggered to the bathroom and spat in the sink. In the mirror was a man with stubble and bleary, unrested eyes, in desperate need of a haircut. I groomed myself quickly, although the barber would have to wait. I had a missed call from Abayomi Abayomi. No voicemail. I watched a toothpaste commercial featuring Western-looking Alcacians with jet-black weaves and fair skin. *Aspire to this*, they said, *try to be like us, to be us. Then you'll be happy*.

I took a taxi to Auntie Blossom's house.

Since the funeral the house had been empty, or so I was told by the gateman who was himself leaving in a week's time. The windows were shut, some boarded over. The leaf-strewn porch seemed lonely. The compound sported tall, green and healthy weeds, which didn't take long to flourish in a moist, sub-tropical environment.

It all had to do with death. Once the owner of a house died Alcacians would often shun the house. It was assumed that the spirit of the owner lived on in the grounds and in the walls. New

173

occupants would have to spiritually cleanse the place or suffer torment. Cleansings were expensive, not for the poor. I did not go in, not because I feared poltergeists, but because my business was with one of Auntie Blossom's neighbours.

To the left was a two-storey house, dazzling white, over which a water tower presided. This was where the Hastruups lived, Nana's parents. A skinny Fulani groundsman swept the driveway lazily with a raffia broom.

Nana's dad sat in a cane chair watching me approach, and dressed in a three-piece suit in spite of the heat, bespoke, at that. Cool, though, not a drop of sweat in sight. He seemed entirely composed of his two piercing eyes. No whites noticeable. I do not remember if he blinked.

When I was a few feet from him I prostrated myself in greeting. Proper traditional greeting required males to be fully pronated on the ground. With time and Westernisation this has been abbreviated. Bending at the waist and touching the floor with both hands, touching the floor with the right hand (never the left) or just bowing had all become acceptable alternatives. The traditional method was reserved for royalty, extremely old people and supplication. It was a bit more complex than that. At times people of the city would make fun of attempts to be traditional, regardless of circumstances. I didn't even know I remembered how until I saw him seated there with gravitas, and I reverted to my childhood mannerisms.

'Is that Elias?' he asked.

'No, sir; it's Weston. Weston Kogi. I was Auntie Blossom's child.'

On his left side was a stool which bore a tall glass of water, a pair of clear-glass spectacles and an empty CD case. A CD player was on the ground, but no music issued forth.

'Stand up, my son. How is your father?' He sipped water and offered his hand, which I shook after brushing off the dust. We made our way through the customary greetings, although to me he seemed restrained.

'Sir, I was just wondering, where is Nana?' I said. 'I am only in town for a short time.'

'Nana moved out, my son. Imagine that. An unmarried woman, too. Her mother hides information from me, but I know she has a boyfriend or man friend, or whatever you people call it these days. Nana has a boyfriend, not her mother. I would not want you to get the wrong impression. I can get you her number.'

'When was she last home?'

'I don't know. It has been a while. She sends me money from time to time, pays for my *Newsweek* subscription. Her mother knows more.'

'Could I speak to Mummy?'

'No, because she is in the village for a funeral and won't be back for a month. You know how emotional these women can get.'

Nana's father was an autodidact. You could see where she got her smarts from. When we were children he would hijack me off the street and inflict learning on me. Herodotus or the Heimlich Manoeuvre, he didn't care which. He dropped out of secondary school age fourteen, but did not tell his parents. At sixteen he took the bar exam and passed *and* took the Alcacian Law Association to court for preventing him from working as a lawyer. And won.

'Weston, don't waste your time. She seems quite taken by whoever this boyfriend is.'

He said this in a kindly voice, not realising that I was the man in question. I did not correct him. He waffled on about something but I was no longer listening. I waited a polite interval and left.

If her parents did not know where she was, then I had hit a dead end.

But I had an idea.

* * *

Diane called, but I let it go to voicemail. I was not interested.

I met Church at a flat in the Reservation Area.

The Reservation Area was not what it said on the tin. Intended as a large tract of land where greenery would flourish along with wild fauna under government protection, it now served as a location for military strongmen to reward sycophants by granting them Leave to Build, which was a kind of indulgence for the sin of defiling virgin land. There was precious little green left, and that existed as wall paint. Because building there was illegal in the strictest sense, there was no real planning in this district, resulting in streets with open sewers on both sides and complete urban disorganisation.

Crime and cholera flourished.

The flat was unfurnished. Church sat on a severed tree trunk in the lounge peeling a pawpaw with a dagger.

'Ore, I'm not entirely sure what you need from me,' he said. He held the pawpaw in his left hand and pared the last bit of skin off, revealing the yellow flesh.

'I need to find my girlfriend.'

'Yes, I heard that. When did you get a girlfriend?'

'Well . . .'

'Never mind. Not my business.' He sliced into the ovoid fruit, cut it into nine segments and emptied the sticky black seeds on to the floor beside him. He did not seem to mind that I had nowhere to sit. 'So, who is this Taiwo person?'

'He works for my father.'

Church handed me a slice of pawpaw and started to eat one. His face was, for once, in deep contemplation. I ate what he offered, though I was put off by his dirty fingernails and the lack of water for washing the fruit.

'I don't understand you,' he said, 'but I'll help you if you'll go with me on an errand.'

'Hold it; hold it one minute.'

'Relax. It's nothing like that business with D'Jango. This is just a delivery.'

I sighed. 'Where are we going this time?'

'We have to go and see the King of Boys.'

The King of Boys has existed in Ede since 1959, but his history goes back further than that. In ancient times there were no beggars in Alcacia or whatever Yoruba settlement preceded the modern nation. There were poor people, but they were always catered to because a percentage of all profits from the barter of goods went to the poor. The fetish offerings were deliberately directed towards cooking large quantities of food for the poor, a tradition called sah'rah. Begging was never really necessary. With the invasion of Christianity from the south and Islam from the north things changed. A beggar class emerged due in part to the selfishness induced by the colonialist society and a mis-understanding of scripture – Islam on the giving of alms and Christianity where Jesus said the poor would always be with us.

In Alcacia beggars were part of a network of intercommuni-cating clans of homeless folks. In 1959 Adeomi Obaleye declared himself Adeomi the First, King of Boys, because King of Beggars did not strike the right tone.

There were those who said Obaleye suffered from paranoid schizophrenia, and that was as acceptable an explanation as any. However, since his time, there had always been a King of Boys.

Church and I took an okada to Imu Egbere, a coastal fishing community to the south of Ede. The land was swampy, with foot-paths constructed of wood and mounted on struts. The okada motorcyclists rode their bikes skilfully (or recklessly from my point of view) on the path and I expected to drop into the blue-green mud any minute, a hair-raising fucking journey. This didn't seem to bother the pilots. Church was impassive, chilled.

The King of Boys was on a fishing boat – what was it with me and boats? The okada dropped us right at the jetty and we passed from one decrepit fishing vessel to another on unsafe gangplanks. I do not have good sea legs but Church went on like he was born in a mangrove swamp.

The fishermen were a docile lot and barely reacted to us walking across. This was the expected way to get around. There was no smell of fish, even though it was overpowering at the jetty. The king's boat was the same as the others. Wiry men went through the motions of fishing, of salting fish, of sorting freshwater bottom feeders and other fauna from sardines, mackerel and sturgeon. There was other marine life that I could not identify, recycled as bait, sent back to the sea.

The king was in the cabin, which was dim. Akpala music played from a transistor radio which he held in his right hand. I hadn't seen a transistor since 1986.

The King of Boys wore a crown to receive us. The crown was jewelled with marbles – children's marbles. It was a band of tin, beaten together from old Burma-Shave containers. His head was completely bald, shining from within the rim of his crown. He had a black tailcoat on and he looked like an impoverished Fred Astaire. He wore white gloves, dirty ones. His shoes were holed, filthy, but courtly. He wore no socks. He did wear a necklace of cowries. A flaky, scaly dark lesion decorated the skin of his neck. I wondered if he had AIDS.

'Kabiyesi,' said Church, but he did not prostrate himself. I followed his lead.

The king had no attendants, but a young, sullen house slave

fanned him. The boy had a unibrow and wore only dirty white Y-front underpants.

'A man called stone,' said the king.

'A stone bearing gifts,' said Church. He gave the king a brown paper bag. The king tore it open, counted fresh bills.

'This is good,' said the king.

'And none of your beggar subjects died in the fires,' said Church.

'You are all my subjects,' said the king. 'You just don't know it. Take some fish on your way out.'

We, Church and I, waited outside my father's office. For Taiwo.

'Why are we paying off the beggar king?' I asked.

'For popularity,' said Church. 'We wanted to send a message with the fire, but if one beggar had died the whole plan could backfire, no pun. Beggars live in the market and they listen to their king. He told them to stay out on the night of the fire. We paid him a lot of money to keep them out. Everybody's happy.'

'So yours is a revolution by bribery.'

'My friend, Julius Caesar and Augustus Caesar were two of the greatest achievers of the Roman Empire. Both used bribery extensively.'

'We went to school together, Church. I read Suetonius too.'

'Then don't make stupid comments. In the entire world Alcacia is only lower than Pakistan and Nigeria on the corruption league tables, and that's probably because they bribed the researchers. Bribery is oil. It makes things go easy. Like the money you carry around in that belt.'

'That's not a bribe.'

'I'm sure you really believe that.'

'There's Taiwo. Getting into the Hyundai.'

'Groovy. Let's boogie.'

This was the second abduction I had ever participated in.
It went smoothly.

Back in the RA now.

Same flat.

More people. Henchmen, minions, outsourced Area Boys, revolutionaries.

Mister Taiwo was hogtied and we all stood around him. He did not look afraid.

Church said, 'Ask.'

I stepped forward.

'Mister Taiwo, where is Nana?'

Silence.

'I know you know who she is. You gave her a message for me the other day.'

Nothing.

'Where have you taken her?'

No reaction.

Church stepped forward. He looked intently at Taiwo, cocked his head, squatted.

'I know your type,' said Church. 'You've seen war and suffering. Old-school style with Sarin gas, white phosphorus and anthrax canisters. You've defiled churches, am I right? I bet you've even tortured a few in your time. It's in your eyes. The way you don't take any of this personal. You're afraid but you know the rules of the game. We have to hurt you first, in a minor but painful way. A cruel way. We do that so you know we're serious, in a cruel but non-lethal way, you understand. This is all almost comforting to you because it's expected, familiar. It's the drill.' He drew his dagger. Flecks of pawpaw clung to the hilt and dropped off as Church began to wave it about in front of Taiwo's face, as if deciding what to cut.

I knew he would cut nothing.

I drew my gun and cocked it, flicked the safety.

I aimed it at Taiwo's head.

'Fuck this Dr Evil bullshit. Tell me where she is or I'll blow—'

'What is wrong with you?' asked Churchill in a low, dangerous tone. 'Holster that weapon.'

Taiwo began to smile.

I replaced the gun in the ankle holster.

Church stood up, disgusted. He shoved me and I took a step back to regain my balance. I slipped on the pawpaw seeds and fell flat on my back.

There was a loud bang and searing pain down my right foot. Then wetness. Church pinned me down, knelt on my leg and carefully removed the gun. He switched the safety back on. Then he took off my shoe and sock and looked at my leg. The outer edge had a small chunk gouged out, but it was not a major injury. It hurt in a terrific, maddening way.

'You're kind of an idiot,' said Church.

'It's been said of me.'

'Church!' said one of the minions.

'Oh, shit. Sege, waka, *motherfuck*!' said Church, and when he moved I saw what he saw.

Blood oozing from a smoking wound in Taiwo's neck.

Sightless eyes.

CHAPTER 18

The skies opened and it rained for four days. I spent the time eating chocolate cake and watching reruns of *Mission: Impossible* and *Hawaii 5–0* on a pirate television station out of Nigeria. Oh, and there was a good documentary about Kwame Nkrumah. I did not leave the flat.

Nana did not call or turn up. The flip side was that I received no ransom demands and my telephone sweep of the local hospitals still yielded nothing. I even called the police, but they had nothing for me. I did not file a missing persons report. I was confused and tried to push the whole thing away. I felt it strange that her landline did not ring once in all that time. Nobody telephoning with an assignment or to complain.

I could feel my muscles atrophy each day, but no way was I going out in the quagmire that Ede City turned into when it rained. I had food and water. I had a TV, a VHS and a DVD player. I had cable. I had books. I could outlast any meteorological obstacle that fate threw at me.

In those rainy days I had a very few flashbacks of Taiwo's death. Not that I was feeling hard, or anything. I just could not bear the thought that I had killed someone. I pretty much forced myself not to think of it, but that never worked.

Church cursed me constantly for around twenty minutes. All

the while he bandaged my foot. When he had finished I tried to speak but this just set him off again, so I kept my mouth shut.

I was worried about leaving the bullet inside Taiwo. It had passed through my foot first before embedding in his neck. My DNA and fingerprints were on it, post-*CSI* world and all that. I needn't have worried. The team Church brought were old hands. They chopped Taiwo into many parts and the deformed bullet dropped from his neck stump.

I did not ask any questions. Might have been my imagination but it seemed to me they treated me with a grudging respect after the death, as if I had joined a club. Even Churchill's bitching was half-hearted.

I had killed a man.

Fine, it was accidental and clumsy, but I was still a murderer now, or at the very least a man-slaughterer. I also helped get rid of the body by waiting after dark and burying the parts in twelve separate quicklimed shallow graves. The floor of the flat we washed thoroughly with water from the well. Then we doused the whole flat in bleach, the strong odour of which drove us all out of the property at four in the morning.

I had killed a man and perverted the course of justice. Conspired with people I didn't even know, not to mention trust.

It was a good thing I wasn't a drinker.

I did not mourn Taiwo the way I did the man I had seen killed in the PLF camp on the day after Auntie Blossom's funeral. I felt nothing apart from apathy. It would probably hit me later. It was not because Taiwo was a prick, which he surely was. It was more Weston Kogi getting used to real-life violence, inured, unaffected.

In the four days I stayed home I had two disturbing dreams. In the first I was back at my secondary school, though fully grown. All the other students were grown up too. One or two had fallen to car accidents or illnesses over the years, and they were represented by rotting *zombi*. It looked like a macabre adult-education scene. I went looking for Nana, who was in the class next door. The teacher did not mind. Nana was there in a revealing black one-piece swimsuit. Her breasts wobbled with each word she said.

'Why are you wearing that?' I asked.

'Go get me a uniform,' she said.

I went downstairs to the student shop, but a mulatto lunatic ran towards me. He wore a torn straitjacket and pyjama bottoms. I started to run, but he chased me up an embankment. I punched him a few times, but this only slowed him down. Then a larger, white-skinned lunatic appeared, similarly dressed, and they both pummelled me until I woke up soaked in sweat. That was from an afternoon nap and I was so shaken that I drank two tumblers of vodka neat. I fear the insane. Lynn, my sister, has always criticised me for this, and I know she has a point, but I can't help it.

The second dream was familiar to me. It was the market scene that I had dreamed of before. The empty market. Tosin's head was gone, but Simon, my deceased brother, sat on the chopping board and Taiwo lay beside him. He bore all the cuts with which we divided him along with the bullet hole.

'Death by a thousand cuts,' said Simon.

Taiwo tried to speak but only gasps and grunts came out.

'That's because you shot him in the neck. He can't draw breath properly, and you need breath to be able to talk. No breath, no sound.'

I looked at the sky. 'The vultures will come soon.'

'Not for this one,' said Simon. 'This one you killed. He stays. There are consequences.'

'And you? I didn't kill you.'

Simon smelled of urine or ammonia. I don't remember which.

'Me? I am just a random element of delight.'

And with that he curled into a foetal position and sucked his thumb.

I woke, but without terror. Just vague disquiet.

On day five I decided to go into town. I needed a barber to control my hair – I had an impending Afro. This is what happens when you kill people. I could not bear to take the gun, not just yet. Could not even touch it. I also left the money belt and took only enough for transport, food and a haircut. I left my phone because I didn't want to speak to anyone. I walked past a mirror and had a vague impression of a thin, bearded vagrant. I didn't care. I thought I should have done the dishes in case Nana returned while I was away. I missed her. The whole thing left me discombobulated and I desperately needed direction.

I walked for half an hour before I was able to hail a taxi. I thought everyone on the street *knew* and stared, because murder walks with me. There were no posters posted or helicopters overhead. I relaxed and the traffic into town crawled along. A town crier warned of an oro procession for the next three nights. Oro was a masquerade that women were not allowed to see. They looked and sounded trouser-soilingly scary. This might have been because they only came out at night and the sound came from a device that looked like a clacker and was akin to catgut being stretched.

I let the taxi cruise along the main street until I found a barber's shop that I liked purely in an aesthetic way. Which means it looked Western, like a barber's shop in America would look. I was starting to miss being home in London. I wanted Cumberland sausages. Not that you couldn't get them in Alcacia, but a Balance of Trade problem meant you had to exchange them for large amounts of cash.

I got dazzled by the barber's shop's interior, with reflected light and images everywhere since all the walls had mirrors. I had at least five reflections. It wasn't large – about ten by twenty feet – with three barber seats, only one of which was occupied by a customer. Another man, whom I presumed to be the barber, welcomed me and pointed to a bench with his clippers, after which he resumed trimming the hair of the customer. The music of Mighty Sparrow boomed from speakers that I could not pinpoint, and the place smelled of various hair products and after-shave. I sat down and waited. The walls had posters of Evander Holyfield victorious and an almanac showing the types of hairstyles the barber could be expected to duplicate. There was a certificate of cleanliness from the city, a framed photo of the barber with someone famous in Alcacia, but unknown to me, and a plaque listing the prices for services from a simple beard trim to a treatment called a Royale.

'What's a Royale?' I asked in Yoruba.

'It's the full service, sir. Shampoo, haircut, shave, basic manicure, hair dye if necessary, scalp massage and stimulating conversation.'

'All that is why you charge premium for it?'

'The stimulating conversation is free, sir.'

I laughed. 'What is your name?'

'Dayo, sir.'

'Dayo, there's no need to call me "sir".' We were about the same age.

'My oga insists that I call all customers this way, sir.'

I tuned out again, flipped through the available magazines, which were old *Ebony* editions featuring actors and musicians whose stars had long dimmed in the celebrity firmament. When Dayo had finished with the customer he called me to sit. I opted for a Royale and it was soothing with the bonus effect of making me look good. I went for a clean shave, taking off the moustache

I had cultivated while in Alcacia, and a crew cut. Dayo found four grey hairs in my beard. I didn't know how to feel about that.

I didn't have time to think about it. A black car pulled up outside the barber's shop and two suited men in sunglasses climbed out. They entered the shop and Dayo backed away. It wasn't the bulge of weapons under their jackets. It was the bearing, the impression of petty power that they wore, life and death power, my sweet, secret police.

'Dayo, it's okay. These men are here for me.' I said this looking at the taller of the two. I aimed my gaze in the general direction of his eyes, but you could never tell with sunglasses. 'I need to reach for my wallet to pay this man. I am not armed. Is that all right with you?'

After I paid Dayo they took me away. A small crowd gathered to watch.

CHAPTER 19

I found detention scary, but so far, for a frightened guy, I thought I was coping well enough. They left me in an interview room after a short drive to police headquarters. The room bothered me because there was one seat and nothing else but white tiles on the floor, ceiling and walls except for the door and the flush halogen light bulbs. In one corner there was a drain. The chair was not bolted down. The room was designed to be easily washed, like a bathroom or an abattoir.

They took my belt and shirt so that I would be unable to hang myself. They also took my shoes and socks. I had a singlet and my trousers which, if I stood, I had to clutch or they would fall. They told me if I wanted to piss I could do it in the corner, near the drain. I was allowed to open the tap to wash the urine away when finished.

The room was expertly soundproofed. Either that or nothing was happening outside. There was no guard, but there didn't need to be. I had seen on the way in that the station was a fort. If I attempted to run I would be leaving in several bullet-ridden pieces. The people who brought me in didn't even condescend to threats.

A man came in without knocking.

He closed the door and stood leaning on it with his legs crossed.

'People die here,' he said. 'We start to question them . . . they fall apart. They bleed and they die. I think it is the burden of guilt.' He paused, stretched his hands forward, and let them fall. 'People die here.'

I didn't say anything. I waited for introductions.

'We've seen everything here. Everybody. Heads of state, prominent lawyers, captains of industry, musicians, coup plotters, fashion models and people we just don't like. Administrations come and go, but we remain the same. We abide. I'm telling you this so that you won't waste time telling me how influential your friends are or how much money or political influence you have. It means as much and offers as much protection as the semen dripping from Lady Macbeth's cunt. Do you understand?'

'Yes.'

'Good.' He took two steps forward and stood with his feet shoulder-width apart. He wore a black suit like the two who arrested me, but without a tie. The first two buttons of his white shirt were undone and black curls of hair reached up towards his neck. He had a flat immobile face, a total absence of emotion, a face that gave nothing away. It was a bony face, skin pulled taut over every contour, veins crawling up his temple towards his hairline.

'Am I under arrest?'

'It would be better if you let me ask the questions.'

'I'm a British citizen.'

'Ki lo kan mi? Did you not hear me when I said your political influence was irrelevant here? Does it look to you like this is the kind of place that cares about the colour of your passport? Or the number of your household gods?'

'Sorry.'

He reached inside his jacket and showed me a photograph of Church. 'Do you know this man?'

They already knew I did if they'd been following me.

'Yes, his name is Churchill Okuta.'

'What is your connection with him?'

'We went to school together. He made my life hell in board-ing school.'

'Which school?'

'Bishop Ajayi Crowther Secondary School.'

'Fee paying?'

'Yes.'

'And Okuta was in your class?'

'No, he was in form five when I was in form one. He was my senior.'

'How did you meet?'

'I don't know if you've ever been to boarding school, but form one students are fair game. The seniors more or less wait for you to arrive in the hostel and they grab you and that means you're "assigned" to them. From that point on you're like indentured or something until they get their GCEs or leave school. Such a senior becomes your School Father. It's a warped version of the Buddy System.'

'How old were you?'

'Ten. Maybe eleven.'

'So Okuta was your School Father?'

'Yes.'

'What was that like?'

'He flogged me with a belt for any reason that caught his fancy.'

'What kind of reasons?'

'Not making sure his water was warm enough before he took a bath in the morning, not cleaning up his corner in the dormitory to his satisfaction, not getting to the refectory on time to fetch his meal, not pressing his clothes, not sharing my con-fectioneries with him, anything really.'

'Why did you not report him?'

'You've obviously never lived in a boys' hostel.'

'Answer the question.'

'If you report anyone to the teachers you get labelled as a snitch. The rest of your life in school will be hell. My life was bad enough.'

'What do you know about Okuta's parents?'

'His father was the vice chairman of a political party, I forget which. I don't know anything about his mother.'

'Did your parents know each other?'

'I don't know. I never saw them together and . . . well, I didn't see much of my father. My aunt sent me to Crowther after my mother died.'

'What was he like? Okuta, as a boy?'

'Pretty much the same as he is now. Vicious, unrepentant, hard. The reason he left school is he took a boy called Ibitoye Omole into the latrines and beat him into unconsciousness. The boy caught pneumonia. Because he damaged Ibitoye's larynx the boy had to have a tracheotomy and talked funny for the rest of the time I knew him. Ibitoye said Churchill laughed all the way through.'

'So he was expelled?'

'Yes. From what I found out while cleaning his clothes Church's father got him out of most trouble, but the Ibitoye affair was too serious. He almost died. I heard Church had to go to remand school after that, but it was a rumour. The other rumour was that he went to prison.'

'Did he ever talk about politics?'

'Just the standard things that everybody used to talk about back then. Black September, Beirut, Reagan bombing the Libyans, Patty Hearst, things like that. I didn't understand most of that stuff because my interests ran to comics and cartoons and the girl next door.'

'Did you feel relief when he was expelled?'

'I did not have the time. Soon afterwards the university strikes began and Crowther was closed because of the violence in the city. My aunt shipped me out of the country.'

'And you recently returned.'

'Yes. I came into town originally for my aunt's funeral.'

'This would be Blossom Kogi?'

'Yes, and Church was there. I saw him at the party. We caught up, and I've met him a few times since.'

The man took another step forward. He was now within striking distance. I couldn't tell if he was pleased or pissed off.

'Do you know that he is wanted for treason?'

'No.' The truth. I didn't know, but I was not surprised.

'Do you know he belongs to the Liberation Front?'

'Yes.'

'Do you belong to the Liberation Front?'

'No.'

'Do you belong to the Christian Army?'

'No.'

'What is your political affiliation?'

'I have none.'

'If you help one side or the other, if you assist anyone against the Federal Government, you have political affiliation.'

'I'm a private investigator.'

'Yes, you are. Your documents were signed by George Elemo, a man who was subsequently murdered. This happened soon after your main rival, also a known associate of Elemo, was gunned down in the bus terminus shootout. It seems you are a dangerous man to know, Mr Weston Kogi, Private Investigator. You are lucky the police have not made these connections and don't even care to check. And that this chain of events does not interest us at this time.'

I swallowed.

'Do you own a gun?' he asked.

'No.'

He turned his head to one side, but kept his eyes on me in a gesture that would be cute on a five-year-old.

'You lie. Okuro. Liar.'

I said nothing. There was obviously very little this man did not know. Some of it must have been conjecture and anything I said might just fill in the blank spots for him. Better to shut the fuck up. Keep the brain empty to minimise body language revelations. Think of snow, of static on TV.

'It's best to think that we know everything. Anything we don't know is not important,' he said. 'There is no point in lying to me. None.'

I noticed his upper lip had been repaired surgically. A slim scar traced his philtrum to the base of his nose. Cleft lip. Harelip. He might still feel deformed.

'I know who you work for,' he said. He leaned close to my ear. 'I know and I do not care. Do you know what I care about?' I shook my head. His breath was stale and reeked of neglect and alcohol. 'I care about information. Useful information. The kind of information that prevents market fires. Information you would be privy to as the anointed PI of two insurgent organisations. It might even earn you a stipend.'

'I'm not sure I follow you.' But I did.

He carefully replaced Churchill's photo and his hand came out of his pocket with a calling card. Telephone numbers. Two: one mobile, one satphone. No name.

'You call me when something interesting comes up.'

'Who are you?'

He straightened up. 'I'm glad we had this talk.'

He walked towards the door and opened it.

He said, 'For black eyes use a cold compress, although it should sort itself out in a few days.'

'I'm sorry, what? Why are you telling me this?'

He left the room and two other men came in.
They escorted me into hell.

They took me to the cells where I was beaten carefully by other prisoners for what seemed like hours. That kind of beating, you have to go to a mystical place to survive with your mind intact. *The earth also was corrupt before God and the earth was filled with violence.* Genesis chapter six, verse eleven. This verse kept playing in a recursive loop in my mind. Just playing over and over again. The earth was filled with violence. The blows no longer hurt. I was getting too many of them and I imagine my nervous system decided I wasn't taking care of business and wanted a divorce.

The earth was filled with violence. My lungs were filled with blood.

I hoped I would not piss blood. I got enough kicks in the kidney to make it likely.

Thirty-six babies had to die for me to be released from detention.

How it happened was a brand of baby milk sold in Alcacia became contaminated with an exotic chemical – I forget which one. Within twenty-four hours seven babies had died. By day three the count rose to thirty and the authorities swung into action and identified the culprit as Sweet Mother brand. Pressure from the Head of State galvanised the secret police and they swooped down upon the board of directors of Carnacot PLC, the company responsible for producing the baby milk. They had more suspects than they could cram into the cells and they released me and a few others without charge.

I spent forty-eight hours in detention. Despite my very expensive haircut I looked like untreated sewage.

* * *

A few things that the potential victim of beatings should bear in mind: the most painful moments were the first few seconds after the beating started and twenty-four hours after the last blow landed home. It was not magic. Once the punches began the body pumped the blood full of adrenalin and endorphins so that it could fight back and not feel pain. And run without getting tired or feeling muscle fatigue. A day later the healing process had begun. Any movement would dislodge newly knitted body tissue with dolorous results.

With this in mind I took a higher than recommended dose of codeine phosphate and paracetamol. I was in a haze of euphoria and terminal constipation when I checked my messages. Diane had called many times. Church. Abayomi three times. Someone who did not leave a message and from a withheld number. Abayomi again. Nothing from Nana. I was angry at her for . . . whatever. Why did she leave? What was she playing at? Whatever the fuck, or wherever the fuck she was.

I had not been cleaning. The house was filthy, disorganised and uninviting. No clean dishes in the kitchen, the bed unmade for days, a layer of dust over every surface. I felt and moved like an old man; no way was I cleaning anything up.

I called Diane.

'You are a bad man,' said Diane. 'You do not return telephone calls. I should not even be talking to you.'

'Send a car for me,' I mumbled.

'What? Why do you—'

'Just send the car, all right?'

The doctor Diane press ganged was thorough. He came to her house with his own diagnostic equipment and invited me back to his private hospital for a little MRI or CT scan action, but I declined. He checked my vision, probed my skull, looked at my teeth, ultrasounded my abdomen, bent my limbs into strange shapes for the purpose of confirming or ruling out dislocations or fractures. He even stuck an uncomfortable cold, moist finger into my rectum.

He made notes in tiny illegible script on a pad. All the while Diane stood by the side of the bed, concern in the slight wrinkle on her brow.

'You like me,' I said.

'Not as much as you think,' she retorted, but she stroked my head where it wasn't bumpy.

The doctor ignored us both. He received the results of tests from his assistant and nodded.

'There is no permanent damage done. You have a few malaria parasites in your blood, but that's normal for the environment. You are a bit anaemic, but it looks like this has been there for a while and is not due to the blood loss from physical trauma.'

I hadn't been taking my proguanil pills. In all the excitement, I kept forgetting. It was a wonder I didn't have malaria.

'Take the pills. Get bed rest. You'll be fine.' With that he was gone, paying scant attention to Diane's effusive gratitude.

She closed the door to her room and locked it.

'Now, you,' she said.

'What?'

'Let me see how much I can ride you in this state without breaking you.'

'I know him, you know,' said Diane.

We were talking about Abayomi Abayomi. She lay face down on the bed, naked. Even after sex, after everything, the smoothness of her skin made me want to lick her all over.

Diane was showing interest in my investigation. I figured she wanted me to talk as part of my recovery, or she was just curious, or she just wanted to talk about anything.

'How do you know him?'

'He used to build villages.'

'Excuse me?'

'He used to build villages. He even caused an international incident once. That is when the government asked – ordered – him to desist.'

'How does one go about building a village?'

'In the mid to late nineties the north-east of Alcacia had semi-nomadic tribes scattered all over the place, living in ramshackle tents like cut-price Mongols in the Gobi. They had poor education, zero infrastructure and absolutely no representation in central government. Abayomi went evangelistic, speaking to the tribal heads and chieftains, getting drunk with them, explaining how taking root would be a good idea, a thing of the future. They staked land and he designed simple, grid-pattern villages for them, made petitions for local government, attracted teachers for schools, initiated work programmes, earned himself oodles of respect.'

'And the incident?'

'The last village he built inadvertently crossed the Nigerian border. It was an honest mistake, picked up by the drones in Town Planning when he submitted plans. He would have adjusted his plans and resubmitted, but there was a leak in the office and by the next day Nigerian troops bore down on the nascent village, which was really only a few tents at the time. Our troops had to respond to the "impending invasion" by our neighbours. Big hoo-ha. Big pow-wow. Big intervention by interdips.'

'"Interdips"?'

'International diplomats. They love to fly in from Western nations and make their portfolios fat by brokering peace among the savage tribes of the Dark Continent. I know the type well. I married one, after all.'

'So how'd he get from philanthropy to rebel mouthpiece?'

'Who knows? The episode with the Nigerians soured him. He disappeared. Next time he emerged it was to voice the martyr-dom videos of PFC suicide bombers in the Red Summer of 2002 when that sort of thing was fashionable.'

I massaged her neck while lying on top of her. My soft penis nestled between her bum cheeks. 'You still haven't told me how you know him.'

She turned her neck to look at me meaningfully from under insanely full eyelashes.

'I see.' I was jealous. I stopped kneading her muscles.

'He was talked about everywhere, just back from university in Oxford or Cambridge. I do not know which.'

It occurred to me that her husband must have still been alive at that time.

'When did you last see him?'

She made a brushing gesture, dismissive, creasing the bed linen. 'I only saw him a few times. A long time ago.'

'How were things between you and your husband when he died?'

'Pretty shitty.'

It was the first time I had ever heard her swear. I resumed the massage, but my heart accelerated.

She said, 'This happens in any marriage, though. We just happened to be in mid-quarrel when he died.'

'How were you relating on the day he died?'

'We were not speaking. I just chatted with his bodyguards. I did not say goodbye to him.'

'What did you fight about?'

'I cannot remember.'

I didn't push.

'I've been to see one of the guards, the survivor. In Arodan.'

'I had forgotten about him,' she said. 'I was closer to the other one. What was his name? Wale?'

'Wallace,' I said. 'Special Agent Idris Wallace.'

'Do you love me?' asked Diane.

'I don't think so,' I said. 'I love Nana.'

'Your girlfriend?'

'Hmm.'

'You frighten me, Weston.'

'How so?'

'You can say all this with a straight face. You can talk about loving Nana while making love to me, while your sweat is dripping on to my back.'

'—'

'Your blankness is worrying. No, blankness is not the word . . .'

'I am worried about her.'

'Yet you are here with me.'

'Yes.'

'—'

'—'

'Faster.'

CHAPTER 20

New summons.

The People's Christian Army looked worse for wear.

There were more ruins than my first visit, but in addition the buildings smouldered and there were craters everywhere. The place had been shelled recently and repeatedly. There was a profusion of wild dogs roaming about. The children were still there, but they did not chase after the car. They looked haunted and even dirtier than before. Many were injured and bore filthy dressings. The tank in the square was so much twisted metal.

My escorts had to drive a long way to get to a building in front of which we parked. Men wearing fatigues cradled rocket launchers and smoked weed. My escorts took my gun and mobile phone, then led me down a suspect stairwell. There were no railings and a drop into darkness on both sides. At the bottom there was a large chamber, like a garage. An overhead light lit an area where Abayomi Abayomi stood waiting.

'You look like Mike Tyson tried to bite off your ear,' he said.

'And you were supposed to take care of the Men in Black, remember?'

'This is true, this is true,' he said, shaking my hand. 'It's hard to keep track of things when I have American-made Chinook helicopters firing missiles at my office block. It makes one lose concentration. Things slip the mind.' He had none of his mirth and there was an edge to his voice.

'You want an update on my investigation?'

'No.'

'Then why—'

'I have new orders from His Excellency.'

A church bell rang somewhere above us. I wondered who would be left to worship.

'Am I to stop investigating the murder?'

'No, by all means, continue that. The new orders involve you delivering a package.' He snapped his fingers and a man appeared out of the darkness and handed Abayomi a briefcase, which he gave to me. 'Open it.'

I went down on one knee and placed the case on the other. Then I popped the catches open. Rows and rows of crisp American dollar bills. I closed it and stood.

'How much?'

'A quarter of a million.'

'Where does it go?'

'Oh, I'm sorry, that's not the package, that's the payment. The money is for you.' A different man from the shadows stepped forward and handed him a shiny, polished-steel cylinder. Abayomi held it up for me to see. 'This is the package. You are to go to the Front's headquarters and give this message to their leader.'

'For which you propose to pay me two hundred and fifty thousand dollars in cash, in advance.'

'Yes.'

'What's in the cylinder?'

'Don't open it.'

'I won't. What's in the cylinder, Abayomi?'

'It is a weaponised version of a haemorrhagic fever virus similar to Ebola or Lassa fever, but with a more controlled spread capability. It's called Epoch. I think because after deployment so many people are dead that everything needs to start afresh. But, yeah. Epoch.'

I swallowed. 'I need a minute.'

'Take your time,' he said, but his body language contradicted this. He still stood legs apart, staring right into my eyes, waiting for a response. The church bell kept ringing. Were there armed people in the shadows, waiting on my response?

'Who goes to worship at this time on a week day?' I asked. My voice sounded hoarse.

'That's not a call to prayer. That's the air raid signal. But don't fret; this place is safe as long as the Feds are not intent on exterminating us, which they aren't.'

'I may have some questions.'

'What are they?'

'Do you not think the delivery of a biological weapon into the heart of the Front will escalate hostilities between you?'

'I know it will. I want it to happen.'

'Why?'

'Because by destroying the largest and most popular open market in West Africa the Front has provoked the government and is responsible for the shelling that we are now experiencing, Weston. They've also scored a major point with the people. By carrying out a hit like that they're announcing that they still run shit. His Excellency does not agree that the Liberation Front runs shit and he does not like his bunker being bombed. It frightens his concubines and interrupts his relentless search for the G-spot. We need to ensure that after the bombing, the inevitable political negotiation takes place with us, not the Front.'

'Is that what you believe?'

'It's what the PCA is doing now.'

'Then why not take the fight to them with conventional weapons? There's really no need to open the Seven Seals on them.'

'No time. They are stoked from burning the market, we are demoralised by the same thing and depleted in numbers from this infernal bombing. This virus will be the great equaliser.' His voice echoed in the chamber. There was no way of telling how many soldiers he had, but it was irrelevant. I would not leave the camp alive if they did not will it, if he did not will it.

'I am not a mass murderer,' I said.

'Maybe not, but you did have a large part to play in the disappearance of one Mister Taiwo. That information could find its way into the hands of the authorities. You think the secret police were harsh on you. The regular police are just as brutal, but without the brain power that drives the other agencies.'

'How did you—'

'Know? Weston, we have people watching you as much as the Front does. I can tell you how many times you pissed on Wednesday night and how many dabs of aftershave you used this morning.'

Fuck.

'A lot of money in the briefcase, Weston. Nothing causes amnesia like American dollars.'

Fuck.

'And on completion I'll tell you where to find your Nana Hastruup.'

CHAPTER 21

'You know where Nana is?' I asked.

'That's correct,' said Abayomi.

'You have her?'

'No, but we do know where she is. I know you're looking for her. We'll let you know when the job is done.'

'Is she safe?'

'It wouldn't be much of a bonus if I gave that away, would it?'

'And Pa Busi's murder?'

'I think the Front has taken things two steps beyond that. I don't think the cosmetic investigation is at all necessary in the current climate. Do you?'

'Are you officially taking me off the case? Off the payroll for that?'

He took time to consider this. 'Not officially. Until the Front does the same our official position is for you to continue to search for truth. In actuality, I want you to discontinue whatever it is you are doing to search for his killers. It is academic at this point.'

'But what you're doing is asking me to take sides. In a most horrific way, I might add. You know I am as Switzerland in this thing.'

'How, now, Weston. I'm not asking you to take sides. I'm asking you to make a delivery for a fee. What do you say?' said Abayomi with finality.

There was really no choice in the matter.

The canister was a ten-centimetre-long cylinder. Thin. Shiny. It came in a carry case like the kind used for spectacles. Light, weighed practically nothing. Epoch. It would maintain hermetic seal for three weeks after which nothing could guarantee Epoch particles wouldn't start leaking out. Particles is what you call individual viruses, I'm told. The cylinder had a mauve button on one end. Press the button and in fifteen minutes Epoch would be released.

Not a lot of time.

Plus, there was no going back once the button was depressed.

On TV four women in Ankara wrappers performed synchron-ised dancing with bowls of fruit balanced on their heads.

I strongly considered running away. I could just go to the British Embassy and tell them to get me the fuck out of Alcacia.

I typed up a highly edited account of the mess, altered to remove any serious personal culpability, and then attempted to email it to Lynn in London, but it kept bouncing back. I sent myself a blank email and it arrived safely. I tried to send a single paragraph about the fiasco and it bounced. I sent a single line saying 'hi, Lynn' and it went though. In desperation I opened several bogus email accounts, but they would not send the infor-mation either.

I switched off Nana's computer and picked up the canister case.

On the side, there was some text in relief: STORE IN A COOL DRY PLACE.

I wrote in my journal for four hours, getting it up to date in as much detail as I could. It was difficult, my concentration was shot.

I'd be writing one sentence and my mind would drift to the virus in my possession.

I was still contracted to find Pa Busi's murderers, but the thin veneer of righteous indignation from the PDF was gone. LFA fire-bombed Ede market and the PCA wanted to unleash a plague. The two factions were or soon would be at war again. Not cold war, but an all-out shooting war. The assassination was falling into the background.

But.

Diane had fucked Abayomi Abayomi and probably Idris Wallace. I thought of that and her sweat mixed with mine and sixteen million dollars. I wondered, felt jealous, wondered some more. Aaron Wallace mentioned Idris had a lover and that the same lover stopped calling after Pa Busi died. Idris had the strange paranoia before his death. Diane was all over this. Was she just an opportunistic sexual predator or was there a design?

I had to look at the photos I got from Diane's house, see if there was anything interesting. I had to speak to the insurance people.

All of which was bullshit. I had to get out of the country is what I had to do. Take Nana and run. Except to do that I'd have to deliver the virus to the LFA headquarters. I may have killed Taiwo, but I did not consider myself a murderer. I wasn't going to do it, no matter what. Death on that level makes one think of one's immortal soul, and I didn't even believe in the soul or gods.

I could always just say I delivered it and say it was a dud.

Or go without Nana. Again.

No way.

Later I showered, dressed and went out to eat.

It was a mistake to eat out. Most of the eating joints played loud music with the food. I was in a place called China. Juju music was

207

their weapon of choice. Two of the server girls were having a drag-out altercation right on the 'shop floor'. I ate rice and beans with beef stew. Sections of ox tail were placed on the mound of rice and I worked my way through them.

The food, plentiful and delicious, made up for the noise. One of the fish-wife servers came to clear my dishes and I asked for a beer.

China was a workers' eatery, and it was lunch hour. The seats were arranged so that everyone could see everyone else. Workers were on their own or in groups of two to five. Loud conversations, business lunches, arguments over one pop star's superiority over another, politics, loud mobile phone conversations, one-sided, monologues that were not monologues.

My seat backed the entrance, so I was surprised when a white man came to rest by my side.

'Howdy,' he said. 'Weston, my ol' buddy, my old pal.'

I sipped my beer to compose myself. 'Who are you?'

'Cal Steinhurst.' He offered a moist hand, which I ignored.

'State your business, Cal Steinhurst.' He knew my name, so he must have had a specific reason for being beside me. I wasn't even surprised at this kind of thing any more.

'I like that. Straight to business. I wish everyone in Alcacia was like that. Make transactions a lot easier.'

'Get to the point or go sit on the empty table yonder.'

'Be calm.'

'What the fuck do you want, Cal Steinfuck?' I dropped my hand to my lap and shifted it to the handle of the gun in my waistband. Cal's eyes flicked there and back up to my face.

'I'm the unofficial representative of a foreign government.'

'What does "unofficial" mean?'

'It means I don't have a desk at the embassy, but I'd be evacuated in the event of a major crisis. I perform various advisory duties.'

Deliberate vagueness. He either was or wanted to be seen as a member of the intelligence community.

'What agency do you work for?'

'Nice try. Listen: I'm here to offer advice. Friendly advice for now.'

'Friendly.'

'Yes.'

'And what's the advice?'

'Go home, Weston. Alcacia does not want you any more.'

'Thank you for your advice. Now, piss off.'

'Fearless. I like that. I like you, Weston.'

'See, I don't even know you and I hate you. *¿Habla inglés?* Fuck off. I do not want what you're selling.'

One of the girls dropped a bowl of sliced guava and Cal picked one. His fingernails were clean, but bitten. I was sure they bled from time to time. Index and thumb were ink stained. No rings. The cuff of his right hand was blackened, but not the left. Plaid shirt. Not usual for a white man to wear long-sleeves at this time of day in Alcacia. Tanned, but not burned. Cal had been here a while. Hairy. Light brown. Five o'clock shadow, but otherwise good haircut. Not military. The ink did not come off on the guava.

'I like you,' he repeated. 'Not a trace of fear, even given the apocalyptic fuckers you are fucking with. I'll bet you went through idagba soke before going to London. You did, didn't you?'

'I couldn't get a sponsor,' I said defensively.

'I know. Father declined, as I recall. But you still did the ritual, didn't you?'

Idagba soke is the coming-of-age ritual for Yoruba males in Alcacia. Yoruba elsewhere do not have this. It takes thirteen weeks and begins in June, in the thirteenth year of a boy's life, starting

209

the day after the first rains. It's a good time since the planting would have finished and harvest would be far away.

A boy's father is the usual sponsor. He brings the boy to the hall of the warrior class in the wrestling ring along with the other prepubescents. Six warriors take them into the rainforest with nothing but machetes and their dangling foreskins. In the first twenty-four hours finding an animal skin for clothing is of paramount importance. By the end of the thirteen weeks the boy has learned to fight, to hunt, to kill and generally to survive.

On the last day the boy emerges as a man ready to be called into battle by the tribe should the need arise. The occasion is marked by ritual circumcision and scarification of the neck in a manner that symbolises a cut throat, meaning the warrior does not fear death since he has already died.

My idagba soke was long ago. I fear death now.

'My aunt vouched for me,' I said.

'Yes. And all the other little nigger boys made fun of you, didn't they?' He reached for the guava bowl but I slapped his hand away. I saw a red welt form.

'You don't need to bait me, Cal. I already hate you.'

'The nigger thing? Relax, Weston. It's reflex. I'm not prejudiced. I will ask you to reconsider my advice.'

'And I will tell you once more to fuck off. What does it matter to you?'

Cal spread out his hands. 'There are forces at play here, son. Tectonic plates that are shifting and they will crush you because you choose to surf the fault line.'

I clutched his groin and he grunted, squirmed. I tightened my fist. 'This is Africa. We have a single continental plate. There are no fault lines, there are no shifts and there is no surfing.'

I left him there, paid for my food, tipped the girls and mimed spitting at Cal's feet.

Sweating, red in the face, clearly in pain, he mimed tipping a hat to me.

'CIA?' asked Church. Bad, crackling phone line.

'Or allied. What is the CIA looking into me for?'

'The PCA is more Whore of Babylon than Lamb of God, aburo. They're in bed with everybody from the People's Republic of China to Havana. They're versatile that way.'

'What do the Americans want?'

'Who knows? He could be printing propaganda for them – hence the ink – or he could be building roads. This guy Cal has been in position since the Reagan administration. The Yanks are just hedging their bets as usual. They want to be sure neither the Front nor the PCA can act as fertile ground for Al-Qaeda indoctrination and that should either one of us achieve primacy Uncle Sam would have a well-heeled foot in the door. They are monitoring all sides. You, my friend, are a wild card. They don't like wild cards.'

'He called us niggers.'

'He didn't mean anything by it, or he was gauging your reaction. He's probably not racist, but he is a pro. I should know. The "advisors" who trained me were ex-CIA among other things. They say that kind of thing, but save your life in a fucking heartbeat. Have you found your woman?'

'No.'

'I have some time to kill. Let's look for clues.'

'I'll call you back. I have one other matter to take care of.'

'I'll meet you at the market gate.'

'Okay.'

* * *

I dialled the number. It rang once, then silence.

'Hello?'

'Speak.'

'We need to talk. I went to the PCA camp . . .'

Blinding, retina-shattering sunlight dazzling me, heating me up so that I wanted to take off my shirt but didn't because of the gun in my waistband where it was much easier to reach than the ankle holster.

So hot that I could hardly breathe. So, so hot.

I bought three sachets of iced-water and broke them over my head one after the other. The market gate was sticky, sweaty and crowded. A murder of the most motivated traders on the planet pressed against me, tried to sell me items. The most outrageous was a Barack Obama dildo, for which the seller could be jailed – Alcacia has draconian obscenity laws.

Area Boys postured at me; I postured back.

Just outside the gate there were four piles of books and a 'five cent per copy' sign. There were very few bookshops in Alcacia. Pupils bought their textbooks from the market. These were usually bad photocopies of originals, bound and sold at one-hundredth the normal price.

Commotion. A Toyota honked its way through the crowd at two miles per hour. There was, officially, a road in front of the market gate, but nobody ever used it. Except Churchill. Old women moved their stalls, cursing his family line with exotic poxes.

I was embarrassed to get in the car.

But I did.

CHAPTER 22

The drive home took an hour because I had to keep describing the way, and to be fair to Church my descriptions were below par. Church was good-natured about it, at least to me. He cursed many other road users.

He thought I was lucky to live in England and told me so. 'Those white women, what are they like? I've heard they can be wild.'

'Some of them are,' I said. 'But it isn't that simple. You can't just walk into a party and assume. You have to wait, watch reactions. You see white faces, most of them are okay, but some of them are racist. You can't tell. So you wait. You don't know for sure the people who are just casually xenophobic and humour you by talking to you. Attempt to take it further and they freeze you out.'

'Seriously?'

'Understand, they don't mean any harm. They just . . . I don't know, at times, when you use words of more than three syllables they look at you like you're a performing monkey, with surprise and amusement. They think you're clever. Like that Carter book.'

'Who?'

'Stephen L. Carter. He wrote a book called *The Emperor of Ocean Park*. Black law professor in America. He wrote a complex—'

'Man, all I wanted to know is how those English women are.'

'They're wild, Churchill. Wild.'

'I knew it,' he said, without irony.

There was no parking on the street. The local government had decided to regrade the surface and all the cars were either in driveways or garages. We parked two streets away from the flat in front of a general store whose owner erupted at us.

We walked back.

'So this is where you've been hiding,' said Church.

'It would appear so.'

'And this belongs to your lady friend.'

'As far as I can tell.'

I unlocked the stairwell.

'And this is that girl who drove that Mercedes the other day? The hooker?'

'She's not a hooker.'

'I hope not. Nasty, nasty pestilence in these parts, aburo.'

We went up the stairs. I led. It was dark on account of having no windows. Light bulb must have blown or burned out. Except . . .

'The front door is ajar,' I said. I hurried up the remaining stairs. 'Nana?'

I called out, but the apartment was a mess. Inside there was a guy wearing denims, holding my folders and sporting dreadlocks. He looked as surprised as I felt.

A yammering began in my brain, telling me to draw and use the gun at my waistband. Before I could act on it, Church pushed me down and to the left, then he leaped over my legs with a grace that belied his shape and the size of his belly. The man dropped the papers and engaged Church.

My neighbour and his two wives were angry again, quarrelling, sounds coming in from the open window.

Church punched the Rasta twice, a right hook and a left uppercut – two cracks that made me wince. The Rasta kneed Church and kicked him on the side of the head, then spun the other leg into Church's side. Church fell down but grabbed a chair leg and hit the Rasta around the ankles. He continued to hit the Rasta on the legs from his position on the ground. He rose while the Rasta tried to evade the blows. The Rasta backed down for a step, and then came forward in a flurry of punches that Church took on his forearms which he held up in a boxer's stance. The Rasta was ferocious, relentless. Church feinted, then hit out with a straight left that landed on the Rasta's chin, dead centre, dazing him, making him cry out in a female voice.

The Rasta was a woman.

One of my neighbour's wives screamed, said she was returning to her father's house if this is how she was to be treated.

Church bled from the mouth and nose, but the Rasta looked more unsteady and punchy. I had my gun out, but they kept circling each other, stepping over overturned furniture and broken pottery. Church dropped the chair leg.

'Church, get out of the way.'

He spat blood and sputum. 'Stay out of this. It does not concern you.'

He jabbed at the Rasta, easy for him given his simian reach. Each jab hit home. The Rasta cried out with each impact in her all-too-obvious feminine voice. Her denim jacket fell open in parts and her stagger was more visible. Church closed in on her. They scuffled, and Church exhaled sharply.

'You sneaky bitch,' he said. There was blood on his left side, which he held with his right hand. No blood seeped through his fingers. 'Ifa teju mo mi ki'n laya.' A prayer for courage.

The Rasta held a short blade in her hand.

This created some distance between them, and I aimed. 'I'm going to shoot.'

'If you fire that gun I will hit you so hard that your neighbours will think there's been an earthquake.'

Church picked up the chair leg again and swung it, missed, took a knife scratch on his arm, ignored it and smashed his elbow into the Rasta's temple. She went down limp and heavy.

Church followed, slumping down beside her. He knelt and hammered her head repeatedly with the chair leg until the only movement from the Rasta was convulsive twitching of her limbs and the transmitted shocks from being hit.

Church roared and smiled. Bloodstained teeth. The Rasta was supine on the floor, head bleeding, making shifting random and useless arm movements.

Church rolled on to the floor, breathing heavily, laughing.

'That was the most brutal thing I have ever witnessed,' I said.

'Which part? The part where I saved your life? Again?' said Church.

He was showering. Blood oozed from the wound in his side, but he did not seem to be in pain.

'She was already dead. There was no need to keep hitting her.'

'She was a professional who was here to kill. I did it for you, stupid.'

'Church—'

'Make yourself useful and search her,' he said. 'We will not discuss this again.'

The Rasta had twenty-five dollars and sixty-eight cents in cash, a bus ticket from 1975 to God knows where, two spent shells, a packet of gum half-full, a smoke grenade and a mobile phone.

I wiped the phone clean of blood and checked the recently dialled numbers.

I hit redial.

'Hello? Ikem, where the hell are you?' said the voice of Abayomi Abayomi.

I rigged up the television. There was a crack across the screen, but apparently plasma TVs can still run with cracks. There was a third-rate werewolf movie showing, American, with lots of stylish gunfire, dark-haired women with piercings, Gothy, Emo men feeling conflicted. Shit, really.

'I have some people coming to take out the garbage,' said Church. He poured vodka on his wound, dribbling some on the upholstery.

I sat on the righted sofa and watched lycanthropes.

'Do you know her?' I asked.

'Nope.'

A long-haired man transformed into a werewolf. It appeared painful and he screamed for longer than it seemed possible considering the size of human lungs. He grew in size. I hate it when that happens in films. Where does the mass come from? Where were the laws of physics when it came to making wolf?

'That woman killed Pa Busi, you know,' I said.

'So I guess you solved the case. I'll drink to that.' Church took a swig of vodka. 'And I'm a national hero for executing her.' He smiled, crossed his legs on a broken stool and watched fang and claw rip a SWAT team to pieces.

'I haven't solved anything,' I said.

'People's Christian Army shooter, People's Christian Army paymaster,' said Church. 'That's solved enough for me.'

'What did she want with me? In my flat?'

'She wanted your files on Pa Busi,' he said, pointing to the folders the Rasta was holding when we came in. 'And it's not your flat.'

Footfalls. People were coming up the stairs.

217

'That would be people with sharp implements and miles of plastic wrapping to dispose of our assassin.' Church drank vodka again.

Except when the door opened three men and one woman came in.

The woman was Nana.

CHAPTER 23

'Her name was Ikem Okafor,' Abayomi Abayomi said. 'She was an assassin and, yes, she did work for us.'

'You guys killed Pa Busi,' I said.

'No, we did not. There was no such mandate. Just let me finish what I have to say.'

'Go on.' I twirled the Epoch canister in my left hand, holding the phone in the right. A mournful wind rattled the shutters on Aunt Blossom's sitting-room windows. It had been three days since Church killed Ikem Okafor.

'You realise, Weston, that this means you should move up the Epoch timetable.'

'How so? Your assassin was revealed in the presence of a high-ranking Front member. My guess is that they're putting that information into the public domain as we speak. You can't use Nana as far as leverage is concerned because, heh, Nana's turned up.'

'How about these two words: *remote detonator*. You like them?'

'Interesting words.' I dropped Epoch. It bounced and rolled to a stop about a foot away.

'I thought you might find them interesting.'

'Tell me about Miss Okafor.'

'It's *Mrs* Okafor, actually. Husband deceased. She was about forty years old.'

'About?'

'Birth records lost. The Liberation Front burned down her village years ago, killed her parents and family. She was used as a sex slave in the camp. In those days we had frequent skirmishes, gained and lost ground, killed some of theirs, lost some of ours.'

'I notice, Abayomi, that your legal detachment is missing from our last few talks.'

'We took Ikem's village when she was twenty. She volunteered to work for us. Although we held that ground for fourteen days, when we pulled back she came with us.'

'You seem passionate when talking about this war now. Involved. Engaged. I would go as far as to say invested.'

'At first she did what all the captured girls did, namely cooking, cleaning, running the domestic engineering side of things. There was sex, of course, but it was at least semi-consensual.'

'I don't think you've been totally honest with me. I don't think you are being honest with me now.'

'Nobody remembers much about her before what I'm about to tell you. She was also completely lacking in the curve department, looked like a man.'

'Are you ignoring me?'

'Men going to war will fuck anything with a wet hairy hole, though. She was with a new recruit one night and he took his rifle with him to her quarters. He fell asleep as you do. She got up to take a shower. Just as she went to the well our boys brought in a batch of prisoners, one of whom Ikem recognised as her rapist.'

'I wonder why this sudden surge of emotion.'

'Pay attention. This is important. Ikem calmly walked back into her room, picked up the rifle lying next to her lover who was still comatose. She had never used any kind of firearm up to this point. She walked outside, took aim from what onlookers said was about twenty feet away and shot. Took the top off her target's skull with the first burst, split a banana tree behind him as well, but it survived. He did not.'

'Understandable.'

'You need to imagine the shot. The target was moving and surrounded by agitated revolutionaries. It's confusion at such times in the camp. Lots of shouting and tumult.'

'Rowdiness, disorder, general disruption.'

'Yes. And through this a woman who had never handled an AK picked her target with no collateral damage except for a vegetable cluster. That's beyond amazing.'

'A gift, extreme talent, an affinity for the gun.' He ignored my mocking tone.

'She almost got herself killed because of the abundant enthusiastic soldiers swivelling on her. We thought it was a fluke.'

'Beginner's luck.'

'Yes. Except she was tested. Mastered any gun or rifle our Chinese instructor threw at her in record time. Up to ninety per cent of the time she'd hit dead centre. I'm exaggerating, but only a little.'

I had seen evidence of her accuracy in the bus terminus, and she must have been good to make the Pa Busi shot while strapped to a palm tree.

'I believe you, but only with respect to Ikem's accuracy. My previous suspicions remain intact.'

'The Russian advisors just about had an orgasm when she demonstrated her skill. She was fast tracked for as much training as possible. She ate it all up. Ikem Okafor loved weapons, hated the Front and had no regard for human life, hers or anyone else's. She was also nigh invisible. Quiet. The exact opposite of a showboat. She cared about nothing other than when it came to the Front. She killed dozens, maybe hundreds. I don't know. Not privy to all of it. She worked best in a semi-autonomous way. We used her as a gun. We pointed her in the general direction of an enemy and said "kill". Let her loose in a jungle and the enemy will be pissing their pants in twelve hours, wondering who would be shot next.'

'Who pointed her at Pa Busi?'

'Nobody. She pointed herself.'

'Bullshit.'

'Believe what you want. When I first heard of his death I thought it was a mistake. Landmine. But I also knew that she was in the area at the time. Since her death I've searched her things. She had a diary. She did not like the peace process and wanted things to return to the way they were.'

'Attrition, internecine aggression, hostility. Kill, kill, kill.'

'Instead of standing down as ordered she jump-started the war. Or so she thought.'

'And the landmine?'

'Coincidence.'

'—'

'Look, you can read the diary, access her room if you want. I can arrange it.'

'You're too kind.'

'Weston, this makes it all the more important that you deliver Epoch soon. The Front will be—'

'Relax. I have an appointment with the El Jefe in two days. I'll take your engine of war then.'

'Good to know. Weston, I—'

'What do you know about Nana Hastruup?'

'Everything. What do you need to know?'

'How did the affiliation with the Liberation Front start?'

'At university. She got kicked out for "fomenting unrest", which is the administration's term for headstrong communist radical.'

'Wait. She told me she left university voluntarily. There was a randy professor who wanted blowjobs for grades or something.'

'Weston, I have a carbon copy of the letter. She was rusticated. She and a few others set fire to the campus zoo and released all the animals.'

Which just made sense. Was everything she told me a lie?

'What else?' I asked.

'She wrote a few self-published pamphlets about her beliefs. Brilliant, but strident. She seemed angry that when the colonial powers were here they created a bureaucracy headed by privileged whites but that after independence Africans did not dismantle the structure, which led to all kinds of corruption. The inequity continues to this day and, according to her, needs to be brought crashing down in the fireball of revolution. Maybe four people read the pamphlet. One of them was obviously from the Front because they approached her for propaganda work. In the Red Summer she wrote the sheet that dissected the suicide bombing phenomenon and exposed it for the rubbish it was. You heard of that? 2002?'

'I've heard of it, but I don't know the details.'

'A new school of thought. The brains behind the People's Christian Army decided to borrow a page from Islamic fanatics and blow themselves up. A whole doctrine was dreamed up to justify this and susceptible young fools streamed into marketplaces and cinemas and political rallies just to blow themselves up. Her essay on the topic is credited with ending the phenomenon. Fucking sharp mind, no argument about that anywhere.'

'How long has she worked for them?'

'Ten years.'

'Romantic involvements?'

'Ah . . . many. I don't know how to say this, but she was used to gather information at times. This meant getting close to people of power, sexually in many cases.'

'Anybody special?'

'Not according to the information we have. I'm sorry to be the one telling you this, ore. It's the *Forest of a Thousand Daemons*; you will run into them whether it's Churchill Okuta or Nana Hastruup. She—'

I cut him off. The phone was losing charge so I jacked it in a wall socket.

I made some notes in my journal.

I tried not to think of Nana, and obviously she was all I could think of.

You really haven't looked after my place, Weston. That was what she said. I said nothing. What do you say when the woman you love does not rush into your arms but instead kisses the homicidal psychopath who has just killed someone right next to you?

I tried to focus. I could end this soon.

It would have been a good time for the gods to stand up for Holloway bastards, but they didn't.

She kissed Church. It was a lingering, wet, tongue kiss with his hands moving all over her body and squeezing her bottom. It couldn't have lasted more than a few seconds but it was hours to me. I was unable to speak and there was this loud tinnitus in my ears. My forehead hurt, real discombobulating shit.

Church broke off the kiss and looked at me, smiling, one side of his mouth twisted downwards. He still held Nana around the waist. She looked like a rag doll in his hands, all floppiness and double joints, eyes glazed over. Her hand was over his zipper, stroking. What the fuck?

'Do you feel beaten? Do you feel a great sense of injustice? Impotence, yes? That is how we feel every day in Africa. You are a tourist and understand nothing. Did you really think we would just hand you money to spend and a pussy to fuck and a gun to fuck people up with for fun? You think we have funds to spare?'

'You know each other, then?' I said.

'Know each other? I sent her to Blossom's funeral, my dog.'

'No,' I said, stupidly.

'You're an idiot,' said Nana. 'You think anyone could live exclusively on writing essays for university students? With the kind of starvation and oppression we're going through, how many people do you think even care about higher education any more? How is it that you even remember to breathe in and out? I swear, you're so stupid.'

'Who are you?' I asked.

'She is a revolutionary,' said Church.

Around us Ikem was rolled on to plastic wrapping paper and machetes rose and fell. I learned that as long as you slice around the joints you can cut a body into ten portable parts before your sharp implements get blunt. The body generated more blood than I imagined, but the 'cleaners' knew what they were doing. One man shaved the dreadlocks off.

Nana had nothing to say to me.

'Relax, aburo. You did your job. Your darling Nana will write up a wonderful propaganda piece in which you will be the hero of the republic having solved this heinous crime. My part would not make it into national press but then people like me . . .' He shrugged.

'Nana,' I said.

She stared blankly.

'It was all a lie?'

She frowned. 'Weston, you . . . How can I say this? You and I, we were in love and if you remember certain promises were made. I waited and waited for you to contact me, to send a letter, anything. You, on the other hand, fulfilled the cliché to a letter. All those long talks about how nobody else really knows how to conduct a long-distance relationship across the Atlantic and how we would show them. How we would write a letter a week and have a telephone call every month. Phone sex. Care packages. As soon as you settled down you were meant to invite me over. Do you remember any of this, Weston? Do you know how long I waited, checking the post office box, checking your aunt's house for packages, straining myself for any word from you? And there was nothing. Not one line. You touched down in Heathrow and forgot all about me. You said you'd call from the airport to tell me you were okay and I believed that shit! And I felt stupid for a long time. I wouldn't date. I said there must have been some kind of mistake, perhaps you didn't have the right address, perhaps you were too busy, some fucking thing which was just me making excuses for you, me being daft, slightly soft in the head. But now I have to wonder who is more stupid. I'm thinking, after all this, any idiot would know that a woman would find it difficult to forgive. Hell hath no fury, and all that. Wise words, you know. Simple, oft repeated, but seriously wise. But you, Weston, you came back after all this time and believed that I would just forget all that pain and become the biddable lover that you left behind. You believe that. Are all Holloway Babies soft in the head, or is it just you?'

'You love me,' I said.

'No, I really don't. You cured me of that,' said Nana.

'Aburo, you want to let this go,' said Church.

'I'm sorry, Nana,' I said.

'I do not want your apology. I don't even know who you are. The Weston I used to know no longer exists. You think we're detestable, right? You think our actions are abhorrent and that Church is an incarnation of the Antichrist. Yet you have no idea about our reasons for being so, nor do you care. You have no drive yourself other than survival. At least we are about something; we have taken a stand. You stand for nothing but yourself.'

She left the room, but came back shortly with cleaning materials and began to work on the spilled blood.

I did not know what to do next. Church was speaking but I wasn't paying attention. I searched for and found my journal, the

Epoch canister, the money and the details of my investigation. Nana did not look at me or speak to me and I ached inside. A lot of what she had said was true. My acknowledgement of this was met by indifference from her and laughter from Church. I left, not exactly knowing where I was going, but ending up in Aunt Blossom's house after wandering for five hours. It was dark when the taxi dropped me there and I had to break in via one of the back windows. The electricity was not on, but there were blankets and beds and furniture draped with plastic, reminding me of the disposal of Ikem Okafor. There was dust everywhere, but that didn't bother me. I re-sealed the window and fell asleep on the couch. I did not dream.

My life at Aunt Blossom's house was fairly systematised. I had electricity now. There were a few unofficial ways to source juice in Alcacia depending on your expertise. Power tends to be served by overground cables strung up on poles. In front of each house a feeder cable branched off to be shared among several properties, usually terminating in a meter. A skilled person could tap electricity straight off the branch before the meter and not pay for the supply. The power company was considered fair game and a perpretrator would not be grassed. The only drawback is the occasional fatal electrocution. An alternative would be to covertly position an extension cord in a neighbour's property and bury or hide the cable. This was effectively stealing and was frowned upon. I stole it from Nana's parents' house next door. I only used it to power a fridge, television and fan. Aunt Blossom had a generator, but I did not want to announce my presence. I had a small lamp but I kept it off most of the time.

I stayed home all day and left the property at night, lurking around for food and beer on one occasion. The mosquitoes were pernicious. They bred in pools of stagnant water scattered in the luxuriant weeds around the house.

Throughout the day I stared at what I had on Pa Busi's murder, thinking, sifting, cajoling my brain into action.

The slow pulsing of green light on my phone charger was hypnotic. As I stared at it I realised there were four things I needed to do before my meeting with the Liberation Front.

CHAPTER 24

To get to Arodan a second time I had to pay a taxi driver one hundred dollars in advance, with the total return fee being three hundred. This time I haggled because not haggling is what gives them the impression you're fresh off the boat. As usual the weather was sunny, but this time a warm shower dripped through the rays, throwing up rainbows all over the place. It was psychedelic.

The drive over was lonely this time. There was no Nana to provide horror stories about abandoned villages. He was a stone-faced southerner who drove without speaking. His stereo was broken and the air conditioning spurted out hot air sporadically. We had to keep one window open when it rained to prevent the windscreen from fogging up.

Between the parking lot and the main door I got drenched, but that didn't bother me. I dripped water on to the floor and approached the reception nurse.

'Eku ise, o,' I said.

'Ek'asan,' she said. It was the same girl, Bola, and I saw her eyes examine the puddle I was creating on the floor.

'Eku ojo yi o,' I said.

'Ahh, ki l'ama se si?'

'Do you remember me?' I asked.

'Of course. I can't forget a Holloway face. You're here to see Afolabi?'

'Yes, thanks,' I said. I counted off fifty dollars and placed it near the magazine she was reading.

She looked troubled. 'You know, sir, the patient deteriorated after your last visit. It took a lot of work to settle him down.'

I peeled off an extra twenty.

'Eniyan gidi,' she said, and leaped off her stool. 'Follow me.'

I spent forty-five minutes with Afolabi Akinrinde.

The Ede market was back in business with very little evidence of the fire left. I negotiated the stalls and found the mobile phone unlockers. I selected one at random and dropped Idris Wallace's phone.

'This is a very old model,' said the proprietor.

'I know. I want all the phone numbers that are stored on the SIM card and if you can show me the last numbers called you get a bonus.'

He smiled.

On my return to Ede I went to the offices of Gentian Alliance. The receptionist in the claims department was pretty, perky and unimpressed by my wet clothes or my offers of seventy dollars. My inanity didn't help matters either.

'I need to speak to someone about a claim handled by your company.' I made it a hundred dollars and added an edge to my voice.

'One moment,' she said, whisking the money away. She pressed a button and spoke quietly into the phone. Her name card read Emiola Onanuga and underneath the lettering she had taped 'JESUS SAVES'. She did not invite me to sit down, but then given my general appearance I wouldn't invite me to sit either.

Presently a man walked out of the office to speak to me. He

was fat and sweaty. He was the claims advisor, which is what claims investigators were called in Ede.

We talked.

Ireti Olubusi opened the door to their flat and glared at me. He was a younger, hipper version of his father. I did not understand his hostility, but comparing the property and area they lived in to Diane's gave me a hint.

His mother was seated, an aura of calm around her. She was Iranlowo Olubusi, first wife of Enoch Olubusi. I found her from processing the digital photos I took of correspondence in Pa Busi's house. She was about fifty, large in an elderly Yoruba way, suspicious. I sat opposite her.

We talked about Pa Busi for two hours.

At ten past midnight the docks were empty barring the occasional policeman to whom I was invisible after a hundred dollars tax. I stood there leaning against a lamp-post that gave no light. I chewed on a corn cob while watching an okada make its way towards me. I dropped the corn and put my hand on my gun, but the cyclist just dropped a book and screeched away. It was the diary of Ikem Okafor.

I went home.

I spent time thinking and drinking coffee and thinking and reading the diary. Mosquitoes feasted on me. In about eight hours I would be meeting Church and he'd be taking me to the Front headquarters where this whole odyssey began for me.

'Fuck it,' I said, and dialled Diane.

★ ★ ★

TADE THOMPSON

'You are filthy,' said Diane. 'Get in the shower. Do not even come near me. How is it you always come here when you are filthy?'

'I'm finding it's an occupational hazard in this country,' I said.

I took a bath instead of a shower. I pampered myself with aromatic bath oils and whatever salts I could find. I had to change the water twice – it got so dirty.

I was in the tub with my eyes closed feeling no pain when I heard the door open. Diane came in with no clothes on.

'That was different,' she said. 'You are usually more timid, more tender. I am not complaining, mind you.'

Three thirty a.m. Post-coital garrulousness from Diane, out of character for her but perhaps triggered by my unusual moodiness. I stood naked in front of her aquarium following carp with my eyes and a finger on the glass. Fish are meant to be calming. I felt calm. Might be because I had just had sex, of course.

'Do you want to go to the theatre today? I can get us into *Man and Superman* at the National.'

I tapped on the aquarium glass. The carp scattered.

'You made her feel even more ugly than usual,' I said, without looking at her.

'What?'

'I said, you made her feel uglier. Uglier and uncouth and uncultured. You made her acutely aware of it.'

'Who are you talking about now?'

'Ikem Okafor.'

'Who?'

'You don't know her?'

'I do not seem to recall—'

'I know you killed your husband, Diane.'

I heard the bedclothes rustle as she sat up. I turned to face her.

232

'You have been listening to absurd rumours,' she said. Her eyes were narrow slivers.

'No rumours. You killed your husband. I know that much, but I'm not sure of the motive. His first wife thinks he was a bit of a shit, you know. Was that why you killed him?'

'This is a joke, right? A fantasy?'

'Not a fantasy at all, Diane, but I can tell you a story if you like. On the day your husband died, Alao drove out to the PFC camp, lost control of the vehicle on the way and stopped. Almost simultaneously Pa Busi took a shot to the head and the trunk. The body shot was from inside the jeep and the shooter was most likely Idris Wallace. The head shot was taken by Ikem Okafor from a palm tree that she must have climbed hours earlier. The jeep then exploded. I think Ikem mined the road or placed some remote detonating grenades around her kill zone. Either way, I'm fairly sure she was responsible for the blast.'

'What does all this have to do with me?'

'I know why Ikem pulled the trigger. She wanted to restart the hostilities, but then there was something odd about her diary. There were entries relating to you. Her paymasters have told me that she pretty much worked on her own. Long rope, loose super-vision, all that. When she decided to kill Pa Busi she spent a lot of time observing her target, and in the process she observed you. She thought you were beautiful, charming, otherworldly, every-thing she was not. She also felt sorry for you, which I could not understand. She saw something that she felt she had to put a stop to, which gave her a second reason to kill him.'

Diane was getting dressed. 'What are you talking about?'

'She killed Pa Busi for you. She saw something and felt she had to get him out of the way. For you.'

'She was mistaken. And her misconception does not mean I ordered my husband's death. I never spoke to her!'

'No, you probably did not, but that's not why I said you killed him.'

'Then why—'

'Because of Wallace.'

She was silent.

'You can't say you don't know Wallace, can you? You told me he was the only bodyguard you talked to. Afolabi noticed the relationship between you two. You see, he's the kind of straight arrow who likes a clear demarcation between duty and leisure. He did not approve of fraternising at work. He saw some undue cosiness between you and Wallace. Have you ever spoken to Afolabi? Remarkable case. Totally brain dead in everything but the day he was blown apart. Amazing, really. Anyhow, where was I? Oh, yes, Idris Wallace. I don't know if you were lovers—'

'Oh, please!'

'—or if you promised to pay him when the insurance came through only to find him conveniently blown up after the event. Then you simply stopped taking his calls, after which he is meant to have killed himself. Did you start a fight with your husband to reduce the guilt when you "discovered" his assassination?'

'I want you out of my house.'

'In a minute. You lied to me. I went to the insurance company. Gentian Alliance. The claims department is virtually one investigator and an extremely busty secretary. He told me there was no investigation into your claim. You said it had been fully investigated when I asked you. Why would you say that? The investigator said there was a wave of sympathy when Pa Busi died and he was instructed "from on high" not to bother with a close look at the circumstances of his death. Sixteen million dollars, wasn't it?'

'Get out.'

'I will, but not yet. I want you to know something: I don't plan to share this information with anybody. Ikem Okafor has been found and killed. It doesn't matter how. The official story will be that she was a lone gunman and that will be that. You and I will know the truth, I suppose, but that doesn't matter. I've found out recently that I have no real morality or politics.'

'You were fucking me while your girlfriend was missing, Weston. That should have been a big clue.'

'Yes, yes, my powers of detection only work for the benefit of others. Blah, blah. Diane, I know you did it, but I don't know why. I don't buy greed as a motive, although sixteen million is sixteen million. Yet Ikem saw something while she was watching you.'

'—'

'What did he do to you?'

'All you have is conjecture.'

'I know.'

'But the kind of thing that could theoretically drive a person like me to murder would have to be an insult against my body. It would be something I consider to be defilement. For example, if my husband were to drug me one night, to drug my food, and undress me, and scoop some of the low-fat butter from the refrigerator and smear it inside and around an orifice which we had not previously agreed was open to him and insert his erection and take me again and again until the bed linen is stained with blood and semen and excrement, all to satisfy his urges and needs. It would probably take weeks in the hospital to heal. Wounds would open up between the bladder and rectum, which would mean incontinence and persistent urinary infections since faecal matter would leak into the bladder. Hospital staff and servants would have to be paid off to keep quiet but the victim of such savagery would always know that they knew. Such a victim would feel dirty no matter how many times she washed, not just from the rape, but from the incontinence and fear of incontinence. Theoretically, if he were to do that, then the shame might be enough to drive a person like me to murder. Not me, mind you. A person like me. Not me.'

'No. Of course not.'

We were both dressed now. I gave the aquarium a final tap. I remembered the extreme porn I found in Pa Busi's locker when I roamed the house. I nodded at nothing. A few tentative birds started experimenting with dawn song.

'Do you even care, Weston?'

'Not really. I was just curious as to your reasons. It makes no difference to either of our destinies.'

'I mean about me. Do you care about me?'

She seemed vulnerable for the first time. Her hair was all wet and floppy and the anger was gone. Just resignation and sloped shoulders.

I walked over and kissed her in lieu of an answer. Then I left.

CHAPTER 25

I was sleep deprived again.

I had worked everything out and there was no fine man-oeuvring to do, but I had to remain alert. I felt slightly dizzy whenever I stood up quickly and I had a layer of cold sweat on my back. I asked for strong black coffee while I waited for the Supreme Commander in his lounge.

The Liberation Front of Alcacia had moved headquarters since my last visit on account of government shelling. It was smaller and the commander's quarters weren't as grand.

Rather than the old camp where the revolutionaries pushed back the forest with a bulldozer, this one secured a gentler place, more in tune with the countryside. Even from inside I could hear wind shaking up the trees. Nature was winning this time and there was an impermanence to the place. It was still early enough in the morning for cocks to crow.

There were both gas lamps and kerosene lanterns on shelves although the distant hum of a generator guaranteed power.

There was a dining table covered with a white Red Cross blanket instead of a tablecloth. There was bread, open bottles of olive oil, tea cups, dodo, ogi, empty glasses, bottled water, a boiled egg, salt and pepper shaker and a cooked, half-eaten fowl. Nothing steamed so I guessed it was all cold. The table lacked vitality – these were leftovers.

Inexplicably there was a bootleg poster of a young Leonardo DiCaprio on the wall.

There were windows with vulgar bars across them. I spied two men sitting under a tree, sharing a meal and laughing; a delayed guffaw. One would throw back his head and the dopplered sound would hit later.

I was here to be officially congratulated. This time I had not been kidnapped or even blindfolded. I simply waited at the market gate and a car came for me. I was not searched, even though I wasn't armed.

Sing a happy tune.

A door opened and Supreme Commander Osa Ali came in with Churchill and another man whom I didn't know. I was slightly disappointed; I had hoped Nana would be there too. Not that it was necessary. Church was in a buba and soro, which is a modified caftan made of local fabric. He smiled at me with an eyebrow raised and cocked his head to the side with his hands spread out. As if to ask, *No hard feelings?* I nodded at him with a scintilla of a smile. Osa Ali did not have his glasses on, but he seemed rather benign and wore a white shirt with jeans. The unknown man was Chinese and wore a suit.

'Your Excellency,' I said.

'Weston Kogi, we owe you a debt of gratitude,' he said. He hugged me, drew me into himself. Very expansive. Hardness in the muscles under his layers of fat. Smelled of Old Spice. 'May I present Mr Tian Rui Han? This is our private investigator Weston Kogi.'

Han shook my hand. Ali did not volunteer what exactly Han's role was and I did not ask. He handed me a sheet of A4.

'Press release,' said Church. 'It's going out later today. Nana composed it, but it will appear under a different byline when published.'

Indeed.

After many years of uncertainty the murderer of Pa Busi has been unmasked. The investigation was carried out by private detective Weston Kogi working in conjunction with the Alcacian Government. He has disclosed that the killer was Ikem Okafor, a People's Christian Army agent. It appears clear that the PCA's intention at the time was to stoke conflict between rebel factions and disrupt the peace process sought by other groups, particularly the Liberation Front of Alcacia. In an attempt to apprehend the assassin she was fatally injured and did not survive. Mr Kogi was not available for comment. This draws a line under a case that has baffled authorities for . . .

'What do you think?' asked Church.

'You said "fatally injured" and then that the person did not survive. Tautological.'

'Nobody cares, Weston.'

'This is going to become the official version of events, isn't it?' I said.

'Pretty much.'

'It would be a pretty good advertisement for me if I were planning to stay in the country and work.'

'True, but you don't have to worry about funds for the time being. We have remuneration for you,' said Ali. He handed over a briefcase. I didn't look inside. 'Do not give any interviews about this affair. That could make things inconvenient for us. It is over.'

'I have a gift for you,' I said. I took the Epoch canister out of my hip pocket and offered it to Ali.

'What is this?' he asked.

'It's a nasty little synthetic virus that the PCA wanted me to release in your camp. My gift to you. Do with it as you will. I'm out of this business.' I stood up.

'Wait,' said Church. 'Let's confer.'

They asked me questions about the virus and how to release it and who specifically asked me to bring it. I answered honestly most of the time. Han was most interested in the parameters of the disease that Epoch induced. They got into agitated whispers which did not interest me in the least.

'Not that I'm any good at strategy or anything, but what are you planning to do with it?' I asked.

'We are going to shove it right up the PCA's collective asses,' said Church. 'It's just what we need.'

'You'd unleash it on them?'

'They were going to do it to us,' said Church.

'Goodbye, Mr Kogi. We'll think of you again if we have business,' said Ali.

'Please do not,' I said, and left the room.

From the car I telephoned Nana. This time she picked up the phone. 'We have nothing to talk about, Weston,' she said.

'My passport?'

'It's at my parents'. I've told my papa to give it to you if you turn up.'

'Thanks. Listen, I really am sorry for—'

'Yes, yes, I know.'

'One last thing: are you in the camp?'

'Yes. Why?'

'Get out.'

I hung up the phone and dialled another number.

'It's me. I did what we agreed. They also planned to use Epoch once it was in their hands. My part in this is over.' I hung up and tapped the driver of my escort jeep.

'Stop the car. I need to take a piss badly.'

I went into the undergrowth and ran as fast as I could. I was still running when the rumble of bombing began.

* * *

After an hour I began to hallucinate. Nordic frost giants melting in the noon sun of Alcacia. Watermelon monsters battling over the corpse of a Jabberwock. A dozen monkeys babbling Shakespeare's sonnets. Orange-red Martian landscapes with corpulent African fertility gods running marathons. Giant bats, jaws dripping blood, swarming around me. Yet in all this I was not afraid. I was walking or running through it, trying to get away from a conflagration behind me. Or in front of me, it was difficult to tell. I drifted, floated off the ground, dissipated into nothingness.

I woke up in a bed that was cold and wet with my own sweat. It was night-time judging from the crickets and the darkness outside. I had no idea where I was. The ceiling had this dusty netting strung up across it and random objects like books and toothbrushes were caught in it. Mine was the only bed in the room, which was small with a single window. Someone had scribbled 'Stand Up For Jesus!' on the wall beside me. The other walls had a one-foot crucifix and a painting of shepherds. It was too dark to determine colour other than a dull brown. A gas lamp hissed in the corner in front of me turned low to provide a night light. I sat up, felt dizzy, steadied myself. I was naked.

Near the door there was a chair, as if someone had been watching over me. The bedside desk had a King James Bible and an empty glass. Perhaps a hospital? I wondered what had happened.

There was one cupboard and I aimed myself for it, feeling a fresh wave of dizziness. My clothes were inside, clean but not pressed. Also, my briefcase of money, which surprisingly still contained the cash Ali had given me. I dressed, but very slowly. I spent a few minutes looking for my shoes and found them under the bed. I tried the door. It opened into a hallway with nine similar doors on each side with mine in the approximate middle. Lamps hung at intervals from hooks in the ceiling. I stepped into the corridor and blacked out.

When I came to I was in bed again, clothed this time, with a kindly nun standing over me. She was South Asian, fiercely furrowed face, benevolent smile. I generally hate nuns, but I was glad to see this one.

'It's good to see you awake,' she said. 'My name is Puja.' She didn't sound Indian, or even Alcacian.

'Where are you from?' I asked. I needed water. My throat was parched and I sounded like a frog in mating season.

Puja laughed. 'Usually, people in your condition want to know where they are or what day it is. You have questions about my accent. Huh.'

'What's with the . . . aren't you a nun or something?'

'I'm a reverend sister.'

'Okay, so shouldn't I be calling you "sister" or some other reverent noun?'

She laughed again. I was learning she laughed easy. 'Some call me Sister Haq or Dr Haq. Puja's fine also.'

'Am I dreaming you?'

'No.'

'Good. What's wrong with me?'

'Malaria. You were delirious and dehydrated too. I had to give you quinine.'

'Malaria? But I was taking proguanil.' Except I hadn't taken it for God knows how long.

'You have malaria. You're better, but you need to take meds for a while.'

'I feel itchy.'

'Yes, quinine does that.'

'Right.'

'What's your name?'

'Weston.'

'Weston, how is it that you were wandering in the forest with just the clothes on your back and a sizeable briefcase full of money yelling about pterodactyls?'

'I fell in with a bad crowd.'

'You were asking for your gun.'

'It was a very bad crowd.'

'Hmm. That will have to do, I suppose. Are you hungry? Thirsty?'

'Not really hungry. Thirsty, though.'

'Does your bad crowd . . . are they . . . ?'

'Not criminals or gangsters. They are revolutionaries, patriots!'

'You mock them. What did you do?'

'Let's see. I don't want to be a mass murderer so I swapped something harmful for something harmless.'

'What are you talking about?'

I telephoned the number, I told the secret police guy about Epoch, he asked for a meet. He took it from me and gave me another cylinder. Harmless, with a tracking device. Asked me, told me, to take it with me to the Front meeting, and I did, knowing it wouldn't be long before the helicopters arrived, knowing the existence of Epoch guaranteed the obliteration of the Christian Army, knowing the choice made by Ali would determine its own survival.

If he had opted to destroy the virus I wouldn't have led government troops to his headquarters.

I hoped that Nana got out, that Church was dead. But I knew better. Church would survive nuclear holocaust and still have time to dance bata on the radioactive corpses of his enemies.

As for Abayomi, who knew where he would wash up? I didn't care.

★ ★ ★

'I'm worried about myself, Sister. I don't care about anything. I have no ethics, no code of conduct.'

Puja pointed to her own chest. 'Not a psychiatrist. Just a physician tending to poor Alcacian folk in the middle of nowhere.'

'You're a reverend sister.'

'You want me to discuss the Word of God with you? The Risen Christ?'

'No, thank you.'

'Then what do you want?'

'To feel intensely about something. I want to want to take a stand.'

'What's stopping you? You are mistaken if you think I will recommend God. My God is a refining fire who will burn away the impurities of self. You are still devoted to yourself, I think. You want a purpose, a mission statement for your life, and it does not include God or the Holy Mother or service. I cannot help you with that.'

'I have this recurring dream, you know. I'm walking through a marketplace, only it's empty. All the stalls are open, the beans and grain stands with their measures ready for trade, but there are no humans. I usually end up in the butcher's stall where a dead person will speak to me and then a flight of vultures will come down and eat them up.'

'Hmm.'

'Is that it? Don't you have some words of wisdom for me?'

'There's certainly a loneliness theme in there, but I cannot help you. I'm the least wise person I know, Weston. I'm a doctor. I am here to heal your body. I can tell you that every person who heals you gives birth to you in part, but I'm not your mother. Get better. You cannot stay here.'

'How long have I been—'

'Three days before your fever broke, but I think you were

wandering in the forest for at least twenty-four hours judging by the degree of dehydration.'

'Do you have any newspapers? Or a radio or television?'

'I think there is a transistor somewhere. I'll have it brought in.'

'Thank you.'

The letter I sent to my sister in London went like this:

Dear Lynn,

I feel like shit.

As I write this my skin itches all over from quinine injections.

My nails are shiny from scratching and I have marks all over me, some from mosquitoes, some from itching. I should have trimmed my nails, shouldn't I? Before you ask, yes, I have malaria; yes, I did take anti-malaria pills, but they didn't work; yes, that's because I'm in Alcacia. In fact, I'm looking at that famous painting, the one after Poussin, by Gbamileke. *Et in Alcacia ego.* It's at the end of my hospital bed. Oh, and yes, I am in hospital. I'm in the mission hospital, though I might not be by the time you get this. They tell me I've been owning malaria for four days now and the fever just broke. The ink smudges on the letter are from my sweat. I've tasted it and it's curiously without salt.

I'll explain why I couldn't email in a minute.

~~There isn't enough water for me to take a decent~~

Do not fret. And don't blame me either. I didn't come to the home country for an adventure. I came to attend Auntie Blossom's funeral. Then I got caught up in something . . . icky.

What I've sent you constitutes diary entries. I've scribbled everything that ~~happend~~ happened up till this point. I don't know if it'll get to you or if I'll be able to send more. We'll see. This should get to you via the ~~xxxxxx~~ embassy. ~~Every other commis-~~

~~sion appears to have an interest in impeding my progress.~~ That's why I couldn't send the emails – my account's being monitored.

I think I should have stayed in London, making *faux* armchair-revolutionary noises with the Yoruba diaspora. Spilt milk, in any case.

Do not come here. I am fine. Apart from the parasite eating my red cells and the poison that is meant to kill the parasite but is trying to kill me as well, that is. Read the report for your information, but don't take any action. If I need something I'll make a loud noise, okay?

Sorry, forgot to ask! How are you? Still pining away after the research job? I hope you're well, my sister.

~~Lot of love.~~

Weston

Xxx

Which sums up my current situation. I put the letter in an envelope which I sealed with the parcel formed by the copy of my journal entries and handed it to the waiting boy. I gave him a dollar for himself and twenty dollars for the courier service that the nuns had engaged for my use.

When he had gone I settled back into bed and scratched myself with a corn husk. I remembered talking to Lynn about Auntie Blossom. I had ideas of how to get her out of Africa, far-fetched schemes. I said Alcacia wasn't kind to Blossom.

'Alcacia isn't kind to anyone,' Lynn had said.

The story I told in the letter was rather incomplete, but I felt sure the journal would fill in any gaps. I drifted off to sleep.

I harvested information from the transistor. The charge had run out of my phone and there was no charger in the mission.

The government had announced the complete crushing of

both major rebel factions. The army was in the countryside mopping up stragglers and exterminating the minor groups to prevent a power vacuum. This had been 'an elaborate operation meticulously planned over two years by Special Forces in conjunction with the secret police'. Craig was dead, Ali in custody, but there was no mention of Church or Abayomi. Or me. I don't know what I expected.

I had to get back to civilisation. I was way past due to leave Alcacia.

'Is that young Weston?' said Nana's father.

'Yes, sir,' I said. 'What are you reading?'

'An unbelievably dull paper on Lagrangian Mechanics. Are you here for Nana?'

'She's here?'

'Yes.'

'Then I'm here for her.'

'Nana!' he yelled.

I was wearing seventies-style clothes, which is all Puja could find for me. My shoes were still serviceable, but my beard growth made me look like a hippie in the wild. There was a bad taste in my mouth which I had forgotten, but it happens with malaria. It would pass. I gave the Portuguese mission five thousand dollars considering they were so decent towards me. A truck brought me to Ede after which I caught a taxi to the Hastruups' place to get my passport.

'This is a new look for you,' said Nana.

'It's retro. It's what all the cool kids are wearing these days.'

She looked softer in a way, less intensity around the eyes. Perhaps it was the homely loose linen she wore or the Ankara wrapper under it. Maybe it was because she was home. She wasn't hostile to me, although not in love. Her father made an excuse and went inside the house with his Lagrangian Mechanics paper. His porch chair remained empty since Nana and I both preferred to stand. It was like he never left.

'How have you been?' I asked.

'All right, considering everything. I'm alive, aren't I?'

'Yes, there is that. I'm glad you got out.'

'You turned out to be a cold bastard.'

'"Bastard"?'

'You know what I mean. You're the only one who's bothered by all that Holloway shit, anyway.'

'That's not true, and you know it. I think you just wanted to get a dig in. It's okay since your lover is probably dead and I caused it. Partially.'

'If you're talking about Church we were only occasional lovers.'

'Why didn't you tell me?'

'What, you thought I'd spend all this time pining over you? My main work over the last few years has been with the Front. You were an assignment. I just had to keep you in line, keep you controllable, keep them informed.'

'And there's nothing left of us?'

She sucked her teeth. 'Please.' She reached in the folds of her wrapper and gave me my passport. 'I should warn you: Church cloned it.'

'I know. I figured that part out a few minutes after I saw you kissing him.'

'He's probably alive.'

'I don't care.'

'You should. He'll be slightly upset with you.'

'Then he can look me up. We'll talk.'

'—'

'Goodbye, Nana. I really did love you.'

Did I, though?

I left her on the porch and went next door to Aunt Blossom's house.

Girders shifted in the house, sounding like the bowel sounds of a dinosaur. They ticked and creaked with the rapidly increasing heat of the day. The dimness was slashed by several shafts of sunlight finding gaps to shine through. I wanted to spit; my saliva was still bitter from the malaria. I plugged my phone charger in one of the illegal sockets and then went to the kitchen to drink some water out of a ceramic pot that I had filled from the well.

I climbed up the stairs to my old room, which I'd colonised. I placed the briefcase on the bed and started gathering my meagre belongings. I had been at it for about twenty minutes when my phone rang. I rushed downstairs, running my hand down the banister. Withheld number.

'Hello?'

'Open the door,' said the secret police agent I had been dealing with.

'What?'

'I'm outside. Let me in.'

'The door's locked. I don't have a key. You have to step over the fence, walk by the left side of the house and go to the fourth window. There's a loose board that you have to manipulate—'

'Never mind.' He hung up on me. I went to one of the windows, trying to see the gate through the gaps, but there was a resounding crash and the front door swung open, lock shattered.

'Mr Kogi,' he said. He had two other men with him but it was difficult to tell if they were the ones I was familiar with. He wore sunglasses too this time.

'Isn't it a bit hot for black suits?' I said. I realised I was still holding the phone to my ear. I dropped my hand. One of the men closed the door as best he could seeing as the hinges were now off alignment.

They fanned out in the living room and one went down the corridor into the kitchen and up the stairs before returning and nodding to the leader. 'Clear,' he said.

'Why are you here?' I said. 'I mean, I'm not going to ask how you found me, but our business is over.'

'Sit down,' the leader said. 'I still have to debrief you.'

He removed the sheets from some of the furniture and we began.

Our shadows grew long. We went over the same ground several times. What route did we take to the base camp? How many soldiers did I see before getting to Ali's headquarters? Who was Han? What did he look like? What was he wearing? Was he armed? Who first handled the Epoch canister? Who liked it the most? Do I think they would have wanted to destroy it? Did I get injured at all?

The other two both took notes and there was a recorder on the table they had placed in front of me.

When it was over they packed up. The leader gestured to me, indicating I should give him something.

'I did what we agreed,' I said.

'You did. And you are out of trouble in that regard. But this is still Alcacia and there is still the matter of a briefcase of money in your possession. Or did you think I wouldn't know?'

'I was going to mention it.'

'It's good that I saved you the trouble, then. Give it here.'

I gave the case to one of the other agents and stood back. The agent opened it and nodded to the leader.

'Don't I deserve compensation for the work I did?' I had to ask the agent for a cut otherwise he would have suspected there was more money somewhere. Which there was.

'Ibi a ti n'sise l'a ti n'jeun,' he said. He took two bundles of cash and threw them my way. 'Do not be greedy. With the fame from the newspapers you'll have more investigative work than you can ever complete. Your business will be booming from now on.'

'Business?'

'Make sure you do not mention this money to anybody, you hear?'

'Yes.'

They were gone. I sealed the front door as best I could, but I had no hammer or nails.

I looked at my watch. It was six thirty. How could they have kept up the interrogation for so long? But then I supposed they had had a lot of practice with political prisoners. I went to get more water.

While I drank I reflected on information I had obtained through reverse-engineering of the questions the man asked me. The Epoch canister had a tracer in it which was activated on my signal. The helicopters homed in and let loose their missiles. There were no prisoners taken, although a lot of Front personnel were unaccounted for, but this was apparently normal in the crushing of insurgencies. The rebels tended to escape by blending into the surrounding villages, renouncing their association with the organisation. The same thing had happened in the PCA camp, but most of the fighting there was hand-to-hand and room-to-room because they had bunkers underneath the buildings which protected them from the aerial bombardment.

It was getting dark, but I only had to gather my things and go to a hotel. I would have to bank the money and convert everything to pounds. It was a decent sum considering the rest of my expenses in the money belt and the Epoch fee. It was more liquidity than I had ever had in my life. I could take it easy for a while, contemplate my life. I packed.

When it was all done I looked out of one of the gaps in the boards on the window. There were lights on in Nana's house. I thought I should say goodbye to Nana's parents at least. And possibly see Nana again. I did wish and hope that she would still fancy me, or at least forgive me.

I went over. The streets were dark, patchily lit by the lamps. Moths were doing their kamikaze thing. No party this time, no coloured lights. Nana's gate was ajar, no gateman in sight. I walked past her father's chair, which had been overturned. I eased the gun into my hand and opened the front door, which was unlocked.

'Weston! Come in! Come in and drink from the overflowing cup of my fucking vengeance!' said Churchill.

CHAPTER 26

I don't know what the date is.

That was all I could think. It seemed important that I know the date of my own death, a nagging Ides of March vibe that would not let me go.

'Churchill,' I said. 'What have you done?'

'It does seem a bit much, doesn't it?' he said.

The entire lounge was in disarray. There were spindle-shaped drops of blood leading from the front door to an unconscious Mr Hastruup who was in the middle of the room. There was blood all over his clothes and in a pool under his head. The leather sofas were torn up, the television screen broken, the ceiling fan ripped out of its moorings. The carpet was crumpled up like a used handkerchief and there were books strewn everywhere. The heavy wood bookshelves and cabinets that Nana's dad had had made by a famous carpenter were all broken up. How had I not heard any of this from next door?

In his left hand he had Nana's hair. In his right hand he held a knife with which I assumed he had shorn her. Nana herself was sobbing at his feet, with patchy hair.

'After the Second World War the French and Italians used to do this to collaborators. Women. Whores who fucked Nazis for biscuits and cigarettes and petrol rations.'

I pointed the gun at him. 'Drop the knife.'

253

'No.' He scattered the hair over Nana's quivering form, then he seemed to consider her head. 'You know, I think I might have missed a bit.'

Church himself was wounded. He was bare-chested, with black denim trousers and combat boots. His left arm was bandaged, dressing dirty and bloodstained. He also had dressings on his head and belly. He swayed slightly, but held the knife firm. There was no tremor in that hand and the muscles worked just fine. His eyes were slightly glazed, perhaps drugged, but he smiled that perpetual smile of his, uncaring, unbothered.

'Nana, are you all right?' I asked, stupidly.

'She's fine, aburo. Hair grows back, broken teeth can be fixed, fractured jaws sewn back together. She will still be beautiful,' said Church. 'Now, take off your money belt and give it to me.' He stopped smiling and studied me as potential prey. I could see it in the set of his chin, the slight narrowing of his eyes and the change in the angling of the blade.

'I have the gun.' But did I? I was more afraid of him than he was of me. If he was even afraid at all.

'Weston, I've had RPGs and hollow points and white phosphorus-bearing cluster bombs trying to kill me all day. I am not afraid of your gun and I know you don't have the cullions to pull the trigger. Wa kan je iya l'owo mi. Stop the useless posturing and give me the fucking money belt right now.'

'I killed Taiwo.'

'No you didn't. That was a mistake. I was there, remember?'

'—'

'There is no shame in this, Weston. It's not your area of expertise. Stop wasting my time while them out there continue to search for me. Se kia kia.'

I looked at Nana.

'Don't worry about her,' said Churchill. 'She still cares about you. She didn't tell me where you were even after I did that to her father. What does that tell you, hmm? I was about to start really going to work when you dropped by.'

Fuck it.

I loosened my belt with my left hand, holding the gun uselessly with my right, feeling continuous waves of shame and fear and self-loathing. I pulled off the money belt. He could have it. I just wanted the nightmare to be finished.

'Throw it over here.'

I did.

He examined it, saw the money and donned his smile again. 'Good boy. Good boy. I need this for *my* expenses now, all right?'

'Just get out,' I said. I didn't know if Nana's father was wounded or dead, but his body did not move.

'I'm leaving.' Church said. He fastened the money belt around his waist and rooted around the mess. 'You know, the Israelites used to do this thing once a year. They'd get a goat or a lamb, I can't remember which. They'd lead it outside the city gates, abusing it, flogging it, swearing at it all the way. Innocent animal, but they'd do this. Then, outside the gate, they'd put the animal to the blade, kill it. It was supposed to take all their sins on itself and die for them.' He finally found what he was looking for, a grey shirt and white singlet. He started to dress. 'This country needs me, Weston. Me and D'Jango and people like us. They need us to place their sins on us so that we can take their transgressions outside the city gates and die for them. Our rebellion may not have worked, but it will drive the government in power to some kind of change, even if it's just to avoid the emergence of other groups like us. We are part of the path to democracy, Weston.'

'So you commit rape and mass murder so that we won't have to? Do you tell yourself that so you can sleep at night?'

'I sleep fine, Weston. That nonsense about murdering sleep is for the storybooks.' He spat on his boot and wiped off some dirt. 'How is your slumber?'

He stepped over Nana towards me, swapped his knife over to the side nearest me and winked, walked past. I turned around and he was at the door. A few more seconds and he would be gone.

I shot him in the back. I pulled the trigger, but the gun misfired. Church heard the click, spun towards me and the gun was in his hand before I could react. He pocketed it and grinned.

He said, 'I understand why you did that, and I forgive you, but don't do it again. You'll break my heart, and I don't want my heart to be broken.'

He stared hard at me, and I was aware of the knife in his hand describing tiny circles in the air. Then he left.

I calmed myself and called the ambulance service.

While I waited at Nana's bedside I wasn't sure how I felt about Church being out there in the wild, but if he had wanted to kill me he would have. I felt this empty spot in my belly – an absence of revenge. I wanted to kill him, to get justice for . . . for what? What did he deserve? What did I deserve?

Nana woke and did not want me there. She pressed the button to summon the nurse and ordered me out.

'I don't need you to save me or avenge me, Weston. I'll take care of my family, you take care of yours.'

Outside the hospital the police turned up and arrested me for assaulting Nana and her father and for burglary. I was able to get a phone call to the agent. It took twelve hours to get me out of police custody. When I finally got out, rubbing the skin of my wrists from the handcuff chafing, the agent was waiting for me with a car. I raised my eyebrows, questioning.

'Part of the service. You get to choose the destination.'

'I like that.' He opened the car door and I got in beside one of his drones. 'I was just thinking since we've been through a lot together and all, you might find it in your heart to tell me your fucking name. Just a thought.'

I turned to him. He was smiling. It was tight-lipped and tense, but a smile all the same. He shrugged.

'If it's that important to you, call me Joe.'

'Thank you. See, I don't think—'

'Shut up; it doesn't make us friends.'

'Sorry.'

In the hotel I soaked in a bubble bath. I felt vaguely human again. I had counted all the money and still came out decently in the black.

When I plugged my phone back in the voicemail was full. The messages were mostly from strangers. Journalists wanting an interview or a comment, one persistent person from the British Embassy, my father, but the bulk were from people with problems they wanted me to solve and enquiries about my fee.

I did see the kernel of a business here. I looked at the boarding pass for my flight. I thought about getting stuck on the underground and the smallness of my flat and chasing shoplifters in the car park and dead or dying dreams and aspirations, and my sister Lynn. I thought about the constant greyness of London skies, the unbelievable number of people who wore black, the hostility of strangers, the drunken youth, the politicians who lie just as much as the ones in West Africa.

I called my father. His PA picked up the phone.

'Tell Mr Kogi that I am interested in buying Blossom's house,' I said.

'Tell him yourself; he's been waiting for your call.' A few bars of Chopin and I was through to my father's phone.

'Weston.' His voice sounded drained of the aggressive undercurrent that usually characterised our talks.

'Father.'

'I . . . eh . . . I've been told about your activities.'

'—'

'I think you should have been more careful. This affair was potentially risky for me, for my business.'

'You mentioned this before, Father.'

He cleared his throat. 'I wanted to let you know that if things had gone wrong and resulted in injury to you, I would have been displeased.'

'Stop it.'

'As you wish. I have a letter on my desk from the widow of Enoch Olubusi. She thanks you for your role in bringing her husband's assassin to justice and offers—'

'Father, I am not interested in that. I want to buy Aunt Blossom's house. Who did she leave it to?'

'I don't think I am comfortable with you owning family property,' he said. Gruffness creeping back in, I noticed.

'Once you've sold it the house will no longer be family property and you can take the money into the family coffers.'

'It's what the image of you living in Blossom's house implies.'

'I grew up there after you left my mother to die in penury. That's image enough. Give me a figure.'

'Where will you get the money?'

'None of your beeswax. How much?'

'What will you do with it?'

'How much do you want for it?'

My hotel suite was high above Ede and I could see most of the city in all its glorious filth. I would have to sift through that faeculence in order to do my new job. Kogi Inquiries. I tested it on my tongue.

'Kogi Inquiries. Discreet, efficient, affordable.'

Not perfect, but I had time to work on it.

I stood dripping water, misting the part of the window I touched. The sun was setting and flocks of fruit bats moved eastward. I felt calm, settled, in sync.

I wasn't happy, but I had a purpose; a goal. I was content with my place in the world.

And that was a start.

Acknowledgements

Thanks to my agent Alexander Cochran for finding a home for *Making Wolf* with Constable, and to my family for putting up with my eccentricities.